"Scott's details are placed in their settings like gems in fine jewelry — each has several facets: the beautiful, the dangerous, the ominous, and the familiar. This is the story of a family that flees financial ruin by leaving the United States for the island of Napoleon's exile: Elba. The father, Murray, is charming and hopeless; the mother, Claire, is constant but passionately in love with her husband; the four brothers are as wild and independent as the children in Virginia Woolf's *The Waves*."

— Susan Salter Reynolds, *Los Angeles Times*

"Beauty and unease, two hallmark qualities of the gothic, are on masterful display in *Tourmaline*. . . . There are many scenes here that are simply stunning, events and moments that shimmer and vibrate long after reading. *Tourmaline*, like the stone itself, reflects the outward surface of things and some luminous quality buried deep inside their forms." — Richard Wallace, *Seattle Times*

"In this Gravesian, introspective novel, the light of hindsight illuminates, as usual, not quite everything." — *The New Yorker*

"Joanna Scott is a worker of wonders, and *Tourmaline* is a wondrous novel, one which should be read and then read again."

— Adrienne Miller, *Esquire*

"Anyone who likes a book with many facets will find *Tourmaline* a real gem." — Kate Finley, *Wall Street Journal*

"In prose that has the luminosity of a light reflected off precious gems, Scott weaves a complex family history. . . . Scott digs deeply into the secret hearts of her characters and comes up with a novel that is richer than diamonds."

— Mary A. McCay, *New Orleans Times-Picayune*

"Joanna Scott is a writer drawn to the peculiar poetry of history. . . . Scott trolls the depths of historical record for the enigmatic characters, turns of plot, and rich, visual details that make her work come alive. But it is not quite accurate to call Scott a writer of historical fiction. Scott is, in truth, more historiographer than historian, because her glorious literary obsession is not really with the minutiae of history as it is with the particular ways history is made. . . . Scott's gorgeous prose and poetic sensibility capture the taste of blue tourmaline, the sensation of loneliness, the sound of the sea, and the beauty of the landscapes that the Murdochs encounter on Elba. . . . Scott is a thoughtful storyteller, armed with a technical expertise that, in places, rivals her many 19th-century models. Like Claire, who is haunted by Hawthorne's owls and Tolstoy's Anna and who tours the grand Tuscan landscapes with Keats and Alexandre Dumas by her side, Scott has an intuitive understanding of the complicated dance between literature and life."   — Laura Ciolkowski, *Chicago Tribune*

"Napoleonic history, geology, and a father's folly are woven together in this captivating novel. . . . This is an absorbing picture of a family rediscovering themselves in a foreign land."
— *Publishers Weekly*

"An engrossing tale of familial stress and thwarted passions on a Mediterranean island. . . . *Tourmaline* maintains the elegance and intensity readers of *The Manikin* or *Make Believe* might expect. . . . Scott's Elba, with its eccentrics, brooks limitless drama and depth."
— Max Winter, *San Francisco Chronicle*

"A novel that Scott makes as prismatically complex as the gem that provides her title."
— Michael Mewshaw, *Washington Post Book World*

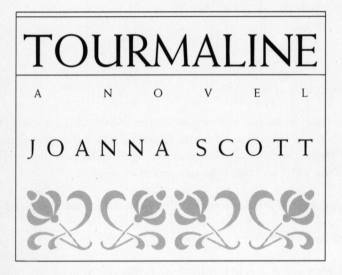

TOURMALINE

A NOVEL

JOANNA SCOTT

BACK
BAY
BOOKS

Little, Brown and Company
Boston   New York   London

For Maureen Howard

and Mark Probst

Originally published in hardcover by Little, Brown and Company, September 2002
First Back Bay paperback edition, September 2003

ISBN 0-316-77618-1 (hc) / 0-316-60848-3 (pb)
LCCN 2002102895

The Back Bay Books name and logo are trademarks of Little, Brown and Company.

10 9 8 7 6 5 4 3 2 1

Q-FF

Text design by Meryl Sussman Levavi/Digitext
Printed in the United States of America

October 1, 1999

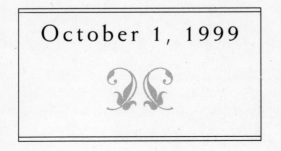

WATER LAPS AGAINST THE QUAY OF PORTOFERRAIO. HUN-gry dogs blink in the sunlight. A grocer stacks oranges. A carabiniere checks the time on his wristwatch. A girl chases a cat into a courtyard. Men argue in the shade of an archway. A woman rubs a rag over a shop window. Heels click on stone. Bottles rattle in the back of a flatbed truck. A boy writes graffiti on the wall above the steps leading to the Liceo Raffaello. German tourists hesitate before filing into a bar. An old woman, puzzled to find herself still alive at the end of the century, sits on a bench in Piazza Repubblica, her eyes closed, her lips moving in a silent prayer to San Niccolò.

I have seen the faded frescoes of San Niccolò in the church in San Piero. I drove to this little enclave yesterday in search of a grotto that is supposed to be full of tourmaline. After wandering through the hills without finding the grotto, I returned to San Piero to explore the village and the deserted ruins of the Appiano fortress. The emptiness felt so complete that the shadow of a man on the granite wall startled me — my own shadow, squat in the light of late morning.

Inside the church, Niccolò has watched the world with knowing eyes for six hundred years. Bloodied Niccolò, who knows everything about everyone and will never be surprised.

When the earth's ancient fire cooled and shrank toward the core, it left behind a hard, uneven shelf of land along the west coast of the peninsula of Italy that was extraordinarily rich with minerals — with hematite, magnetite, pyrite, quartz, agate, and tourmaline running in pure veins through the deep folds of metamorphic rock. Millions of years later, the fire inside the earth flared, tremors vibrated in the glaciers, and the Tuscan Archipelago broke away from the continent. Vents opened in mountain peaks. Basaltic lava flowed over the land. Rain cooled the lava into rock, storm winds wore the rock smooth, rivers cut channels, dust turned to soil, soil softened to fertile mud along the deltas. New forests grew, diverse species of plants and animals evolved. A unique species of poisonous snake made its home on Montecristo. Each island had its own kind of beetle. At one time, small brown bears lived in the caves of Elba, a prehistoric species of rhinoceros roamed the fields, and lynx hunted the newborn foals of wild horses.

Like all bodies of land, the island of Elba would continue to change. Everything on Elba would change, except the minerals. Deep inside the ground the minerals of Elba would remain what they were, pure, intact, untouched by measurable time.

At Pomonte, follow the road to the right of the church beyond the last of the village houses. Continue up the rise. At the fork, cross the little cement bridge and climb the granite steps to the mule track. Follow the track through the vineyards, keeping the stream to your left. Continue past the last vines and into the woods. Cross through a chestnut grove, go forward about a hundred meters, wade through the stream, cross a valley, and continue into another wood of white poplar and oak.

Eventually you will come to an old sheepfold and shepherd's cottage at the top of Grottaccia hill. If you look carefully at the dome of the cottage, you will see that no mortar was used. The skillful builders constructed the dome simply by putting one stone on top of another.

Four thousand years ago, a woman stood in the grotto of San Giuseppe and poured oil from a vase into a bowl. She crumbled dried rosemary into the oil and pounded it to make a paste. She rubbed the paste on the forehead of her sleeping child to take away his fever.

Three thousand years ago, two Greeks, who happened to be brothers, tended a smelting fire. When the burning wood suddenly popped and sparked, the brothers lurched back with a gasp. The fire burned on. The ore melted. The brothers laughed at their cowardice. They decided to name the island Aethalia after the sparking fires. They knew these fires would burn for centuries.

Twenty-five hundred years ago, an Etruscan patriarch stood on the steps of the acropolis on Volterraio and admired the island's beauty. He decided then and there to deliver an edict moving the smelting furnaces to the mainland territory of Populonia.

Two thousand years ago, a Roman mapmaker wandered the island, recording the contours of land, the presence of rivers and streams, the size of villages. The most prosperous villages belonged to the Ilvates — settlers who had come from Liguria — so the mapmaker decided to name the island Ilva.

The name of Elba, replacing Ilva, first appears in Gregory the Great's *Dialogues,* written in the second half of the sixth century A.D.

Hair tangled by the salty seabreeze. Sparkle of quartz dust. Pigskin ball sailing through the air. Clamor of American soldiers in pursuit. Confusion, laughter, protest, happiness, youth.

Still the men in the shade of the archway are arguing, still the old woman sitting on the bench in Piazza Repubblica in Portoferraio is mouthing a silent prayer. The boy who was writing on the wall has left. French tourists stand outside a bar, trying to decide whether or not to go in.

Follow the path from Marciana toward the San Cerbone monastery. At the little lay-by area beyond the woods, take the steep narrow track through the shade of tree-heath. Climb over the broad granite slabs and across the screes to the ridge, where the paths for Poggio and Sant'Ilario meet. Keep following the track up the eastern slope of Monte Capanne, through the scrub of lavender and genista, proceed in a steep climb for about half an hour to the summit. If the day is clear, you will be able to see the coast of Tuscany in one direction, the mountains of Corsica in the other.

Five hundred years ago, a mother hid with her three children in the family's dank lightless cantina in Marina di Campo. The father had locked the door from the outside and left to fight with his neighbors against Khayr ad-Dīn, the pirate known as Barbarossa. The mother sang to her children, and then the children took turns telling stories. They had only a loaf of bread between them and nothing to drink but wine. When the father unlocked the door three days later, his family tumbled out, dissolute, overcome with hilarity.

Four hundred and fifty years ago, twelve young men and women were dragged from their homes in the township of Fabricia onto a boat bound for Tunisia, where they would serve as slaves for the rest of their lives.

Two hundred years ago, the young British painter John Robert Cozens, son of the painter Alexander Cozens, looked out through a window of the chiesetta di Madonna di Monserrato and tried to mix colors on his pallet to match the color of the hills above Porto Azzurro. He decided the best he could hope for was honorable failure.

Follow the road to the right of the Fortezza pisana for about a hundred meters. Turn left onto the mule track that continues into the woods. Continue past the bronze statue of the angel to the paved road that is flanked by the fourteen Stations of the Cross. Follow this through the woods and up the rocky slope to the shrine of Madonna del Monte.

According to the legend, shepherds discovered an image of the Virgin painted on a chunk of granite. They carried the rock to their valley, but the next morning when they woke the rock had been returned to the exact place where they'd first found it on Monte Giove. The shepherds took this as a sign that they should erect a church at the site.

It was here that Napoleon stayed for two weeks during his exile in 1814.

The sun. The wind. Fragrance of rosemary and rock roses, lavender and beer. Sound of pebbles sloshing in the lazy waves. American soldiers breaking from a huddle. Run, jump, twist, crash, fall, get up again, and hike. Yessirree, we could get used to this place! Touchdown!

After the short reign of Napoleon, the island reverted to the Grand Duchy of Tuscany and, in 1860, to the Kingdom of Italy. During the Risorgimento, the mines of Elba were expanded to meet Italy's growing demand for iron. During the First World War, more than two hundred young Elban men were killed fighting on the mainland. After the war, labor unrest escalated on the island. In 1920, miners occupied the administrative offices of the Alti Forni of Portoferraio, demanding an improvement in working conditions and a reduction in prices for food and dry goods. An agreement was reached after a two-month standoff.

The Cinema Moderno opened in Portoferraio in 1924. The Festa dell'Uva was initiated. Mussolini visited the island on several occasions between 1928 and 1936.

The Second World War arrived on Elba in September 1943. On the sixteenth of the month, beginning at 11:30 A.M., seven German bombers buzzed across the sky above Portoferraio. By 4:00 in the afternoon, more than one hundred civilians were dead, and the people of Elba had surrendered.

Nine months later, the Allies attacked in an invasion called "Operation Brassard," planned by General De Lattre de Tassigny. A group of "commandos d'Afrique" led the way early in the morning on the seventeenth of June, followed by French marines. During the night between the seventeenth and eighteenth, Portoferraio was bombed sixteen times. The fighting was swift and severe. The Ninth French Colonial Division lost hundreds of men but managed to take twelve hundred German soldiers prisoner.

What had begun as an apparently minor Allied operation reawakened and reinforced German fears of Allied landings behind the Germans' western flank. The Germans retreated into the

Appenines. The Allies instated a military government on Elba. And in July an obscure American Division arrived to oversee the distribution of supplies.

The Americans, with their chocolate and cigarettes, Spam and rice. The American boys turning war into a holiday. The Americans wanting to do nothing but strip down to their shorts and play football on the beach at Le Ghiaie. Bare toes curling over hot gravel. Shining faces and salt-bleached hair.

The men are arguing about the war. I know because I started the argument. I'd fallen into conversation with one of the men, stopping to ask for directions and then going on to ask more probing questions in hopes of learning something about the history of the island. I asked him if he remembered the American soldiers who came to Elba in the summer of 1944. He said he'd been serving in the Italian navy in Puglia at the time, but he'd heard about the Americans and their games. We were joined by his friend. The two men got to talking about the occupation of the Germans and the invasion of the Allies. The men disagreed about the value of the Liberation. Other men joined us. They talked rapidly, but I could make out the gist of the argument. Some believed the Allies had saved the island; others thought they'd come close to destroying it. One man ripped up a receipt he'd carried from the grocer and threw the pieces on the ground. *Eccola.* That is what the man would have his friends do with the past.

They seemed to forget me, and I withdrew without a word. I walked from the archway into the piazza and saw the old woman sitting on the bench. I was about to go up and ask her for directions when I noticed that her eyes were closed and her lips moving in silent prayer.

I spent the morning wandering the island. Walking back through the piazza later, I saw the same old woman on the bench and the men still arguing in the archway. I saw an English couple coming out of a bar, balancing cones topped with towers of gelati. I read the graffiti on the wall above the stairs leading to Liceo Raffaello: "Michela è un sogno."

I returned to my hotel room and opened the window. The hotel is adjacent to the vineyard of La Chiusa, and I can smell the ripe grapes. I hear doves cooing in the palms, a rooster crowing up in the hills, motorcycles buzzing and trucks rattling along the main road.

On the table in front of me I've set out the faded deed I found among my father's papers last month when I was helping my mother get ready for a yard sale. The deed names my father as owner of five hectares of Elban land. I flatten the worn creases with my thumb. Though there are many signatures and a stamp on the last page, the claim is worthless, local officials have already informed me. Why, then, don't I just turn around and go home?

The woman I lived with for seven years called two weeks ago to tell me that she is getting married. When I invited her to come to Elba with me, she laughed, her tone one of easy fellowship, as if she'd just chucked me on the shoulder.

This is my first visit back to the island since the mid-1950s, and though I've only been here for three days I'm already looking forward to returning again soon. I consider myself lucky to have the liberty and resources to travel. My brothers agree among themselves that I'm indulging in nostalgia and remind me that there are better ways to spend my money.

Our father had been to Elba himself during the war and stayed long enough to play football on the beach and swim in the tepid sea. Based on his firsthand experience, he could assure us that the sun always shines on Elba, wildflowers bloom year round, Elbans will give away the jackets off their backs, and pirates know it is a good place to bury stolen treasure.

Where on earth is Elba? we wanted to know. It is an island not far from the coast of Italy, our father said. Napoleon once reigned in exile there.

Where is Italy? we asked while we watched our parents pack for the journey. Who is Napoleon? What is exile?

Forty-three years later, I am like a blind man feeling my way through a house that has appeared repeatedly in my dreams. I recognize everything, though nothing is familiar. Much has changed, of course. When I came here with my family, Elba was still dependent on its mining industry. Now it is an active tourist resort. It is just after the high season, and the island seems tranquil to me, but it is overrun in summer, people say. I have been warned to stay away from the main centers of Portoferraio and Porto Azzurro during July and August. Hotel reservations should be made far in advance, expect traffic jams, don't bother with the crowded beaches at Bagnaia and Procchio and Marciana Marina, forget about getting into the Villa Demidoff or hiking to the top of Volterraio or riding the Monte Capanne cable car. Better yet, avoid Elba altogether and go to Corsica.

The soft breeze of the scirocco. The rustle of palm fronds. Piping of a nightingale. Two girls riding bareback on the same brown horse. The granite cap of Monte Capanne shining like snow in the distance. Dust rising behind a jeep as it climbs a cart road to Buraccio and disappears beneath the holm oaks. Mouflons grazing on the grassy slope of Monte Calamita.

The war might be continuing elsewhere, but it is over on Elba, and the American soldiers are leaving. Mementos are traded. The Americans give the Elbans matchbooks and dollar bills. The Elbans give the Americans quartz crystals and polished hematite. My father comes away with a small chunk of a dusky mineral tinged at the center with blue, identified for him later as tourmaline, which he will carry back to New York and sell to a jeweler for twenty-five dollars, telling himself as he walks away from the shop that he'd just made the best deal of his life.

The Casparia

ABOUQUET OF RED BALLOONS BROKE FREE FROM A VENDOR on the pier and fell upward through the haze as the ship's whistle blew its deafening farewell. Our cat yowled in her cage. From the deck below someone threw a cap into the water. We noticed one old woman dressed in black linen blotting tears with the remnants of a tissue, but the other passengers cheered and waved at the dispersing crowd.

It was all so splendid that we never stopped to miss what we were leaving behind. We were heading out to sea on a ship so huge it dwarfed the tankers in the harbor. We watched the city's skyline shrink to nothing. Our father looked more pleased with himself than ever, and we shared with him the sense that we were at the start of an adventure far grander than anything we would have allowed ourselves to imagine.

While our parents lingered at the rail, we explored the maze of upper decks and corridors. Everywhere we went, there were doors we weren't supposed to open and pranks easy to devise. We snuck into the kennel and fed a puffed, nervous poodle a handful of the saltines our mother had given us to forestall seasickness. Through straws we'd found in a deserted saloon we blew paper peas at passengers dozing in deck chairs. We let Meena the cat roam free in our cabin, though after Nat pushed her from the upper berth, she took refuge in the shower, where she deposited four neat little turds for the steward to discover when he came to deliver fresh towels.

We were traveling first class, an extravagance paid for with borrowed money. To our father, luxury was a deserved reward. To our mother, luxury was an awkwardness, and the wealth of her fellow passengers seemed an amusing secret which she could only fail to guess, while surely they would see right through her to the truth of our prohibitive debts. We were living a sham life onboard the *Casparia,* and Claire told herself that she'd participate in the ruse only because it was temporary.

From the bow we watched the hull split through colliding waves. From the leeward deck we saw sun pillars shining on the horizon. From the promenade at the stern we watched seagulls soar, dip toward the wake, and then wheel around in what we presumed was defeat and head back toward land. We felt sorry for them. We wished we could have collared the birds and pulled them along on leashes.

I picture my parents that first evening sitting in oversized chairs in the ship's grand dining room, Murray veiled by the smoke of his cigarette, Claire holding herself stiffly, elbows pressed against her sides, fingers clutching the edge of the table as the passengers traded introductions. Beside her was a man named Walter Fugle, a retired banker with a round belly curving neatly inside his three-piece suit, a round, bald head, and a round face tipped with a shaggy white goatee. Teresa Fugle, a seventy-year-old woman with hair tinted an odd, rusty red, sat opposite, with Murray on her right. At the end was the fifth passenger at the table, a young engineer from Ohio, whose name Claire would go on to forget.

My brothers and I had been fed earlier. Thanks to the indulgent Italian stewards, we were free to roam around the dining room in search of fun. Or my brothers roamed while I toddled after, losing them, finding them, and losing them again.

Claire says she doesn't remember how the conversation began. Probably with idle chat about the menu followed by an exchange of information concerning work and home. At some point Murray wanted to talk about the glorious island of Elba. "Able was I . . ." Walter Fugle joked. Murray shot back defensively, "Go ahead and laugh, but I tell you, life there will cost you next to nothing." Mrs. Fugle asked if Elba was close to Capri. The Fugles had been to Capri. They'd thought it lovely, though inconvenient. But Mrs. Fugle was wondering about the weather for tomorrow. Her husband wanted to talk about storms. Claire recalls that it was the engineer who turned the conversation to the subject of great ships lost at sea.

Walter Fugle said he'd had a gardener long ago who had been a crew member on the *Carpathia,* the ship that had made the forced draft run to rescue the *Titanic*'s survivors. The engineer explained that if the *Titanic* had hit the iceberg head-on, the bulkheads would have saved it. Mr. Fugle and the engineer moved into a more heated discussion about the disaster, while the others at the table listened. The engineer mentioned the *Normandie,* which had caught fire and capsized in the Hudson in 1942. Mr. Fugle spoke of seeing the burned-out hull of the *Morro Castle* off the Jersey coast. Murray, to prove his own knowledge, reminded them that the *Lusitania* was sunk with just one torpedo.

The engineer asked if anyone at the table had ever heard of the *Eastland.* Walter Fugle had a vague memory of it. No one else knew anything about the ship. The engineer offered to tell the story — a story my mother can still recount almost word for word.

The *Eastland* was an excursion steamer taking two thousand passengers from Chicago across Lake Michigan — this was in the summer of 1915 — and she was being loaded at her pier on the Chicago River between LaSalle and Clark Streets when a deckhand noticed she had a list. The passengers were told to move to the other side. The ship resumed an almost even keel, and more passengers were allowed to board. Then a woman screamed and slipped on the tilting deck. That's when people on land noticed that the ship was listing again, and they watched in horror as the great ship slowly rolled and capsized. Hundreds of people, mostly women and children, lost their lives, the engineer said, adding that a salvage diver went insane after investigating the submerged parts of the steamer.

The group sat silently as a waiter cleared their plates. Teresa Fugle asked to see the dessert tray before choosing her main course. Walter Fugle suggested a game of rummy after dinner. Claire wondered aloud how many people were onboard the *Casparia.*

"Nearly two thousand," the engineer said.

"Are there enough lifeboats onboard for two thousand passengers?" Claire asked.

The engineer said yes indeed there were enough lifeboats onboard, and he reminded Claire that people were more likely to die in their own bedrooms at home than on a ship. "The most dangerous thing you can do . . ." The engineer paused to sip his water. "The most dangerous thing you can do in your life is to get out of bed in the morning."

"All the more reason . . ." Murray began. But Claire's attention had shifted. She started to rise from her chair and called to Nat, who had been skipping between the tables and right then slammed into a steward's elastic belly. The steward stepped back, his full tray wobbled, the china clattered, the crystal chimed. Conversations stopped abruptly as everyone turned to watch. But the steward, an experienced seaman, nimbly steadied the tray and marched into the galley without a word. When the doors swung closed behind him, the room exploded in applause.

"What happened?" Nat asked, running up to the table.

"You're famous," Murray said.

"You're stupid," Patrick said.

"What did I do?"

"Nothing at all, son," Walter Fugle said. Nat took a few hop-skips and climbed onto Claire's lap; but Mama's lap belonged to me, and I began to cry because Mama was my mama, no one else's mama, and Nat was a big fat —

"You have charming boys," said Mrs. Fugle. Her husband squawked with laughter and Mrs. Fugle tilted her head and smiled at Claire, her expression conveying something close to pity for the poor woman who dared to pose as a first-class passenger.

Later, Claire imagined meeting Teresa Fugle's ridicule with a cold stare. At the time she'd been flustered and could do no better than join Walter Fugle in weak laughter, but afterward she wished she'd been icy and dignified. A woman should always have an extra supply of dignity on hand, especially a woman in our mother's position, lacking as she believed she was in *background*. She felt as if she'd come to an elegant party dressed in a cheap gingham sundress — a charming dress, and she was the mother of charming children.

In our cabin Nat and I fell asleep before Claire had finished reading us a story. While Harry and Patrick whispered in the top bunk, Claire cleaned her face with cold cream and lazily brushed her hair. She turned out the overhead light and shed her dress — not a gingham dress, not cheap, just an inappropriate light polka-dot rayon that would have been more suitable for a secretary heading off to work. She slid naked between the cool sheets.

Murray had stayed in the saloon to play cards with the Fugles. One more round, he'd said, though Claire expected he'd play for another hour or two. She wanted to be awake when he returned.

Once she was certain all of us were asleep, she turned on her bedside lamp to read. She started the novel her sister had given her that morning — Hawthorne's *The Marble Faun.* "Four individuals, in whose fortunes we should be glad to interest the reader . . ." She read and reread the first page, pondering the images: the swooning marble Gladiator and the Lycian Apollo, women hanging out their wash in the sun, the Alban Mountains, the great sweep of the Colliseum. She let her mind wander and found herself picturing white sheets billowing on a clothesline strung over a street.

"Side by side with the massiveness of the Roman Past, all matters that we handle or dream of nowadays look evanescent and visionary alike." Claire read on. She was half asleep when Murray lay down beside her, still fully dressed in his suit, the smell of cigarettes overpowering the lingering fragrance of Claire's own perfume, signaling to her that he'd been among friends and had enjoyed himself. She liked the smell of his cigarettes. She liked the way his body on top of the bedspread tightened the covers around her. She yawned so he'd know she was still awake. He floated his hand lazily along her shoulder.

"I wish we didn't have Teresa Fugle at our table," she whispered. "I could tell she'd gotten your goat. He, on the other hand —"

"He seems decent."

"He's a cheat. Took me for five dollars."

"You placed bets?"

"It was his idea."

He stroked her lips and dipped his fingertips into her mouth. She tasted brandy, salt, tobacco. He withdrew his hand, traced the curve of her chin. She tried to forget that Murray had lost at cards. She asked herself how much she was prepared to lose and for a moment felt only a surge of dejection, until she remembered the sum: five dollars. Maybe she didn't mind if Murray lost a little money at cards now and then. He may not have had much winner's luck, but he didn't play often.

She rolled over and locked her mouth against his and began

unbuttoning his shirt. He peeled her free of the sheet, followed with his open hand the rise of her hip, moved in a smooth familiar spiral around her thigh.

Later that night Patrick was woken by the wind shushing against the thick glass of the porthole. He put on his glasses, which he'd left hanging on the headboard of his bunk, and peered into the night. A creamy brown halo surrounded the moon. The mist had thickened; stars were visible only as occasional glitter behind the haze. And as though in reflection, whitecaps sparked across the water and then disappeared, folded back into the darkness. Patrick says he remembers this like it was yesterday.

Harry says he remembers playing miniature golf and Ping-Pong. Nat says he remembers our parents tossing him between them in the pool. He remembers his shrieks echoing off the metal roof. Patrick remembers the sink in our cabin overflowing because Harry forgot to turn off the water. Harry insists that it was Nat who left the water running.

The voyage from New York to Genoa took a week. But somehow we became convinced that while the ship was surging forward, the ocean was flowing backward and we were going nowhere. We didn't mind. If we'd been offered the choice, we would have stayed on the *Casparia* forever, and forever looked forward to reaching Elba.

After breakfast we'd go to the rec room. After lunch we'd go to the pool. After the pool our parents would take us to the nursery, and our father would play cards with the Fugles while our mother claimed a deck chair for herself and read until someone came by and engaged her in conversation.

Usually it was the engineer from Ohio who would pull up a chair. He was eager to talk, and when he learned that our mother had never before taken an ocean voyage, he was eager to tell her what he knew. It turned out he knew a lot. He explained the tug of the Gulf Stream and the constituents of salt. He explained how bromine could be extracted from the sea and used to make ethyl gasoline. Magnesium hydroxide could be filtered and used directly as milk of magnesia. Uranium could be extracted, and silver, and even gold. According to the engineer, a troy ounce of gold is found in every eight million tons of sea water.

Whenever the engineer sat down in the chair beside her, our mother would close her book and listen politely, because that's what she'd have done with anyone. He seemed trustworthy. And he was more interesting than she'd expected him to be. She found herself intrigued by his mix of information and disclosure, and she looked forward to their conversations.

He said he planned to go first to Florence and spend a week there seeing the sights. Then on to Venice for another week, and then to Turin, where he would serve for three months as a site planner — a *field dog,* he was called — for an expanding textiles mill. He'd return to the States by December and spend Christmas with his brother's family in Ashville.

He mentioned his ex-wife only once, when he spoke about selling his house in Cincinnati the previous spring. He didn't mention any children, and Claire didn't ask. He complained about his insomnia and confessed that late at night he'd sneak to the pool and swim alone in the dark. He said that sometimes, leaning against the rail, he'd feel close to overwhelmed by the desire to dive into the sea. He spoke about the responsibilities of his job and the inspirations of travel.

As the days passed, the afternoon meetings between our mother and the engineer became routine. She would arrive on deck first, and he'd appear within ten minutes. He was pleasant, she thought. Perhaps a bit pedantic. The knowledgeable engineer from Ohio. She listened to him. She looked at him. Each day she looked at him more closely — at the delicate curl of his nostrils, the slight peak of his upper lip, his long lashes, the pinhead pupils in his eyes, the spray of dandruff on his shirt. She noticed that his breath smelled of peppermint, and the thumbnail on his left hand was a bruised purple. She was about to interrupt him — he'd been talking about Darwin, Darwin and pigeons — and ask him what he'd done to his thumb. But just then Mrs. Fugle came up to complain about the breakfast, from the soupy eggs to the cardboard bacon.

Claire and the engineer murmured in agreement. Mrs. Fugle settled in a chair beside the engineer and tilted her hat to keep the sun out of her face. Claire let her thoughts drift away from the conversation for a few moments. She experienced the kind of peace she associated with waking up from a good dream.

She decided that she'd misjudged Teresa Fugle. And the engineer from Ohio — was there anything he didn't know?

Only minutes later, they were all laughing because Mrs. Fugle admitted that Mr. Fugle had poured salt into his jacket pocket at breakfast after he'd overheard a man at a nearby table saying that a pinch of salt was considered good luck onboard a ship.

"And when you sneeze," said the engineer, "sneeze on the starboard side —"

"And not on the port side, or you make trouble," finished the first officer, who'd come up quietly behind them while they were talking.

"Ah, sir, welcome," offered the engineer.

"Officer, sir!" Mrs. Fugle snorted with laughter; she'd worked herself into a giddy mood and was finding everything and everyone ridiculous.

"Of course, you might have nailed a horseshoe to the mainmast for our protection, sir!" joked the engineer.

"All you need to do is cross your second finger over your first, ecco!"

"Or a hunchback. You should keep a hunchback onboard, sir."

"Or you can spit into your hat — that will bring good luck. Or strike your left palm with your right fist."

"Or break a piece of wood, here" — the engineer took a pencil from his shirt pocket and snapped it in two — "and you'll have a lucky break."

"A lucky break!" echoed Mrs. Fugle with another burst of laughter.

The officer touched the peak of his cap and strolled on, leaving the engineer and Teresa Fugle and Claire to sigh and acknowledge one another with friendly smiles. Claire felt as if she were sitting outside on a summer evening with neighbors. The engineer and Teresa were her neighbors on the ship, and Claire was grateful to both of them, to the first officer as well, to the other passengers, the captain, the stewards, to everyone who was making this trip so safe and wonderful.

First there were petrels wheeling overhead. Then porpoises swam for a couple of hours alongside the *Casparia*. Then the barometer dropped, the birds and porpoises disappeared, rain balls gathered overhead, and the squall began, sheets of rain lashing the deck, waves colliding across the stern, the wind whistling, the ship's bell clanging. At dinner the engineer told the others at the table about a North Atlantic storm so powerful it tore apart a breakwater on the coast of Scotland by ripping away an 800-ton slab and the 550-ton foundation to which it was bound. He said he knew the engineer who worked on the replacement section — a 2,600-ton block of concrete, which was promptly swept away by another storm.

Talk turned to tsunamis and tidal bores, gales and hurricanes. Mr. Fugle put a handful of marbles on the floor and sent us in pursuit when they rolled away. The vertical lights around the room flickered, making the bright walls look as if there were flames spreading behind the hammered glass. The motion made Mrs. Fugle queasy and she left early for bed. Claire drank too much wine. Murray did some card tricks for my brothers and me.

The storm passed without incident, and by the next morning the air was cool, the skies gray over the turbulent water. Shortly before breakfast, Claire took Nat and me out to get some fresh air, and we found the engineer on the sundeck. He was smoking a cigarette and watching passengers stroll by. When Claire saw that he hadn't spotted her yet, for some reason she couldn't have explained she started to move away in the opposite direction.

But just then Nat tugged loose from her hand and ran ahead, calling us to hurry up and come on. Claire carried me toward Nat, and a moment later the engineer joined us. Nat was already scrambling over the partition dividing the first-class terrace from the second-class promenade. Claire yelled at him to stop. The engineer climbed over the partition and grabbed Nat, who squirmed in his arms and tried to slip away. But when the engineer murmured something in Nat's ear, Nat abruptly calmed, as if he'd just been promised an extravagant toy. The engineer carried Nat to the far rail at the stern, and they stood there, watching the wide white expanse of the wake disappear into the mist.

That's when I felt my mother tense. She held me in the usual fashion, propped against her jutting hip, one of her arms supporting me, and I felt the hand resting flat against my belly tighten into a fist. I might be picturing what my mother has described to me, or maybe I do have some real memory of it: the salt spray, the wind, the rough sea, the knuckles of my mother's hand, the broad white wake spreading out behind us like ribbons of taffy. And a man in white trousers and a black jacket standing with his back to us, my brother in his arms.

Claire set me down on the terrace and hoisted herself over the partition, her knees stretching the tight cap of her skirt hem. She ran toward the engineer. I started to howl, for it seemed clear that my mother had discarded me. Claire skidded to a stop a few yards short of the engineer, who pivoted slowly. His expression was somber. His arms were outstretched in front of him.

There he stood, palms turned inward, my brother no longer between his hands. That's what my mother saw: a man in the pose of a priest who has just made an offering to the sea. Where my brother had been was the invisible outline of his form.

And then the engineer turned another degree and Nat was

there again — my brother, Claire's third son, a boy overjoyed at the thrill of flying high, effortlessly, over the open water.

Iron rings clanged against the flag mast. A dog barked on the deck below. The wind carried the sound of someone's cough. I heard all this through the sound of my own crying. Something awful had happened, I thought, and something worse was about to happen.

The wind. The sea. Shifting bodies. Shifting moods. Accidental minglings. *Pretend you're a bird. Pretend you're flying over the ocean. Like this!* The infinite water. *It's a small world,* my mother liked to say. *Sometimes,* she would add as an afterthought.

And then the man pivoted another notch, his arms like the gun of a tank, and lifted Nat back inside the boundary of the rail, setting him safely on deck.

Nat wanted to keep flying. He stomped his feet and beat his hands against Claire when she tried to pick him up. Nat wanted the mister to pick him up. But Nat must come with Mama. Wasn't it time for breakfast? Claire flashed a weak smile, unwilling to stir up new trouble by telling the engineer what she really thought of him, murmuring inaudibly that he'd given her quite a scare, muttering a little louder, "I almost thought . . ."

"What?"

"Nothing."

And that was that. Nat forgot about the thrill of flying and remembered he was hungry, and I forgot that I was useless. We left for breakfast. The engineer stayed behind to smoke another cigarette.

The rest of the day passed uneventfully. After breakfast Claire felt a headache coming on, so she retreated to a cozy chair in a deserted salon. She skipped lunch, and though she made an appearance at dinner she only ate the soup. The engineer seemed as animated by his knowledge as ever, but Claire made a point of avoiding any direct exchange. She decided it would be best not to tell Murray about how reckless the engineer had been with Nat.

By the next morning Claire felt better. She was buttering a piece of toast when she noticed both the captain and the first officer moving from table to table. They'd pause to speak quietly to the passengers and then raise their hands in a calming gesture. The murmur in the dining room grew louder as the news spread ahead of him. One woman shrieked. Men echoed each other: Good God, good God. One elderly man led his distraught wife from the room.

A woman at a nearby table communicated the news to Claire and Murray. Apparently, a passenger had jumped overboard during the night. Who was it? Murray asked, though by then Claire had already guessed it was the engineer from Ohio. The first officer approached their table. When he spoke his voice seemed to come from behind him. A terrible tragedy, he was saying. Yes, it is, it is.

Claire's face had drained of color. She could only shake her head stupidly as she imagined the engineer leaping off the rail of the first-class deck into the darkness, his heavy body gaining velocity and tumbling past the cigarette he'd tossed ahead of him. *The most dangerous thing you can do . . .* what had he said? *The most dangerous thing . . .*

Murray stared at the officer. Later he would confide to Claire that he couldn't help but wonder if at the last conscious moment, when a man is breathing in a lungful of saltwater, he'd have the wherewithal to feel regret.

OLLIE, FORGIVE ME FOR SAYING SO, but I wonder why you haven't learned from past mistakes. Your penchant for melodrama. I can tell you that no one shrieked that morning on the *Casparia.* No one was even visibly distraught. In fact, the concern passed quickly, and people sat and finished their breakfast. The stewards came around and refilled our cups with coffee. Newspapers were opened and read. I overheard two men arguing about Khrushchev. The news of the engineer had been noted. Those who had spent any time with him traded stories. Murray and the Fugles recounted conversations. Only six of us joined the chaplain for a memorial service that afternoon.

You say you've lost the ability to make up stories. You're done with novels, eh? I doubt it. You say you might as well write something that's true. Go ahead. I don't mind the disclosures. I have no use for embarrassment in my old age. But you don't mind, do you, if I correct some of the inaccuracies? The description of me shaking my head stupidly, for instance. Stupidly, indeed! It was almost forty-five years ago, but I remember exactly what I was feeling. I was feeling the opposite of stupid. I saw everything too clearly. The man who had thrown himself off the ship had almost dropped your brother overboard. He'd wanted to drop him. He would have dropped him if he'd stood there another minute. That's what I was thinking.

But I wonder, Oliver, if you really want to hear what I could tell you about this particular period in our lives. You are trying to understand what happened to our family on Elba, to sort out fantasy from fact. You say you remember the island as a place where your brothers and you had magical powers. But how much do you actually remember? What should I tell you, and what do you already know?

Here's something: did you know that I didn't learn to swim until I was a teenager? I was terrified of water. I had no reason to be terrified, no frightening experience behind me, yet for whatever reason, I had an intense fear of drowning. Then when I was fifteen my mother forced me to take swimming lessons, and I learned to stay afloat in deep water. But I didn't learn to enjoy it.

From my window here at home the lawn slopes to the seawall, which blocks my view of the narrow beach. When the tide's out the sand is full of driftwood and broken shells, seaweed and sponges — the yellow dead-men's-fingers kind that smell like sulfur when they're burned. The dock behind the Hunters' house is stained with guano from the gulls. The terns are back, nesting in the hedge between our yards, and they dive at me when I go to pull weeds. From Cannon Point sometimes I see the fins of bluefish passing in schools offshore. Emily, the little Hunter girl, said her father saw a Portuguese man-of-war floating in the water last week.

Every morning from May to the end of September I still take my swim. When I'm swimming or just walking along the beach, breathing in the sharp smell of the water, I remember my gratitude. I'm in good health. You boys look out for me. You see to it that my bills are paid, my gutters cleaned, my car serviced. You're fond of me, aren't you, the way people are fond of an old pet? I am lucky. Some mothers must continually prove their merit. My sons don't expect much from me. But you expect me to tell the truth, don't you? Family history as it took shape on the *Casparia.*

I told you the story of the engineer a few weeks ago at dinner. How for a terrible instant I thought he'd dropped my son into the ocean. The mistake of my perception. What I didn't admit was my own complicity. Not for spending time in conversation with the engineer, but for ignoring him. I was too self-absorbed to hear what that troubled man was trying to tell me. With each day on the *Casparia,* I felt happier, and pleasure made me complacent. I wanted to do nothing more than watch the color of the water change with the changing light and let the motion of the waves lull me into oblivion.

I'd been opposed to the trip. With Murray between jobs, it wasn't the time for us to go away. But on that grand ship I shared with your father a new sense of possibility. I could fill the emptiness around me with thoughts of the kind of life I would have lived if I had no responsibilities. And when that man held Nathaniel over the rail, some demon in me saw it as my punishment. If I thought he'd dropped my child into the water, it was because that's what I expected him to do.

I often dream of falling. Even if I wake without the memory of it, the ache in my bones tells me I've had the same dream again. When I push myself up out of bed, I'm still dizzy. I haven't told you about the dizziness before now, Ollie, because I didn't want you to drag me to the doctor for a checkup. I'm feeling fine enough to take a swim in the brisk cove water every summer morning, to go crabbing with my grandchildren off the Hunters' dock, to build a bonfire of driftwood and seaweed at dusk. Did you know that I'm the local expert on the origin of the waves at Morrow Beach? Waves with steep choppy peaks are young waves churned by storms off Block Island. If the waves advance in stately intervals, the rear bulging in a crest, curling, plunging into the foam, then they come from the South Atlantic, born on a far-away fetch.

Superstitions are the riddles we make out of mystery. And the mystery of the sea has to do with death. A person dies on land, takes a bullet in his heart, has a stroke, chokes on food, and his body, whole or torn, remains behind long enough to prove that he was once alive. A person falls overboard — he's there beside you, and then he's gone. When death is disappearance, you can't be sure there was life preceding it. One moment the emptiness in front of you offers any possibility you care to think of, and the next it is full of ghosts and monsters and angry gods.

But maybe it's easier for you to return to the past, and I'm mis-remembering the details. I consider myself adequately lucid, though there are some people who have a different opinion. Emily Hunter informed me that her father believes I have Alzheimer's. What is Alzheimer's? she wanted to know. Alzheimer's, I told her, is what happens when an old lady throws away her clocks and mirrors. Did I have Alzheimer's? Not yet, I said. Do old men get Alzheimer's? she asked. They do. Old men start seeing things that aren't there and confusing one thing with another — for instance, they might see a clump of seaweed and think it's a Portuguese man-of-war. Chew on that one, little Emily. She did, in contemplative silence. And then went home for the day.

There's something else I'd like to point out, Ollie: while it's true Murray wanted to take us to Elba because he remembered it as a place of great beauty, by the time we set out from New York on that muggy July day (the heat, Ollie, the stifling city heat — the white sun burning through the haze of clouds, a ventilator cowl nearby blowing hot air on us . . . ask your brothers if they remember the heat. . . .), by then, the seventh of July, 1956, it hardly mattered where we were going, as long as we were going far away.

SAY THE NAMES. Hold them in your mouth like polished stones: *Leviathan, Titanic, Queen Mary, Ile de France, Normandie, Mauretania, Conte di Savoia, Casparia.* There was a time when three quarters of their space was reserved for the upper classes. "The English Lines," wrote the travel writer Basil Woon, "perhaps have a more distinguishable air of disciplined smartness. . . . 'efficiency' is a word which fits United States Lines boats; Italian Lines err rather on the side of too much servility. . . ." First-class passengers could swim in Pompeian pools or drink chamomile tea beside marble fountains. They could play boccie or shuffleboard or miniature golf. The women could take turns dancing with the captain while the men enjoyed their cognac in the saloon.

My father's first experience on a luxury liner was as a soldier heading to Glasgow on the *Queen Elizabeth* in the early months of 1942. The six miles of carpeting had been stripped from the ship, along with the china, crystal, and silver, and in their place were twenty-millimeter Oerlikon antiaircraft cannons, rocket launchers, and range finders. The ship had been painted battleship gray and girdled in degaussing wire. The restaurant had been turned into a mess hall. Instead of stewards there were chow lines. Instead of brass beds in the staterooms there were bunks crammed on every wall. The ship had been built to carry 2,100 passengers. Lifeboats were provided for 8,000 men. Sixteen thousand troops were onboard. They sailed alone to the Firth of Forth, without convoy. Every man onboard knew that Hitler had offered the equivalent of a quarter of a million dollars and an Iron Cross to any U-Boat commander who could sink the *Queen Elizabeth.*

The ship made the voyage without incident, and Murray spent

most of the remainder of the war at a base in England overseeing the distribution of supplies, except for the one expedition in 1944 trailing the Fourth U.S. Corps up the west coast through the rubble of Grosseto and on to Piombino and then, after the island was liberated by the Ninth French Colonial Division, to Elba, where he stayed for over a month, not because there was work to do but because the army command simply forgot about Murray's insignificant division.

Lasting peace came first to Elba — or so it seemed to Murray during that lost month in '44, and when he needed a refuge ten years later, it made sense that he would return.

We were somewhere near the Azores when we almost lost Nat to the depths. Nat says that though he has no recollection of the engineer from Ohio, he remembers the sensation of being dangled high over the open sea. He remembers the tingling on the surface of his skin and another feeling more difficult to express, a feeling in his bones, he says, an impression that he was in danger, a sense of joy, a sense that he was experiencing a forbidden freedom. He remembers how the wind tugged at his earlobes as if to get his attention. And far below him he saw the churning, foaming, boiling water. He perceived the water to be deadly hot and had a passing impulse to escape the hands holding him and return to the safety of the deck. But somehow he knew that he should be still. For danger to be any fun at all, you have to trust the person in charge — he understood this instinctually and knew better than to try to squirm free.

I don't remember passing through the Strait of Gibraltar, but my brother Patrick does. Or at least he remembers watching two identical steamers surging past us, the ships so minute they looked like toys from the heights of the *Casparia,* their plumes of smoke like the white feathers of cockatoos.

And Harry remembers sneaking from the nursery and making his way to the galley, where a cook put him to work drying pots and then showed him some of the extra treats — hominy grits, cranberry sauce, and malted-milk powder — items so special they were only dispensed upon a passenger's request. Then the cook gave Harry a spoonful of tangerine sherbet and made him promise to go back to the nursery. Harry says he remembers lying across a soft leather ottoman in an empty salon, though he's not sure whether this was before or after he left the galley. He remembers watching our mother repack a trunk. He remembers asking for cranberry sauce at breakfast and being laughed at by our parents.

Our first day on the Mediterranean was unusually stormy, and the ship "rolled like a sick headache," as Mrs. Fugle described it. But among our family, only Meena the cat suffered the effects. She left little puddles of vomit in corners of the cabin, and Claire scrubbed the floor clean and then hid the dirty towels in a bin by the pool.

Our mother didn't let us out of her sight for the last part of the voyage. She ate her meals quickly and paid little attention to the conversations at the table. The Fugles and Murray talked at length about the engineer, speculating about his reasons for suicide. Teresa Fugle noted his obsession with stories of disaster. Walter said he'd seemed well-read. Murray had considered only after the fact that his wife had spent her afternoons in conversation with the engineer, but he decided he'd accomplish nothing by asking her what she really thought of the man.

The weather cleared, and we approached Genoa at noon on a bright, warm July day. After they'd packed and closed the trunks, our parents took us to a terrace to watch as the port slowly acquired form and detail. Beyond the clutter of masts we saw the black and white of buildings, the dark gaps of windows, the bulge of a cathedral's dome. The *Casparia*'s whistle bellowed salutes. A man in a glen-plaid ascot strummed a banjo. Stewards walked dogs along the third-class deck. It seemed as if most of the passengers hadn't noticed that our voyage was almost over, and my brothers and I, knowing nothing about the engineer's death, all shared the wordless disappointment that one feels when a party starts to peter out. Shouldn't there have been fireworks and a band gathered onshore to welcome us, after all the trouble we'd gone through to come here? Murray held me in one arm and carried Meena's cage with his free hand; Claire held Nat's hand, and she ordered Patrick to keep hold of Harry.

The gangway was jarred loose and lowered to the shouting of a dozen men, their commands neatly synchronic, as if joining in song. The sound was a welcome of sorts. But even better was the bagful of streamers Mrs. Fugle gave us. We flung the streamers over the rail and watched them unravel in long ribbons of color that stuck to the hull.

Once the ship had docked, the passengers began collecting their families and appointing stewards to take charge of their luggage. On a crowded stairwell Harry announced that he had to pee, so we returned to our cabin. Later, as we waited in the crowd funneling onto the gangway, Patrick started to whine that he was thirsty, which reminded me of my own thirst, so I began wailing, the cat began howling in sympathy, Harry yelled at Patrick to shut up, Murray yelled at Harry to shut up, and Claire told Murray to stop acting like a child. The faces of adults in the packed crowd were flushed and drenched with perspiration; one woman swooned; someone yelled for help, and at the front of the crowd the first officer called instructions through a bullhorn.

Mr. Fugle appeared beside us, his wife nowhere in sight. "It's not like the *Ile de France*," he said. "On the *Ile de France* you were inspired to live merrily, if only for the moment."

"Mr. Fugle, I wanted to say . . ." Our father hesitated, and Claire peered at him angrily, as if she thought he were going to reveal some humiliating secret about our family. "To ask, rather, if you knew of a decent hotel where we might put up for a day and rest." Claire rolled her eyes and looked away. Mr. Fugle gasped.

"You have nothing booked, Murray? You have your whole family here and no place to stay?"

"I thought . . ."

"You didn't think is the truth of the matter. You'll have to come along with me, stick close, we'll need a fleet of taxis with your luggage and the five boys. . . ."

"Four. We have four boys."

"Four then, no matter. Now stay close. Teresa! Where is she? Teresa?"

We followed Mr. Fugle down the gangplank, followed his muttering voice when we lost him for a moment in the crowd, found him again standing miraculously beside Mrs. Fugle — *miraculously,* I say, because Mrs. Fugle had apparently lost twenty or so pounds in a matter of minutes and had dyed her hair black, powdered her face white, and shrunk in height a couple of inches.

Mrs. Fugle was, in fact, Mrs. Fugle's sister, Ida, who, Mr. Fugle explained, lived half of each year in Florence and was perfectly fluent in Italian. She would keep us from becoming gypsies, he said. They conferred for a moment, then Ida instructed us to take a taxi to the Hôtel Luxembourg, where the Fugles had already reserved a suite; we'd rendezvous in the courtyard, she said. Mr. Fugle secured two more taxis. He'd wait for the luggage and bring it along directly.

We left the Fugles just as Teresa arrived and embraced her sister. We crammed ourselves into a taxi with corduroy seats ripped at the seams, broken floorboards, and a driver who smelled like broiled flounder, and as we rode up the steep narrow streets of the old port, I whimpered because I was hot, Patrick whined because he was thirsty, and Murray remarked at all the stone monsters lounging above doorways, "Will you look at that!"

After nearly half an hour the taxi pulled up onto the sidewalk in front of the arched brick entrance of the Luxembourg, an elegant hotel near the Piazzale Resasco. When Murray reached for his wallet, the driver gestured behind him and said something about the signore. Claire and Murray understood him to mean that Mr. Fugle had generously paid our fare. They gathered us and Meena and the few small sacks we were carrying and headed into the hotel. A fountain graced by a bronze Pan gurgled in the courtyard, and Murray threw in a penny. Then we all had to throw pennies, including Claire. A maid swept the cobblestones, and the swish of her straw broom sounded like the wind onboard the *Casparia.* The broom, the fountain, the fragrance of orange blossoms, the blue patch of sky overhead, the warmth, the stillness, the uncertainty of the future, the certain fact of our safe ocean voyage — everything combined to lull us into calm. I stopped crying, Patrick stopped complaining, Meena curled up in her cage and fell asleep. We sat on the edge of the fountain's basin and waited for the Fugles and our luggage to arrive. We waited serenely for ten minutes, until a concierge approached and in perfect English asked if he could be of assistance. Murray went into the hotel to arrange for a room. Claire sat with her face turned up to catch a beam of sunlight. Patrick quietly counted to twenty in the Italian he had learned from the sitters in the ship's nursery.

Murray appeared, key in hand, and we continued to wait. Thirty minutes turned into an hour. I chased my brothers around the fountain. Murray went to see if the hotel had another courtyard. As each minute passed Claire's features grew tighter. Murray returned, shaking his head as if to shake away the irritating buzz of a fly. Claire coughed, and just as she was about to tell Murray to go back to the harbor to look for the Fugles, they heard the crunch of gravel beneath car wheels. Doors opened and slammed. Voices rose in argument. An engine revved, stalled, and revved again.

The Fugles had arrived, along with one canvas suitcase. The rest of their luggage, and ours, was in another taxi — a taxi that was supposed to follow the Fugles to the Luxembourg, a taxi with a black-eyed, bearded driver who turned off on a side street somewhere back in the centro storico and disappeared without so much as a parting honk.

Ida scolded Walter for not paying better attention during the drive. A bellhop fetched the concierge. The concierge and the Fugles' taxi driver conversed solemnly, while Ida turned her rage upon Teresa. Walter started arguing with Murray, calling him inept and irresponsible. Claire asked the concierge, "Does this mean our belongings have been stolen?" and the concierge, forgetting himself for a moment, started rattling in Italian, then bowed slightly and apologized "for the inconvenience."

The police would be called, the concierge promised, and hopefully the thief and our luggage would be found. Until then he trusted that we would enjoy our stay at the Hôtel Luxembourg. The other adults followed the concierge to the manager's office. No bellhop came to help us, so Claire led my brothers and me up to our fourth-floor room. We had a spitting contest on the balcony while our mother leaned back against pillows wrapped in colorful lace and dozed.

Or, rather, let her thoughts drift through the clutter of impressions — the bearded satyrs and fat-cheeked gargoyles decorating the buildings of Genoa, the delicate green-tipped fingers of the Luxembourg's Pan, the bodies surrounding her on the gangway of the *Casparia,* the annoyed expression on Mr. Fugle's face at the harbor, Teresa's impatient smile. The engineer.

The mysterious, doomed engineer from Ohio. When Claire thought of him now she felt something she wouldn't have wanted to describe to anyone. The engineer had taken the most desperate measure possible to escape his private agonies. That he had spared Nat was cause for a strange, uncomfortable gratitude. Claire wouldn't have called it gratitude. She wouldn't have admitted to feeling anything but sympathy for the unhappy engineer and his family.

Sympathy — and relief. Her four boys were alive. Amazingly, we were alive, safe, healthy, attentive to the world, full of hope, easily pleased. The Murdoch family had survived an ocean voyage, and we would survive the theft of our luggage. Who knows but that it was a necessary loss? In order to leave home behind, we had to lose what we'd brought along with us.

Still, Claire decided that we should postpone our journey and wait in Genoa while the police searched for the thief. In the meantime we'd shop and replace what we'd lost. We were already living off borrowed money. Now Murray would have to wire his mother in New York and beg for more. Convey his desperation in a telegram and wait at the Luxembourg for the reply, which would come eventually, though he'd have to suffer the wait while our grandmother borrowed the money from her brothers.

Such suffering, here at the top of the Luxembourg! The breeze blew through the balcony doors. The hills were the color of new leaves on a sugar maple. Claire could smell the ripe lemons in the garden.

She must have fallen asleep, for when she woke Murray was sitting on the chair in front of the dressing table, his face hidden in his hands. Claire heard Patrick talking to the rest of us out on the balcony. The only other sound was the chatter of a parakeet in a cage on the balcony next door.

"Any success, Murray?"

"We're lucky we didn't lose a thousand dollars' worth of diamonds and pearls like the Fugles did. Though if we're talking relative value, the Fugles lost a couple of shoelaces, and we've lost almost everything."

"Do you want to go home?"

"Yes. No." He rose from his chair and stood with his hands in his pockets, idly watching us through the open doorway. "I don't know. What a mess I've gotten us into. If I'd used the money as intended, I'd have my own office by now. Maybe a client or two — on the condition that I cut my commission by fifty percent. Why do I sacrifice every possibility of profit to incentive? You understand why I needed a break, don't you, Claire? A man who's going nowhere benefits from a change in routine. Some time away to give him perspective."

Of course she understood. We couldn't give up now. We lingered in Genoa. Mornings we'd stroll with the Fugles along Via Garibaldi, led by Ida Fugle, who took it upon herself to distract us all from the loss of our belongings. We dragged our open hands along the cold stone facades of palazzi as Ida told us the history of the local families. We crowded into a funicular and rode above houses built on streets so steep that they had doors cut into their roofs. We climbed up La Lanterna, the ancient lighthouse of Genoa. We shopped for clothes along Via del Campo. Murray treated himself and Walter Fugle to cigars from the Hobby Pipe at Via XII Ottobre and treated us all to marrons glacés. We ate licorice that stained our tongues black. Murray gave Patrick a taste of wine at a bar. We threw the last of our pennies to Pan in the fountain at the Luxembourg. One day in a gentle rain we sifted through the decade-old rubble in an area where new construction hadn't yet replaced a building destroyed in the war. Harry found a leather watchband. Patrick found the frayed end of a rope.

It took five days for our grandmother to wire us enough money to give Claire and Murray both the means and confidence to continue our trip to Elba. The Fugles gave up hope of recovering their luggage and left for Florence on the fourth day. We were content to stay on in Genoa. We were cast as royalty by the smiling, whispering staff of the Hôtel Luxembourg, who made it their goal to convince all the Murdoch boys to try the gianchetti they served as an appetizer at lunch. Gianchetti are tiny newborn fish steamed and coated with olive oil and lemon, and they stare up at you from the plate with the passiveness that comes with condemnation. My brothers and I would wrap handfuls of gianchetti in bits of newspaper and hide the wads in our pockets. We'd nod vigorously when the waiters gathered to ask in English, "You like?"

We fed the gianchetti to Meena, and over the course of the

week she grew strong, regal, fierce. She took to sitting on the rail of the balcony and staring at the parakeet that was owned by a widow who lived year-round in the Luxembourg. The parakeet would twitter — in panic at first, then weakly, helplessly — and Meena's tail would snap back and forth to the rhythm.

Bells rang through the dusk. Swallows fished in the sky for insects. Nat said we were in Fairyland. Harry said we were never going home.

Shortly after dawn on the morning of our fifth day at the Luxembourg we were woken by a scream. Or Murray and Claire and Harry woke; the rest of us managed to sleep as the widow on the balcony next to ours screamed, doors banged, and a maid called from the courtyard below.

Murray and Claire had been sleeping in their usual fashion, back to back, Claire's new silk nightgown bunched up around her waist, Murray in boxers, their rumps touching, one of Claire's legs sandwiched between Murray's shins. When Murray woke he clamped his legs together so Claire had to yank hers free, a movement which, as he'd later explain to Claire, reminded him of her angry, abrupt movements during early labor, and in the blurry haze of sleepiness he forgot where he was and thought that Claire was getting ready again to give birth. How many times had she been through it? How many boys did they have? Four? Or five? He remembered that someone had told him he had five sons. But the someone was a liar — Murray remembered that much. Who was screaming? What was wrong?

Claire had bolted out of bed by then. Murray stumbled after Claire, pulling on pajama pants. Harry followed Murray, dragging a blanket along with him. They gathered out on the balcony and found the old widow on the balcony next to theirs screaming something about a gatto, a gatto cattivo, weeping, shuddering, clutching the sides of the parakeet's cage. Inside, the little green bird lay on its side, button eyes without the flicker of life, legs twisted together like pieces of wire.

Cattivo, Claire heard, a word she mistook to be the Italian word for *cat,* and with her mistake succeeded in understanding the woman's accusation. *Gatto cattivo.* Cat something. Something cat. The parakeet was dead — that's what had made the old woman distraught, a dead bird, nothing more — and our cat, black-masked, velvet-pawed Meena, was the assassin. Or mere onlooker, perhaps, since the door to the birdcage remained closed. Or a medusa, which was the widow's explanation, Claire would understand later from the concierge, Meena having murdered Cerabella with her gaze, simply sitting on the partition and staring had driven the little bird into such a state of inarticulate panic that it had what the concierge called in English "an eruption of the heart."

Nothing more than a parakeet with heart failure on a balcony in Genoa with a view of the rose gardens edging the cimitero di Staglieno and the Ligurian hills beyond. Nothing more than two trunks stolen by a Genoese thief. Nothing more than a few polite conversations with a stranger on an ocean liner. Nothing more than the first two weeks away from home.

OUR FATHER HAD BEEN TRYING TO FIND a suitable job ever since he'd come home from the war. In ten years he'd talked his way into eight different firms — advertising, investment, and real estate — and then somehow managed to talk his way out, leaving behind him a history that his colleagues politely called *mixed*. Finally he decided to open his own consulting firm. His mother loaned him money. But before he'd even rented office space he felt he needed a break from work to consider his options, and he convinced his mother to let him use the money for a trip abroad. He assured her that he would secure a good job upon his return in the fall.

When our grandmother wired the extra money to Murray in Genoa, she warned him that this was it — he'd get no more. But it was enough to let us continue our journey. We left the hotel for the train station on a warm July morning when the clouds were still pink with dawn. We were going to Florence, though in the taxi Murray suggested that we get off the train in Pisa and from Pisa take a bus to Piombino and there catch the ferry to Elba.

"We're going to Florence," Claire said.

"Why not directly to Elba?" repeated Murray.

They argued in the taxi, though Murray knew that Claire would not change her mind. Of course we'd go to Florence, as planned, and Murray would travel alone to Elba to find us a suitable place to stay for the month.

"Wish I didn't have to go alone," Murray murmured.

"The whole point . . ." Claire was in the backseat with me on her lap. She let her voice drift off, leaving the obvious point implied — that Murray had chosen to take us to an island known to the rest of the world only as a place of exile.

When we arrived at the station our train was waiting, the rear cars already packed with passengers. Claire agreed with Murray that if we were going to find seats we'd have to travel first class. Murray, carrying the two new valises, went off to buy tickets. Claire led us toward the front of the train and lifted us one by one up the metal stairs.

The seats of our compartment were upholstered in red leather, the armrests were mahogany, and the perfume of the last passenger still lingered in the air. Harry, always the luckiest among us, found an empty ring-box covered in navy velvet beneath his seat cushion. Patrick offered to trade the rope he'd found in Genoa for the ring-box. Harry declined. Patrick sat on Harry, pinning him down, and tried to pry the box from his fist. Harry screamed. I started to cry. Claire grabbed her umbrella and raised it threateningly. Patrick's terror was fleeting; a moment later he was tugging at the umbrella, wrestling in fun with Claire. No one paid attention to the train whistle. Only when we moved forward with a lurch did it occur to Claire that Murray had been left behind.

"Boys, we have to get off!" But we'd just gotten on, Harry said. Claire gestured as if to wave off his stupidity and rushed to the door at the end of the corridor. By then the train was already moving fast enough to blur the platform, making it appear liquid. As the carriage passed a porter Claire yelled, "Stop this train!" The man cheerfully touched his cap and nodded. Jump, Claire thought to herself in desperation. We must jump. Of course we couldn't jump. It was too late. We were heading to Florence without Murray.

We rode in silence. The train's jerking settled into a smooth forward motion, and Claire sat with her hands crossed over the base of her throat — a position she'd assume in an attempt to ward off panic. The sunlight gave her eyes a milky sheen. She caught the smell of cigarette smoke drifting through from the corridor — Murray's cigarette ... but Murray wasn't there. She jumped to her feet, snapped open her wallet, and poured the contents onto the seat, counting her lire too frantically to keep track. She had begun counting it again when we heard the conductor's sullen "Biglietti, prego," in the corridor. Claire separated coins from bills. She told us to keep quiet, though we weren't making a sound. A moment later the swaying of the train unbalanced Claire, and she tipped toward the door and into the arms of the conductor, who stood with the smirk of understanding on his face, his expression suggesting that he needed no explanation, he knew well enough about le signore like this one, le signore traveling without their husbands. Lonely signore and their clever mistakes.

Claire stumbled away and resumed her frantic search for money to pay our fares. The conductor watched her through the smoke of his cigarette. My brothers and I watched the conductor.

Six carriages back, Murray leaned out a window and watched the landscape, drawing a deep breath in an effort to inhale the scenery — the long single-arch stone bridge, the steep hillside rising above the tracks, a castle's towers in the distance, terraces of vineyards, perfect rows of cypress, a boy walking along a dirt road with a goat on a leash, morning sunlight turning a river gold. He nodded to a conductor and squeezed past with the valises into the next carriage. He opened each compartment door and checked to see if we were inside.

Where were we? If not in this first-class car then in the next one. Murray ambled on — or danced, yes, it felt like he was dancing to the music of the train. He tried to decide whether he wanted a cigarette. He didn't really want a cigarette right then, but he could strike up a conversation by asking someone for a light. How do you ask for a light in Italian? At this point Murray knew only words from a phrase book he'd brought along. *Piacere di conoscerti. Mi vuol passare il sale per favore.*

He looked around. This gentleman in the white linen suit, maybe he'd have time to spare, along with a light. "Pardon me, per favore, signore. . . ."

Of course he had a light. And he spoke a little English. He had a brother who lived in New York. Murray said he was from New York. Davvero? Sì, sì! Murray offered the man a cigarette. The man was from Genoa but was going to Florence to visit his cousin. He wanted to talk. If the signore could wait there, Murray would be right back. He had to find his wife and give her the tickets. *Va bene, va bene* — the man nodded him on. He'd wait there. They could talk about New York. The man had lived for six whole months with his brother in New York!

Murray continued down the corridor, checking the first-class compartments. When he finally located us, Claire had just finished paying the conductor for our tickets. Murray, a few inches taller than the conductor, peaked his head over the man's tasseled shoulder, and said, "There you are!"

"Murray!"

"Where were you?"

"Where were *you?*"

Claire explained that they'd had to purchase five tickets to Florence. But Murray had bought our tickets back at the station. He tried to give them to the conductor; the conductor would only accept a single ticket for Murray. It was too late, apparently, to return Claire's tickets. The five new tickets had been issued. We had eleven tickets for the six of us to travel from Genoa to Florence, at a cost equivalent to a night at the Hôtel Luxembourg, Claire pointed out after the conductor had left.

But she was too relieved to stay angry at Murray. We were together. We were coming from Genoa, heading to Florence, following a zigzagging route to Elba. There was no possibility of retracing our steps. We could only go on, go forward, continue to go away from the past. The speed of the train made our journey feel more than ever like destiny.

MOST OF WHAT I KNOW about my mother's experiences in Italy I know from her directly. We have talked at length. She continues to reminisce. She has shown me photographs and read aloud portions of her journals. Though sometimes she chides herself for her forgetfulness, her memory is far richer than any hazy story I might concoct.

On the other hand, what I know about my father's experiences I've had to piece together from a variety of sources. I've been back to Elba once and plan to go again. I've read history books and newspapers. From my mother and brothers I have a sense of what questions to ask. And thanks to my grandmother, who hoarded everything, I have the letters my father wrote to her from Elba.

As our parents had planned, Murray left us in Florence, in a dark, modest pensione on Via Faenza just around the corner from San Lorenzo, and he went ahead to Elba. In his first letter to his mother, he describes the blue sea cracked with white beneath the blue cloudless sky. He describes the sweet scent of lavender, the linked shale peaks of the mountains, the blue of periwinkles and the red of poppies rippling like scattered bits of silk in the grass. He says the island was even more beautiful than he remembered.

I picture my father standing on a balcony, watching a farmhand named Nino nudge open the door to a shed with his elbow. From another place in the yard came the sound of hammering. A nightingale hidden in an almond tree sang, paused, and sang again. A woman up on a vineyard terrace pushed back her straw hat and called, "Lidia! Lidia!" A small dog yelped in pain, and Murray saw it go skittering across the dirt yard.

Here in a villa on the island of his dreams. Here in the place that after a month-long visit in '44 had filled him with the desire to return. Peasants tying vines, cows chomping on wildflowers, a black dog running across the yard, as weightless as a tumbleweed.

In the distance Murray could see the lopsided orange roofs of the houses in Portoferraio. He considered how little had changed in hundreds of years, how what he saw was close to identical to what Napoleon would have seen during his year of exile. He imagined the little emperor in military garb wandering around the island, plotting his escape. The contradiction amused him: the island of Elba had served as Napoleon's prison, and yet Murray Murdoch had never been as free as he was now.

The summer ahead was like a picture on a screen gradually coming into focus. On Tuesday Murray had lunch with the hotel proprietor, whose friendliness made up for his poor English. Later that afternoon Murray fell into a conversation with a British historian, Francis Cape, when he was browsing in a little stationary shop in Portoferraio. On Wednesday Francis introduced him to Lorenzo Ambrogi, a local padrone, who invited him to stay at his villa. On Thursday Murray borrowed a car and visited Lorenzo's various properties, and by Thursday evening he'd decided upon a house, a sprawling, one-storied house amidst neglected vineyards in the hills midway between Portoferraio and Magazzini. Today was Friday. At one he would have lunch with Lorenzo Ambrogi and negotiate a rent.

Until then, what? Here in a villa on the island of Elba, without his family, with miles of fields and woodland to explore. He would have liked to linger just a little longer at the pocked pinewood table in the kitchen, where Nino's wife, Maddalena, served him a breakfast of hot milk and coffee and panini with fresh butter and honey. But Maddalena, who spoke no English, had chores to do, and she left Murray to finish his breakfast alone.

Afterward, he went for a stroll. He followed a shale path up to the vineyards. He paused at the end of a row and watched two young women tending vines. They glanced at him, turned to each other, and began whispering. If Murray had spoken their language he would have introduced himself. Instead, he left them to their secrets and continued along the path, up and over a verge, and down into a ravine. The broken shale gave way to slippery clay beneath his shoes. The perfume of lilies grew stronger, the vegetation denser as the path leveled. Velvety ferns bordered the path. The sun, still low in the sky, shone through a gap in the ravine's ledge, catching the glint of larkspur and daisies. The rock walls threw back the hollow echo of a trickling spring.

Murray sat on a flat-topped rock beside a pool. He would remember — mistakenly — feeling the tension of expectation, as though he'd been waiting for someone to join him. He listened to the water, the call of a cuckoo, the shush of the wind along the grassy shelves above the ravine. He sat without thinking. He sat for an hour, a day, a week. He had no idea how long he'd been sitting there, how long he'd been listening to the sound of soft humming, how long he'd been watching the girl work. She was pulling handfuls of clover from the flower bed along the opposite rim of the pool. When Murray realized that she didn't know he was watching her he found himself unable to move, as if after immeasurable time he'd grown rubbery roots that stretched around the rock and deep into the soil.

He kept staring at the girl; she must have felt the pressure of his gaze, for she looked up at him abruptly. But she just shook away the startle, shrugged, and went on weeding, as though she didn't mind having an audience. No, she didn't seem to mind at all.

She wasn't beautiful. Her hair was black, with short curls so fine and feathery that he could see the white of her scalp. Murray noticed the line of muscle in her thin arm as she tossed a handful of clover into a basket. She was unnaturally pale, and her cheeks had an oily glow, like marble lit by backwashed sunlight. She wore a simple white blouse and brown skirt, garb that didn't distinguish her from any of the other peasant girls on Elba. Yet there was something different about her, Murray thought, a refinement in her movements, perhaps, or a subtle haughtiness expressed by the tightness of her features. The girl wasn't just too pale, too fragile. Her condition seemed oddly revealing, as if she were sickly because she was selfish or devious or cursed by bad luck. And though she ignored him, she demanded his attention. Murray was certain that she wanted him to keep watching her. She was lonely, and yet — how did he know this? — she was responsible for her lone-liness. She fit the role perfectly. Eve in the garden, leaves floating, falling around her when a gust shook the trees. Just the fact of her presence was a temptation, and yet everything about her warned Murray away.

He stared at her, attempting to settle his impressions into un-ambivalent judgment, telling himself that she was in every aspect a plain peasant girl. He had nearly convinced himself when she stopped humming and spoke.

"You must be Signor Americano." Her voice threw him back into inarticulate confusion. Her English, though clearly a second language, was precise and had a British ring to it. He couldn't bring himself to ask how she knew about him. You don't ask witches and goddesses how they know what they know.

"Yes?" she prompted. Her grin was sly — a response to his con-fusion. He wanted to remind her that she should be careful with strangers. He wanted to pin her to a name but couldn't bring him-self to ask.

She brushed her hands against her skirt. He thought she was preparing to extend a hand in greeting. Instead, she dipped her hands into the water bubbling out of the rocks, and he watched as she drank from the bowl of her palms, his discomfort growing as it slowly occurred to him that her action should have been private.

"Excuse me," he said, pushing himself up. "I must be going." He was amused to hear in his own voice a false accent, an involuntary echo of her refined diction. At the same time he realized he wanted to copy her and cup fresh spring water in his hands. He wanted to linger. He wanted to talk to her.

"Good-bye, Signor Americano."

He hesitated. He didn't want to leave. He must leave. "Arrive-derci." He considered asking her for directions, but on second thought decided this would be silly since there was only one path leading out of the garden, and from the top of the ravine Lorenzo's villa would be in view. He went to tip his hat and then realized that he wasn't wearing a hat. "Piacere di conoscerti."

He left her laughing at him, with him, in sympathy, in ridicule, in spite, in imitation while he walked up the path. He laughed at himself for making this simple encounter into something more meaningful than it should have been. He laughed between puffs of breath as he climbed the steep, slippery slope. He laughed at her laughter. He laughed at his own voice that was returned to him by the rock chamber of the ravine. Echoes of echoes, shadows of shadows. Down in the garden, a girl was laughing. He laughed at himself laughing at her as she laughed at him.

We were in Florence for six days. Murray telephoned every day. He told us that the sea was as warm as a bath, and when he swam out fifty yards from Le Ghiaie he could see through the clear water to the sponges and shells scattered on the sand. He told us about the magnificent gardens and vineyards, the orchards full of sweet yellow peaches, the wild goats grazing on hillsides. He said he'd climbed into the mountains and found quartz, pyrite, and a black glassy crystal that a man at a bar identified as tourmaline. Tourmaline! Tourmaline didn't just come in the blue that he remembered. It came in black, in green and pink and red. The mountains were full of tourmaline. The whole island was a treasure chest for those who knew how to open it!

Murray called to say he'd rented a villa surrounded by vineyards in the hamlet of Le Foci, not far from Portoferraio. The padrone would deliver more beds to accommodate the six of us.

Murray called the next day to say that the beds were in place, and upon the landlord's recommendation he'd hired a cook, an Elban woman from Portoferraio, along with a young woman from the village of Capoliveri to be our nanny. Since when could we afford servants? Claire demanded. Since the padrone had explained to Murray that the fastest way to gain respect on the island was to become an employer. Wages were shockingly low, Murray said, so he'd offered to double them. He hoped Claire didn't mind. The expense was negligible, the advantages immense.

He called to tell us about Francis Cape, the Englishman who was writing a book about Napoleon on Elba. Francis Cape had been helpful in every possible way. He'd even driven Murray to Porto Azzurro, where Murray bought a little motorcyle.

Murray described how the mountains in the early morning mist looked like shadows behind shadows. He said he'd met a Swedish geologist who had done some temporary surveying work for one of the iron mines outside of Rio nell'Elba. The Swede explained to Murray that of all the precious gems to be found on the island, blue tourmaline was the most valuable of all. To find more he should look in the granite outcrops in the mountains. Murray said he was going to buy a rock hammer and chisel and get to work.

Come on, Murray urged. The island was ready for us. Hurry up and come on. Our father would meet us in Portoferraio. He'd take us to play football on the beach.

None of us remembers the uneventful trip from Florence to the port town of Piombino or the ferry ride to Elba. Among my brothers, the first memory of the island belongs to Patrick: he says he remembers waiting while Claire and Murray greeted each other, kissing and embracing as though they'd been apart for months. He remembers staring at the water sloshing against the edge of the quay. He remembers dropping a coin into the water just to hear the sound of the splash and then looking up to face an ancient, gray-bearded man, who scowled and shook a finger at Patrick for wasting good money.

I Fantasmi

ACCORDING TO HIS REPUTATION — SOMEWHAT EMBELLISHED by himself, I came to realize later — our father was a genius at persuasion. He could persuade men to hire him against their better judgment. He could persuade his mother and uncles to lend him money for a vacation they didn't think he deserved. He could persuade his wife to forget the family's debts for a while and enjoy life. And he could persuade his children to spend their time searching an island for treasures left behind by pirates and emperors when we already knew that such treasures didn't exist.

Our father's art of persuasion played upon the contrary temptations of risk and safety. Even as he'd emphasize the thrilling possibilities of an idea, he'd offer assurances and somehow make the paradox seem natural. *Trust me,* his smile would imply. Go ahead, give it a try, and trust Murray Murdoch to manage the dangers.

While my brothers and I only pretended to believe our father when he told us that the island's treasure would be found by those who knew how to look, we sensed that the proposition would make a diverting game. During our first days on Elba, we each searched in different ways, following our different inclinations, escaping from the watch of our new cook and nanny whenever possible.

Patrick looked for treasure by drawing detailed maps of the land around our villa. From an early age he'd understood that learning came more easily to him than to others — an ability that was as much a handicap as an advantage, since it threatened to set him apart from the rest of us. But he couldn't help it — he was our expert. He almost always knew more than we did, and when he didn't, he'd know how to find out.

Harry looked for treasure as if he were hunting for small animals. He'd move stealthily through the vineyards, sift through broken pottery, pick quartz from the gravel drive. He knew how to find whatever had been lost. He was our detective.

Nat, the bravest among us, looked for treasure by roaming. Treasure can't be easy to find, he'd insist. It wasn't enough to draw maps or collect broken rocks. We'd have to go far from home, up into the island's highest mountains. Every day Nat convinced us to go a little farther. Sometimes we went so far — across roads and meadows, through vines and abandoned olive groves — and became so engrossed in the search that we'd lose our direction. But then Patrick would climb up into a tree or to the top of a boulder and orient himself with landmarks — there was the port in one direction, the peak of Volterraio to the west, and there below him, right down there, the villa we already called home.

And since I was the most helpless and least visionary, I looked for treasure by doing whatever my brothers told me to do. Ollie, get me a shovel! Ollie, go find Harry and bring him here! Ollie, hold this, watch that, do it for me now!

We were eager, inexaustible, confident that even if we didn't find treasure we'd manage to prove the worthiness of our efforts. We were sure that there was no place more promising than the island of Elba, no time more appealing than the moment at hand, no adventure more exciting. Not once did we ask to go back to America.

It's as though we've stepped out of time, our mother would say in a dreamy soft-pitched voice. How easily the modern world disappears. She'd close her eyes and listen to the sounds carried like bits of debris by the wind — a ship's horn, the crowing of roosters and chittering of hens, the gabble of servants, the dry rustle of palm fronds, the humming of bees in the oleander. She'd open her eyes and see the scarlet bougainvillea spilling over the terrace wall, the roses filling each frame of the trellis. Inside the villa the marble floors were deliciously cold beneath bare toes. Claire would sink into a chair and stretch her feet out over the floor and ask in a voice rich with irony and pleasure: "What are we doing here? Who gave us the right?"

Murray would say we'd earned the right. Claire would shrug. They'd sip their wine, and when their eyes met they'd laugh a little, as though they were sharing a joke.

After the first quiet week, Claire was ready to spend the second week in the same fashion. She didn't need other company; though, predictably, Murray did. He needed the few hours of distraction that visitors provided, along with an excuse to mix up a pitcher of martinis, so on Saturday afternoon he rode his Lambretta into Portoferraio, where he found Francis Cape watering the geraniums on the stoop of his building, and he invited him to come out to Le Foci for supper.

Of course Francis Cape would come for supper. He would always come to supper, when asked, and he would arrive a respectable ten minutes early.

"He's here!"

"Who's here?" Claire had heard the car coming up the gravel drive but had assumed it was someone coming to visit Lidia or Francesca.

"Francis Cape, the Englishman!"

"What Englishman?"

"Francis Cape. He's the one I told you about. Francis Cape. He's here."

"You didn't tell me you invited him over."

"Didn't I? I thought I did. I meant to tell you. Well, he's come for a visit. You don't mind, do you? He's the one who put me in touch with Lorenzo. Francis lives in Portoferraio, you see. He's lived there for nearly ten years."

It was that soft hour of Elban dusk when everything solid hovered on the edge of transparency. My brothers and I had already eaten our supper and were in a bedroom sorting through the day's booty of rocks. Lidia, the cook, was clattering dishes in the kitchen while she rebuked Francesca for some new fault. Murray's voice trailed behind him as he stepped outside to greet Francis. Claire felt an odd, unsettling presentiment, probably because she'd been so content to have nothing to do and no one new to meet.

Francis Cape the Englishman was here for a visit. Claire heard his voice first out in the courtyard, a barking, confident voice, then Murray's, and then a third voice — the subdued voice of a woman, audible just for a moment before disappearing beneath the clamor of Murray's exuberance.

"Come in, please, come right in, let me introduce you to my wife. Claire, this is Miss Noddi, Adriana Noddi —"

"Nardi," she corrected. Narrrdi. Adriana Narrrdi. She was a young woman of about twenty, with milky skin and black hair clenched in wispy curls. There was something in her smile that struck Claire immediately as deceptive, tinged with private trouble, though when Claire extended her hand Adriana shook it with a confident, delicate firmness.

"Narrrrrrrdi," Murray echoed. "Adriana Narrrrrrrrrrdi, the family who owns the land adjacent to Lorenzo's property, if I'm not mistaken. . . ."

"That's right."

"Signorina, it's a pleasure to welcome you to our house, though you'll have to forgive me for speaking in English. I'm an idiot when it comes to languages. . . . Not like Francis, eh Francis? Francis, I almost forgot! Let me introduce you to Claire, my wife. Claire, this is Francis. He's the one I was telling you about, the historian. He knows more about this island than most people know about themselves, though you could say the comparison necessarily favors Francis, eh Francis? Please, let's sit down, relax, make yourselves at home while I get the drinks."

Adriana Nardi sat gingerly on the edge of her chair, pressed her knees together beneath the cloth of her dress — a plain, V-necked solid navy cotton dress. She played with the braided fringe of her white shawl as she listened to Francis Cape, who launched into an account of the Nardi family — one of the oldest and most notable families on the island, with ancestors who had dined with Napoleon and at one point had owned all of Monte Calamita.

Murray brought out the pitcher, stirring it with a wooden spoon as he explained that he'd picked up the Bombay gin for a song in Genoa. Had Adriana ever been to Genoa? As she nodded Murray rattled, "Of course you've been to Genoa. Genova, rather. Narrrrdi. More proof that I'm inept with languages. There's not a foreign name I don't mangle."

Murray poured four cocktails, but Claire noticed that the girl didn't drink hers after the first difficult sip. Nor did she speak much through the evening. Nor did anyone explain what she was doing there. Was she Francis's mistress? Was Francis taking care of her for some reason? Francis Cape spoke more about the Nardis, moving into a general account of the island's history. Murray joined in to talk about the Second World War and to explain how he'd come to Elba in the summer of 1944 and stayed for a month. "Do you remember the Americans, Miss Nardi? You would have been a child then. The Elban children used to watch us when we played football on the beach. A blissful month we spent in the middle of an ugly war, playing football on the beach at Le Ghiaie."

No, Adriana hadn't watched the Americans playing football, but yes, she remembered the war. Her school had been destroyed when the Germans bombed Portoferraio — a fact she stated with a simplicity that evoked a long, awkward minute of silence.

Francis finally broke the silence with a comment about the island's importance in history as a strategic location, "an island easily ignored until there's a conflict, and then everyone wants to claim Elba as his own. This has been true since the Etruscans began mining Elban ore. Isn't this true, Adriana?"

What is true, Adriana? Claire wondered to herself.

"It is true," she said demurely.

"You speak wonderful English," Murray said with an admiration Claire considered excessive, given how little the girl had spoken. "Your English is better than mine," he continued. "You could teach *me* some English. Maybe some Italian, too. That's if it's possible for an old dog to learn new tricks! I doubt it. What do you think, Claire? Is there any hope for me?"

Claire didn't bother answering, because right then Lidia came to the doorway, her presence announcing that supper was ready and the table set for four, though no one had warned her there would be visitors. Claire took Francis's arm and led the way into the dining room. Murray escorted Adriana with his characteristic gentility, which only ever seemed comical, an effect increased when Murray stepped on one of Harry's toy race cars and his leg swooped forward. He would have fallen if Adriana hadn't caught him and held him upright.

Much later, Claire would mark this evening as the beginning of the end of her idyll, for it had unsettled her, though why and how she couldn't explain, and could only blame herself for craving a tranquillity that excluded others. She didn't dislike the girl, but she found her enigmatic and couldn't entirely believe what she was told by Murray, who repeated what Francis had told him after supper: that apparently Adriana was assisting Francis in his research on island history in exchange for instruction in English.

They were a strange pair indeed. Still, when the visitors were preparing to leave, Claire readily invited them to return — and not just for Murray's sake. She had a sense that she had more to learn from the Englishman and his young friend. The more she knew, the more at home she'd feel. Not that Claire had any intention of settling on Elba. But over the course of the evening, listening to all the talk about the island, she'd become aware of what she'd started to desire in the week already past. She wanted to live on the island as though she belonged, to experience it as if she had no country of her own.

My brothers and I didn't have to waste our time getting used to our grand island empire because, from our point of view, we had earned the right to stay. After our long journey across the Atlantic, we believed that anything we found we could claim as ours and anyone we met was someone we might as well have already known.

After the first week we could gesture emphatically enough to promise Francesca that we wouldn't leave the property, meaning we'd go no further than the dry streambed separating our land from the neighboring farm on one side and the driveway on the other. As soon as Francesca turned her back, we'd take off. We'd cross the sandy ditch and head up into the terraced vineyards and from there into the hills.

On the edge of one field we saw a farmer sleeping in the shade of a cork tree every afternoon. Through the loops in a fence of chicken wire we'd watch an old woman milking a goat in a dirt yard and an old man weaving a basket shaped like a top hat. Every day we waved a greeting to the milkman when he rattled past us in his truck, and he'd honk his horn four times — a honk for each of us. High up on a rocky trail above the villa we'd shout just to hear our echoes. Down at the marshy shore below San Giovanni, Patrick and Harry would jump off the iron skeleton of a dock that had been left unfinished, and Nat and I, who couldn't swim, would throw sticks for dogs whose names we didn't know. The sun turned our freckles black. Salt streaked our brown hair white. Whenever Elbans spoke to us we would nod. Whenever they laughed we would laugh.

About midway through the month the words we'd heard as nonsense began to take on meaning, thanks in large part to the two women who worked for our family. Francesca had a bedroom in the south wing of our villa. At the end of July, Lidia, who'd been living in a house she shared with relatives in Portoferraio, moved into one of the outbuildings — an old chapel that was equipped with a wood-burning stove. She made it clear to our parents that they must surrender all decision. And she made it clear to us that if we wanted to be understood, we had to use her language, not ours.

Lidia, fat Lidia in her voluminous pleated skirts, treated us with the same wariness she demonstrated at the market when she prodded squids in a bucket. She'd poke our bellies after every meal, or she'd make a bracelet of her thumb and forefinger around our arms to measure the size of our muscles. She cared only that we were getting bigger. Children must eat in order to grow, and they — we — never ate enough to please Lidia. She didn't urge us with the typical *mangia, ancora* we'd heard at trattorias in Florence. Rather, she'd stand over us while we ate our meals at the kitchen table, her folded arms resting on the mound of her own belly, daring us to see what happened if we didn't eat every last noodle.

Francesca, our nanny, was far more forgiving than Lidia, more easily delighted by our jokes, and less attentive. It was easy to escape her watch, especially on days when her fiancé, Filiberto, rode over on his scooter from Capoliveri to help with chores.

We didn't need Francesca to watch us, and we could have done without Lidia's fish soup. We were hearty scavengers, as brave as the pirates whose trail we were following. We needed no more than a bit of stale bread and some water to shore up our strength, though a few pieces of milk chocolate didn't hurt, along with a handful of the jelly beans our aunt had sent from America.

Day by day, we learned everything about the sunbaked land that we needed to know in order to find Elba's secret treasure. None of us noticed that somehow, at some point, or gradually over the course of the month, we'd forgotten that the treasure didn't exist.

YOU SHOULD ACKNOWLEDGE the truth of privilege, Oliver. Privilege more than language set us apart from the Elbans. Even though we remained dependent upon Murray's family for money, we were lucky to be able to do as we pleased. We could travel first class on a luxury liner. We could spend an entire summer doing nothing. We could let our children throw money into the sea.

I'll remind you not to forget the privilege of being able to sit with a book. You mention *The Marble Faun* early on and then forget about it. But in those first weeks in Italy I saw the country through the eyes of Hawthorne's Miriam and imagined bearing her burden of secret knowledge, every sight tinged with the memory of a secret crime. I imagined what it would be like to see in the red cast of sunset the red of blood. Donatello's *Amore* made me think of Hawthorne's Donatello. I'd hear Hawthorne in my head as I wandered with you boys around Florence. I'd remember Hawthorne's observations: twilight comes more speedily in Italy than in other countries, the owls hoot more softly, and convent bells ring in a chain from end to end of the priest-ridden country.

And it wasn't just Hawthorne keeping me company. I'd brought along *The Magic Mountain,* at my sister's suggestion, along with *Anna Karenina* — long books useful for long trips, Jill said. I read *Anna Karenina* first. I was reading it during those days in Florence after Murray had gone on to Elba. Not that Tolstoy's novel had light to shed on my circumstances. But I think it's useful to note that at any particular point in our lives our minds are full not just of our own memories but of the experiences of characters from the books we've been reading. That's if we are lucky to have the education and leisure to read at all. And the curiosity. I've always had plenty of curiosity. Too much, perhaps. I have friends who make a habit of telling me I should mind my own business. These are the same people who tell me I shouldn't take my morning swims — not at my age, and not alone.

But I'm wandering. What was I saying? There's lots to tell you, Ollie. The way memory returns with a gentle nudge. You know how it is. Remembering twilight in Florence, Hawthorne's owls, Tolstoy's Anna. Do you need to hear all this? It's hard to know what to tell you.

I am trying to be candid. You shouldn't have to wonder if there's something I'm not telling you, though you'll understand that I must sift through many old memories, some of them vague, some of them irrelevant. Maybe *Anna Karenina* is irrelevant. Also, an awful night I endured back in Genoa, sickened from eating clams. You don't need to know about that.

I suppose I should tell you more about Adriana Nardi, the girl who came with Francis Cape to supper. She was, as I told you the other night on the phone, the same girl your father saw in the garden, though I didn't learn this until much later. When he saw her again so unexpectedly in our courtyard he didn't immediately recognize her, and by the time he did he was already welcoming her as though they'd never met. But I presume she recognized him. She'd recognized him when she'd first seen him sitting on a rock. Signor Americano. The Elbans were already talking about Signor Americano and his *famiglia*, their curiosity about us mixed from the start, I have to say, with some distrust.

We learned Adriana's history from Francis Cape. Adriana's ancestor Renato Nardi had been advisor to the ruler of Elba, Antonio something or other, in the 1790s. Antonio was duke when Napoleon's troops landed in — when was it? Around 1800, I think. French rule deprived Antonio of his territory, and he went to live in Rome, where he died a few years later. Renato Nardi stayed in Elba, and after Antonio's death he led the local resistance in Portoferraio. The garrison held out with support from the British navy. When

France and England signed a truce, Renato Nardi was acclaimed by Elbans as a great hero. And among his rewards bequeathed by Antonio was iron-rich land on Monte Calamita.

Not long after the siege of Portoferraio, Renato was one of the patrons who welcomed Napoleon back as king. It wasn't that he disliked the French any less, but he was hopeful that Napoleon's presence would have great material benefits for the island. And it did: for one year all of Portoferraio became a huge barrack filled with troops and gendarmes, courtiers, servants, adventurers. Napoleon made the Elbans feel like they were at the center of the world, and Renato Nardi, who became a confidant of Napoleon, was at the center of the center.

What does all this have to do with Adriana? Over the years, most of the Nardi family left the island and dispersed. By the mid-1950s, only Adriana and her mother remained on Elba. And they were the ones to inherit the archive — boxes of documents, contracts, elaborate land surveys of the island dating back to the seventeenth century, along with letters from Napoleon, one hundred years' worth of ledgers, drawings, a musical program with Renato's doodlings on the back, and a coffee cup, coarsely glazed — I've seen it myself — with bees painted on a white medallion and *NB* inscribed on the bottom.

It was because of the Nardi archives that Francis Cape became involved with Adriana. Francis, who was writing a book about Napoleon's escape from Elba, had met Adriana when she was a young girl. She would keep him company in the library while he pored through old letters and contracts, and he took the time to help her improve her English. Later, he would describe her to us as *intriguing.*

She arrived in our lives with a significant past, she was one of the very few Elbans who spoke English, and she was lonely. She was Signora Nardi's adopted daughter and her only child. Her birth mother was a Corsican girl who'd fled to Elba in disgrace, left her newborn baby outside the hospital in Portoferraio, and disappeared. We learned later that her father was said to have been a foreign sailor — a mercenary, according to the gossip, or a pirate.

At the age of eighteen, Adriana enrolled at the university in Bologna. She studied English, and after two years was encouraged by her professors to apply for a fellowship at St. Hilda's in Oxford. Her application was accepted. She would have gone to England the following fall, but for some reason no one understood, she began losing interest in her studies and didn't bother to take her exams at the end of the year. She returned to Elba, shadowed by the inevitable rumors about an unhappy romance.

So there you have it — a short history of Adriana Nardi up to the point when she entered our lives. It's hard to describe the effect she had upon people because it never seemed to be the same effect twice. Sometimes I felt she was made up of different people. Other times I thought of her as an empty shell, without a soul or self, like one of those conchs that washes up on the beach and Emily Hunter holds against her ear, mistaking the whooshing vibrations of her own circulating blood for the sound of the ocean.

We had Francis Cape to thank for Adriana's presence at our dinners. Francis Cape was a close friend of the Nardis and took it upon himself to introduce the girl to any English speakers he could find.

I remember one dinner in particular at a restaurant in Porto Azzurro. Francis, as usual, was entertaining us all with stories about the Turks and pirates, and then, in response to a question from Murray, describing at great length the screes of Elba and their yield of crystal and tourmalines, rose-colored beryls, red and gray and honey-colored granite. Francis himself had purchased a serpentine pedestal from a store in Portoferraio — he'd picked it up for almost nothing, he said, because the figure of the saint which it must have once supported was missing. He dated it from the seventeenth century and could tell from the quality of the stone that it came from one of the local quarries. He invited us to visit his home the next day to see it. Which we did, and found the poor man living in a filthy hovel in the shadow of Fort Stella.

But that's another story. I was telling you about the dinner at the restaurant in Porto Azzurro: with Francis Cape holding forth, I stole glances at Adriana. She struck me as frail in appearance and yet rigid in her manner. And she hardly touched the food on her plate, I noticed. Afterward, I found myself thinking more about her, and the more I thought, the more elusive she became in my mind. I asked Murray about his impressions because I needed confirmation that my apprehension was justified. I felt as if I'd met a ghost, or, more realistically, a clever actress who was used to pretending.

Murray felt nothing of the sort. He thought she was shy, or no worse than reserved. He enjoyed her company and worked hard to make her feel at ease whenever she was our guest, which turned out to be a frequent occurrence, since we spent so much time in those early weeks with Francis Cape, and Francis liked to bring Adriana along. Though the girl's ostensible goal was to practice her English, often in the quiet hour after pranzo Murray would encourage her to speak with Francis in Italian, and he would sit across from them with his eyes closed, happily listening without understanding a word.

My job during siesta was to keep you boys quiet and out of the hot afternoon sun. It was the only time of day when Lidia and Francesca did not expect me to be idle. They would retreat to their rooms, and I would read to you, or we'd work on puzzles or play cards before I'd turn you loose. I'd forget that I could hear the soft music of conversation out on the terrace.

For the rest of the day, Lidia was in charge of our household. She spoke a few decisive words of English and made it clear that she approved of me only when I didn't interfere with her work. Do you remember how she smelled of the fresh anchovies she'd cook almost daily? And Francesca smelled of lavender, like the island itself. Lavender grew everywhere — bordering the paths, sprinkled through the hills and in the village gardens. And aloe — you could take a deep breath and pull the silky taste of aloe down your throat. And rosemary, of course, and mint and honeysuckle.

And do you remember the winds? The powerful scirocco that caught the sunlight and shattered it into a glassy, spiraling mist. The damp grecale that followed a rainstorm. The harsh winter maestrale that brought two months of rain. Always the wind scraping against the side of your face. Always the sound of it. Moaning through cracks in the shutters, swishing over the vineyards, rattling the fronds of palm trees.

And the blue glimmer of the sea all around, as if the hills of Elba had been heaped upon a plate. And fresh fish to eat every day, sole and tuna, squid and shrimp. There was the time we came upon fishermen cutting up a manta that must have weighed a few hundred pounds. And one evening after supper in Portoferraio we saw a thirty-foot-long giant squid stretched out on a dock for display. And once Nino brought over a tiny monster, a viper fish, with its huge, ugly mouth held open with toothpicks.

I remember one beautiful evening, drinking martinis on the terrace. Francis Cape was describing in his usual vivid detail how the German and Italian submarines would cut their engines and use the inflow from the Atlantic to drift past the British blockades at Gibraltar. Once in a while they made it; usually they didn't. I remember thinking sadly that the engineer from Ohio would have enjoyed trading stories with Francis Cape.

But I couldn't stay sad for long. The wind would rise and whisk the past away. The sun turned Murray the color of half-polished bronze. My hair was so tangled I wouldn't bother to brush it for days at a time.

You see how happy I was? Go ahead and use the word *magic* to describe those first weeks. You remember wandering with your brothers in the hills. Have you forgotten that almost every morning Francesca would take you boys to a quiet cove where the clear water was as still as glass? Sometimes I'd tag along. You, Ollie, would stare in a trance into tidal pools, watching the tiny mouths of barnacles opening and closing — you thought they were the eyes of the rocks! The other boys would walk in bare feet across the slippery kelp. Harry always found something — a cork, sea glass, a pink anemone latched onto the back of a crab. Nat would inevitably wander off, and Francesca would go climbing across the rocks in search of him.

Midway through the summer, your father and I began talking about extending our vacation beyond August. The dollar was strong against the lira, and even with Lidia and Francesca as full-time help we lived cheaply. Our rent for a month was roughly the cost of dinner out for our family at a New York restaurant. For next to nothing, we could remain on Elba until Christmas. Harry and Patrick could go to school in Portoferraio. We could fish and swim and climb into the mountains to hunt for precious stones. Maybe we'd get lucky and find a big chunk of blue tourmaline. Who knows? Maybe tourmaline would make our fortune.

In the evenings Lidia would make a big bowl of soup or pasta, and we'd eat too much and sit with guests and watch the sun go down behind the mountains. Our circle of friends grew wider. Adriana introduced us to Mario Ginori and his wife, a wealthy local couple. Francis introduced us to Joshua Meredith, from Shropshire, who was doing research for a travel guide.

During those early weeks life kept me too occupied to anticipate any change. This has more to do with the proximity of the sea than with our routines, for the endless expanse of water makes one feel that nothing short of death is important, and nothing important can happen without nature's consent.

Nothing without natural propulsion. It's comforting to believe that our lives follow the patterns of nature. But it's a small comfort when we're faced with the violent outcome of human action.

OUR MOTHER READ THE BOOKS she'd brought from America, wrote letters to friends and family, and occasionally accompanied us to the beach, where she sat on a blanket looking like some sort of foreign luminary, a visiting duchess from the distant North.

Once in a while our father would come along for a swim, but more often he'd wander off on his Lambretta and spend the morning tapping away at boulders with his hammer and chisel, separating feldspar from granite, granite from quartz. Sometimes he'd bring home wishing stones — dusty, egg-shaped rocks belted by a full circle of quartz — but nothing more, nothing of real value.

The dust was rust-colored, black, brown, gray. Our father would return capped and coated with dust. Dust would envelope Francis Cape's car whenever he bumped along in his Fiat up our drive. Dust would hide Adriana Nardi from view until she opened the door and stepped away from the car. If she ever smiled a greeting at my brothers and me when she entered the house, we were too busy to notice.

July melted into the heat of August. August brought us closer to September. We didn't bother to ask when we would be leaving, and my older brothers didn't protest when our parents announced that they would be going to the local school.

We overheard our father describing to our mother what he'd seen in his expeditions. We listened carefully when he turned the subject to treasure. The land, he said, was the island's greatest treasure. The rich stock of Elban land. Land strewn with sparkling minerals, land rising in peaks and sloping down to the blue disk of the sea. Here on paradise, the value of land was rapidly increasing as the island's future as a tourist haven became more certain. While

Murray spoke, he let a match he'd used to light his cigarette burn far down its stem. The shock of heat against his fingertips roused him and he shook out the flame abruptly. We watched him relax into his cigarette as he continued. Claire watched him. An investor could take advantage of the trend, Murray said. He could invest in property. Developers were already scouting, and local farmers were ready to sell. If an investor were clever, he could be a middleman. He'd find the land that others wanted, stake his claim, bide his time, and eventually sell his property at enough profit to make the effort worthwhile.

Murray wandered the island on foot and motorcycle. He circled it by boat. He studied maps and topography charts. He even tried to make sense of the laws relating to property and taxes, but he found them as impenetrable as the rules relating to Italian grammar. He decided that there were some things he didn't have to know.

In order to calculate the value of land, he needed to know more about the island. Francis Cape brought him to the Nardis' villa, La Chiatta, to see the family's extensive archive.

The front drive cutting between Lorenzo's property and the Nardi olive groves was lined with oleander bushes, their blooms brown and faded from the heat. The villa itself was a tired orange stucco, with a high stone wall around the courtyard that blocked the view of the sea, though the shore must have been close — Murray heard the water slapping against rocks when he stepped from Francis's car.

Signora Nardi, Adriana's mother, met them at the door. She spoke English stiffly, self-consciously. She was a small, gray-haired woman with steely eyes that absorbed everything in a cold, consuming glance. Francis Cape had warned Murray about her, describing the woman as aloof. Murray had the immediate impression that she disapproved of him. Before he opened his mouth to speak, Signora Nardi already disliked him.

She said that her daughter had told her all about the American couple and their lively bambini. She hoped Murray would bring his family along for a visit one day. Murray promised to do so and added that he hoped Signora Nardi would come join them at their house for a meal.

The stiff way she smiled in response suggested reluctance. She motioned to Francis to lead the way inside. Murray followed Francis. Adriana met them in the library, at which point Signora Nardi left, having indicated that Signor Murdoch could examine anything in the collection relevant to his studies.

Studies, she'd said, as though he'd been presented to her as another scholar joining Francis Cape in his search of history. He wanted to laugh at the idea. He wasn't even sure what he was looking for.

Adriana showed him whatever she thought might interest him. Signor Americano wanted to know more about the island. Look at this — a cup made by a nineteenth-century Elban artisan for Napoleon. And this — a mine survey of Monte Calamita dating from the seventeenth century. You want to know about our island, Signor Americano? Here is a ledger from the Palazzina dei Mulini tracking the emperor's expenses.

While Francis Cape watched with a possessive pride, Adriana showed Murray brittle yellow documents signed by Napoleon, music programs from the early 1800s, and old maps of the whole Tuscan archipelago.

What else could Adriana show Murray? Could he come visit her again? Of course he could. What could she tell him about the island and its history? This beautiful, mysterious island. Would Adriana tell him that story again, the one about Napoleon laughing so hard he fell out of his chair?

Murray returned on his own to La Chiatta a few days later,

drawn there because the girl had made him feel welcome, though when he arrived he found the shutters closed against daylight and the courtyard eerily empty. He expected to meet Adriana's mother again, but it was Adriana who answered the door. It was Adriana who served tea brewed from wild mint and let him drink from Napoleon's cup. Murray watched her watching him from her chair across the marble-top table, her chin propped in her hands. Her eyes were a dull brown, the whites faintly bloodshot. Her fingernails had a yellowish tinge to them. Only the moist natural red of her lips suggested any vitality.

Adriana spoke briefly, concisely, about the first visit of Cosimo III to Elba in 1700, how he arrived at three in the morning and was carried by two slaves in a velvet-cushioned chair all the way up to the Stella. She told him a little about the Austrian blockade in 1708 and the civil war that ensued. They discussed the French Revolution and even got into a mild, fleeting argument about a statement by de Tocqueville:

"The King's subjects felt toward him both the natural love of children for their father and the awe properly due to God alone."

Murray accepted every word of de Tocqueville. Adriana declared Murray a fool. Murray scoffed at Adriana's arrogance. Adriana laughed at him, and then without warning she leaned across the table and with her thumb rubbed from his cheek what he assumed was a smudge of dirt or ink, her gesture more in the manner of a sister or daughter than a lover, but still it was enough to unnerve Murray. Before he could speak she'd left to refill the teapot in the kitchen.

After that they spoke in softer tones, laughed nervously to fill an awkward silence, looked away when their eyes accidentally met. He asked if he might return, and she just smiled in reply. He did return — a third and then a fourth time. They grew more formal in their exchanges and rarely let opinions clash. When Murray visited La Chiatta he tried to come prepared with specific tasks. He asked for Adriana's help in translating a newspaper article. He asked for her advice about the land. She told him he should spend his money on a boat.

He found himself watching the girl when he thought she wouldn't notice him, not because of any inappropriate desire but because she puzzled him. The deliberateness of her movements and the scripted quality of her voice provoked in him an imitative poise. He wondered if Adriana were suffering from some chronic illness, but she never mentioned it and Murray never asked. He studied her for signs either of deterioration or improvement. He told himself that his interest in her was as harmless and inevitable as his interest in all things exotic.

Though it remained hot through September, the quicker turn of dusk into night foretold the seasonal changes ahead. Our parents talked about staying on Elba long enough to experience the island in the guise of winter. They negotiated with Lorenzo a three-month extension of the Le Foci lease. Patrick and Harry dutifully went off each day to the elementary school in Portoferraio, and we spent our free hours scouring the sunbaked land for treasures. No one asked us to explain why we weren't going back to America.

Every morning Murray rose early and planned how he would fill each empty hour. At the end of the day he'd feel as though he'd passed the time in a stupor. Sometimes it seemed to him that all the islanders were plotting against him, luring him into a trap with their insinuative talk about the future. He kept asking Francis Cape for assurance.

One morning in October he lay awake in bed trying to remember a conversation from the previous day. They'd all had supper together — he and Claire, Francis and Adriana. He'd been listening to Adriana and Francis speaking in Italian. Somehow Murray had intuited that the girl was saying something he deserved to know, but he hadn't been able to bring himself to interrupt and ask for a translation.

Now, the morning after, he couldn't stand not knowing what he'd missed. He climbed out of bed, leaving Claire sleeping, and rode his motorcycle along the deserted road to La Chiatta. Only when he'd turned off the engine and paused to listen to the sea lapping behind the courtyard wall did he consider how early it was and how ridiculous he'd appear if he knocked at the door.

He snuck away as quietly as he could, though as he crossed the courtyard he had the prickling sensation that someone was watching him from an upstairs window. He resisted turning around to check. He pushed his motorcycle back up the long dirt drive. Doves cooed, hidden in the palms. Olive leaves rustled in the morning breeze. A silver moth fluttered around his head, bumping against his cheek as though to wake him.

The first moth in our Le Foci house was found by Nat floating in his cup of milk, its silver wings shaded gray by contrast. He picked it up by its soggy wingtip and laid it carefully on the table, then called the rest of us to come look. Lidia wasted only a quick glance and commanded Nat to finish his milk, which he did with gusto while the rest of us watched in admiration.

I found the second moth flitting above me when I awoke from my afternoon nap. I knew many Italian words by then, and one happened to be the word for *butterfly*. I announced its presence with a shriek of joy — "Farfalla, farfalla!" — causing both Francesca and Claire to rush to my bedside. They laughed when they understood what had excited me. Francesca threw open the shutters and the moth zigged and zagged across the room and drifted out the window.

Francesca, who was given every Wednesday afternoon off to visit her family in Capoliveri, had been about to leave to catch the bus, and now she tied a blue silk scarf around her head and excused herself. Claire picked up and folded my pajamas. I stared at the rectangles of blue sky and watched without a word as three silver moths flew into the room.

Three dancing moths. Before our eyes they became six, eight, a dozen and more. They were a mist of gauzy wings, a cloud filling the room, spreading down the hall like fog through a seaside village. It seemed as though a single moth had only to unfold its wings and release a haze of offspring. There were hundreds of moths, thousands, their silver, pink-lined forewings identical to hindwings, brown furry bodies the size of plum-pits, needle tips for eyes. Claire fanned them away from me with her hand. In such numbers their fluttering should have been thunderous — instead, they were eerily silent. But a moment later the silence was broken when the moths filled the bedroom where my brothers had been playing. They yelped with delight. The enemy force was attacking, quick, radio headquarters, call the troops, load, fire! Nat threw plastic soldiers at the moths, Harry trapped them in his cupped hands, Patrick batted at them with a rolled magazine. The enemy advanced. The allies were outnumbered, but still they held their ground. Duck, jump, run, stop, turn!

"Get out of the house!" It was Claire's order, but this time the urgency my brothers heard in her voice struck them as ridiculous, and they continued their war. Claire held me with one arm and managed to grab Nat and Harry by their wrists, and she pulled us to the door. Patrick kicked the floor as he followed, furious to have the best game ever interrupted.

Inside the house Lidia threw open shutters and closed closet doors. She found an old set of bellows and set about puffing clouds of moths from one room to another. Though she'd never seen quite so many moths at once, she remained grimly calm. The moths came every autumn to feast upon blankets and sweaters. I fantasmi — the ghost moths. They were arriving in multitudes this year. In some later year, they would come in even greater numbers. That was the way life worked in Lidia's scheme. The moths were proof that the future would outshine the past. Next year's storms would be the worst storms ever. Or they'd be the mildest. If the next summer wasn't the warmest, then the following summer would be. Or the one after. Every record set would be broken. Every war fought would be worse than the last. *Bella, horrida bella.* There were no surprises under heaven.

The season of the ghost moths. We loved them, loved to lose ourselves in the thick of their wings and feel the feathery wisps of their touch. We loved to hear them thumping against window-panes and watch their shadows moving like the reflections of rain-drops on our bedroom walls. Meena loved to comb her claws through their midsts or hop up and catch one with a gulp, swallowing it whole. Our parents hated them. They bought little metal fans for each room and set the switches on high to drive away the moths. But the fans only seemed to draw more moths. They'd fight their way toward the center of the air current like fish struggling upriver and then turn on their wings and flit off, as though it were nothing more than a game to them. The best game ever.

No one noticed them leaving. We just woke up one morning in late October, wondered for an instant what had changed, and realized then that the shadows on the walls were gone. Lidia said something we didn't understand about the sea. Francesca said that the little farfalle had turned into cherubini.

We would have been disappointed — rather, we were disappointed for a few hours, until Harry found the spider in the tub. It was black with white dots on its carapace and white chevrons on its abdomen, and it was about the size of Patrick's thumbnail. Harry trapped it in a cup topped with paper and brought it into the kitchen for the rest of us to see. We gathered round, marveling as Harry dumped the spider into a deep crease in the paper. He asked for a toothpick. Patrick brought him a spoon. Harry flipped the spider over, and we were astonished to see it somehow manage to flip back and right itself. Harry touched it with the spoon again. The spider leapt into the air and landed on the table, and it would have escaped if Nat hadn't crushed it with a rolling pin.

Harry pushed Nat in retaliation, pushed him right against the rickety table. The tabletop knocked against the shelf in a wooden cupboard. On the shelf the delicate glass flue of a lantern swayed drunkenly and then fell forward, shattering on the tile floor.

"Che è successo!" We heard Lidia's voice before we saw her. My brothers fled. I was frozen by confusion. Lidia swooped down, spanked me once, and scooped me into her arms, holding me over her shoulder as she marched down the hall to tell Claire what trouble I had caused.

I suffered my resentment in my room, alone, for the next ten minutes or so, until I heard my brothers whispering in the hall and went to find out what important thing deserved secrecy. Patrick was holding a milk bottle; Harry was securing a piece of paper with a rubber band to serve as a lid. "Shut up," Nat said when he saw me. I circled, preparing to kick him, but my attention was soon absorbed by the spectacle in the bottle — not just one striped spider but a whole clutch of them leaping toward the stick, bouncing against the glass and tumbling down upon one another.

My brothers had gathered the spiders from windowsills on the outside of the house. But they were all over the inside of the house as well. Now that we knew what to look for, we saw them everywhere — crawling on bookshelves, up flowerpots, across the tiles and planks of the floors, up walls, along ceilings. When we understood how plentiful they were, we began yelling with delight. Claire joined us on our hunt without understanding what, exactly, we were hunting for. When Harry showed her the mass of spiders underneath the living-room sofa, she herded us all out of the house again, and this time she wouldn't let us go back inside.

These were the zebra spiders — minute spiders that could leap from the floor to a tabletop and were as wily a prey as minnows. They weren't as beautiful as the ghost moths, but they were more interesting to us. To Claire, they were a new and worse kind of pest, somehow expressive of a mute hostility. If the house had an animate spirit, this spirit had taken a strong dislike to us, and with the moths and spiders meant to drive us away. And if the house were just a house, it was proving itself uninhabitable.

That same afternoon, Claire ordered us to stay outside until she returned, and she walked to Lorenzo's villa, where she put to him an ultimatum: he would see to it that the Le Foci house was free of pests or the Murdochs would break the lease. Lorenzo poured her a glass of wine and promised to help. If the villa didn't suit the Signora, he would find her another villa — *una villa più bella,* he assured her. He smiled gently, his mustache flattening across his upper lip. Claire felt startled by his kindness and recognized how excessive her distress must have seemed. She sipped her wine. When he offered her a cigarette she accepted, though she hadn't smoked for years.

The problem was easily resolved, thanks to Lorenzo's graciousness. For the same rent, he provided us with a new house in the hills between Marciana and Marciana Marina, with a magnificent view of the sea. Claire accepted before she even saw the place. And she made all the arrangements to move without even consulting Murray, sparing him from the distraction of life.

Some days the vibrancy of colors on the island astonished him; other days the clouds hung low to the ground, the air was thick with smoke from burning rubbish, and he couldn't understand what the Italians were saying to him. Elba held no certain answers. But Murray grew increasingly resolute. He didn't want to leave the island without taking with him a deed to Elban land. He hired a surveyor, Carlo Giovanni, who had recently lost his job in the local mining industry. Carlo wouldn't give Murray a straight answer. Either the land on the east side of the island was worth more than the land on the west side, or the land on the west side was worth more than the land on the east side. Either Murray would prosper, or he'd fail.

He kept mislaying maps and forgetting appointments. He heard some men in a bar in Portoferraio laughing, and he knew they were laughing at him. Still, he wasn't close to giving up. Often he didn't come home for pranzo and siesta. Instead, he'd trail Carlo over rock croppings and through chestnut woods. Francis Cape tagged along and proved so useful as a translator that Murray offered to pay him, but Francis said he preferred the status of a volunteer.

If Murray could only put a claim down, he'd feel better. There was plenty of land to buy and plenty of islanders who wanted to sell. But where to begin. When to begin. How?

Uncertainty was beginning to make him agitated. He was losing sleep. He rattled lame jokes for his guests in order to keep them at dinners that lasted for hours. He shrugged when Claire announced that we were changing residences. He wasn't home to help pack. And on the morning we were scheduled to move, he left the house early, before the rest of us had woken, he trailed the surveyor all day, and in the early evening he rode his motorcycle right past Marciana Marina and the cart road that led to our new house, and he returned to the villa in Le Foci.

It was a cool, clear autumn night. The light of a full moon filled the deserted rooms with a dim fluorescence; the fringes of curtains fluttered in the breeze. It took only a moment for Murray's eyes to become accustomed to the dimness and another moment for him to realize his mistake and remember that his family had moved to a different residence. The first wave of panic passed, replaced by a puzzling serenity. He'd always preferred chaos to simplicity, noise to silence, society to solitude. But he felt inclined to linger in the empty house and enjoy the inventions of his imagination. To imagine, without much effort, life without a family or friends. The freedom of solitude.

Alone, without responsibility, in a villa filled with moonlight. He could consider what he might do if he could do as he pleased. He didn't want to have to answer for his actions. He didn't want to think about his reputation. For a good long hour he sat there not thinking about his reputation. All the jobs he'd quit since he'd come home from the war. His mother and uncles. The people of Elba. Adriana Nardi.

The truth was, he hadn't seen the girl for weeks, ever since the early morning when he'd gone to La Chiatta. Sitting alone in Le Foci, he was trying not to think about her. He had no reason to think of her. She'd been busy, Francis Cape had said with a vagueness that had secretly annoyed Murray. But of course Murray had no right to know what she'd been doing. He didn't really care about what she'd been doing. Most of the time, she couldn't have been farther from his thoughts. And yet he experienced an odd sensation of unreality when he heard a noise and looked out the window to see the girl stepping from his mind onto the path beside the house, a mirage so vivid that he had to shake his head and look again. And she persisted, an apparition he'd conjured, making her way toward the front of the house, as real as the curtain he drew aside to watch her. He listened to the delicate crunching as she rolled her shoes over the pebbles, saw her wince when she turned an ankle, heard his own intake of breath, and knew exactly when she looked up to see him move back from the window.

He couldn't will her away, nor did he want to. He just needed to compose himself. He was surprised at how boldly she knocked. People who knock like that always have a clear purpose.

Is anybody home? Buonasera . . . Oh, come in, you poor girl. . . . Without a coat, no less. . . . Murray, it's Adriana at the door. . . . Put the water on for tea and fetch a blanket, will you?

She'd seen him at the window. And his Lambretta was parked in the drive. She knew — he knew she knew — that he was inside the house, just as she'd known that he'd come to see her at the break of dawn. Did she know he was alone? She knocked again and again. She kept knocking until he had no choice but to get up and answer the door, greeting the girl with a smile meant to convey calm, inviting her to come inside.

She hesitated, privately struggling to enact whatever scene she'd rehearsed in her mind. All at once he felt sorry for her; he understood why she was there. It's not easy to find the words in any language, Signorina, when you know you shouldn't say what you want to say. Come into the living room, Adriana, come and sit beside Murray on the sofa, talk, if you want, don't talk if you can't, let the two of you enjoy the sense of existing far away from everything that is familiar, let him hold you, Signorina, just this once, and feel you in his arms, the softness of your skin, the surprising strength of your limbs, this strange island creature making him feel at home in this distant place, bringing to mind the shadows of mountains in the mist, the color of the sea, the beach at Le Ghiaie, the brightness of the moon, the deep folds of a skirt, the tenderness of touch, her coyness, his desire, her resistance, his insistence, her building rage.

She snapped her thighs closed, jerked away from him, growled, "Let me go!"

Why, of course he'd let her go. And she was gone, disappearing into the darkness of the hall. But wait, Signorina, he'd thought . . . what? He'd assumed . . . wrongly. Was there ever a man as foolish as Murray Murdoch! All he had to do was open a door and he'd make a stupid mistake.

He hadn't meant any harm. He was a happily married man. He even found himself resenting Adriana Nardi for leading him on. At the same time, he wondered if what he'd accepted as a deliciously mysterious air about the girl could be attributed to a waywardness of mind. Maybe she seemed mysterious because she was insane. The prospect made satisfying sense. He thought of the engineer from Ohio. He considered how confusion can harden into desperate intention. He felt some real sympathy for Adriana but at the same time wished that he had kept his distance.

He returned to the window in hopes of catching sight of the girl leaving along the terrace path. But either she had taken a different path or she was still somewhere inside the house. He strained to hear a floorboard creak, a door close. Outside, a rooster's restless night cry sounded like a voice raised in brief protest. Or a shout sounded like a rooster's cry. He decided he'd heard a rooster. He brushed a bug from his arm, an ant — no, a spider, one of the harmless little spiders that had driven Claire from the house.

He waited by the window for what seemed like hours but would add up to less than half an hour in real time. Eventually he decided that she must have left the house through the front door and headed down the road to San Giovanni. He'd have to follow the same road west, toward Procchio. His Lambretta was low on gas. How low? Could he make it to Marciana Marina?

He decided he would wait for the length of time it took him to smoke a cigarette. He sat on the sofa, watching the smoke spread and disperse into the darkness, and was reminded of watching the *Casparia*'s wake at night. The smoke felt more than pleasant every time it filled his lungs — it felt like a much-needed affirmation of logic after the frustration of an unsolvable puzzle, a round peg in a round hole. And he was glad to find that the Sambuca had been left behind in the credenza. He sipped the liquor straight from the bottle. He smoked a second cigarette and watched the shadows of the curtains on the carpet, shapes undulating like the long hair of a woman swimming underwater. He caught a white bar of moonlight on his open palm, closed his fist, and studied the stripe of light across his knuckles.

As the hours passed he thought about tourmaline. He thought about the satisfaction he'd feel if he could only succeed in proving that all he needed to thrive was freedom from scrutiny. He wondered if there was anyone left in the world who would lend him money.

BEFORE YOU CONTINUE, Ollie, you might consider the influence of Francis Cape. Remember that Francis introduced Adriana Nardi to your father. Remember that Francis wanted to serve as translator. Remember that Francis didn't want Murray to do anything without first asking Francis for advice.

Francis Cape plays an important part in this story, so let me take the time now to tell you about him. He was a tall man, the skin of his face pitted above his beard, his white hair thinning evenly over his scalp, his flesh collapsing into every joint, making him look comically knobby. He had a lovely voice — slightly hoarse, precise in its elocution yet surprisingly gentle, without any pretension suggested in the speech. At first I liked to have Francis around because I liked to hear him talk. Sometimes I'd even let my mind wander and listen to the music of his voice without bothering to follow his meanings. But as I came to know him better, I began listening more carefully for hints that might have revealed something he wasn't ready to say directly.

As I mentioned earlier, Francis Cape lived in a hovel in Portoferraio, in the shadow of Fort Stella. He had a single room, a third-floor walk-up with two grimy windows looking up toward the south wall of the fort. He slept on a mattress on the floor, used the communal bathroom in the hall, and had no kitchen facilities other than a gas bombola. The room stank of his pipe smoke. The blankets were threadbare, the walls crumbling, the shutters warped. The knickknacks he'd collected were jumbled on top of his bureau. And there were piles of books everywhere — books of poetry in French and Italian, travel guides, history books, Shakespeare's plays, an incomplete set of the 1928 edition of the

Encyclopedia Britannica, and too many books to count about Napoleon.

Francis had come to Elba to write a biographical account of Napoleon's year of exile and dramatic escape. Ten years later Francis was still on the island and had written no more than fragments, some closer to fiction than fact, all of it handwritten on pages their author didn't even bother to number. He wanted to write the definitive book about Napoleon on Elba. He would begin writing, judge his effort inadequate, and try again, writing and rewriting for years in an attempt to do justice to a history that was of mythic proportion.

His frustration with his work first led him to Adriana Nardi. He'd been on Elba three years before learning about the Nardi collection. Three long years he'd spent, or wasted, wandering the island, prowling the passageways of Napoleon's villas and scouring documents in the local library, before an Elban acquaintance finally told him about the Nardi collection. The man, a schoolteacher, spoke the name of *Nardi* with obvious reluctance. Although every native Elban knew about the collection, they also respected the family's privacy. But the schoolteacher was a poor man and could think of no other way to return Francis's generosity after Francis had paid for his dinner.

You might visit Signora Nardi, the teacher had said with a shrug, and Francis had shrugged back. Signora who? Nardi, Nardi, in the villa called La Chiatta, on the road to Magazzini.

Signora Nardi received him graciously, even if her manner was cautious, as Francis would later report. Adriana was still a young sprite, not yet fifteen years old, and she was the one who showed Francis the collection — a collection that would have thrilled any historian and that overwhelmed Francis so completely that he had to cut short his visit and ask to come another day.

Was the collection made more exciting because of the presence of Adriana Nardi? The easy conclusion would be that Francis fell in love with Adriana, though Francis wouldn't have put it that way,

I'm sure. He'd have admitted, if pressed, to no more than paternal affection. But whatever the tenor of the experience within those walls, La Chiatta became both the source of inspiration for him and the impediment. After every visit Francis would begin writing furiously, desperate to do justice to the history. And every attempt would end within an hour, the historian's passion exhausted.

This went on for years. By the time we met Francis on Elba, he had a dazed look in his eyes, which I attributed to eccentricity. He didn't strike me as a defeated man. Rather, he seemed barely able to subdue his giddiness. Whenever he spent an evening with us, he would become the center and catalyst for conversation. And at some point he'd inevitably pause, lean back in his chair, and declare loudly, *I love this island!*

I suppose I became suspicious of his happiness when he invited us to his home. A happy man might have tolerated the disorder of that room, but not the squalor. I remember noticing crumbs of food suspended in cobwebs along the window ledge. I glanced at Francis, who looked away from me in what I interpreted as embarrassment.

Afterward, walking through Portoferraio with Murray, I expressed some concern for Francis; Murray looked puzzled. Such a hovel for a home, I said. He's a bachelor — Murray offered only this as explanation. But it couldn't be good for his health to live in such a place. No, Murray insisted, Francis was doing fine.

I didn't understand Murray's indifference. He liked Francis, but it seemed he didn't care what became of him, and he didn't want to know more than Francis was willing to tell. Francis Cape was one of the few men Murray was inclined to keep at a distance, though not because he didn't trust him. He trusted Francis more than I did and didn't feel it necessary to press him to reveal his secrets or even to offer him a room in our house. Which was all for the best, I suppose, since Francis wanted us to believe in his happiness.

Life on Elba was good — so good that Francis thought Napoleon a fool for leaving. Yes, life on Elba was very good, Murray would agree. They spoke with the condescension of men who considered themselves worldly. Their knowingness irritated me. I remember one evening when Adriana had joined us for dinner. I stepped into the kitchen to fill a pitcher with water, and I paused to listen through an open window while Murray and Francis praised the island. Didn't the mountains look like cardboard stencils against the blue sky? And what amazing sunsets. The flowers. The iron ore. The precious minerals. Heaven stored its jewels here, Francis said — porphyry and serpentine, beryls and aquamarines. And tourmaline, of course. And who knows but diamonds, why not diamonds! Carlo had told Murray that a small diamond had been found on the slope of Volterraio by German soldiers during the war. I said it sounded like a rumor to me, but Adriana insisted it was true.

Where there's one diamond, there are always more, said Francis. He yawned, stretched his arms toward the night sky. Isn't that right, Murray?

The Germans made themselves sick digging for diamonds on Volterraio, Adriana said. When they weren't training, they were digging. Day and night, digging, digging, digging. They were sick and weak when the Allies attacked. I think many Germans were killed because of the Volterraio diamond.

She spoke slowly, more in the manner of one who chooses to linger over words rather than as someone who isn't fluent in the language. I used the opportunity to watch Murray watching her. It was clear that she intrigued him, yet even then I was not suspicious. The fact is, I'd already come to the conclusion that Adriana belonged to Francis Cape, his possessiveness being of the mystical kind, the way God belongs to priests, and Murray could only adore the girl through Francis, in Francis's company.

Call me innocent. Or foolish. Or blame the distractions of the sea. In those days all I wanted to do was watch the sunlight dancing on the surface of the water.

I told you at dinner about what happened to Murray when we

moved to the villa in the valley below Marciana. On the first day at our second home, I didn't even finish unpacking one suitcase. Most of the afternoon I spent lounging on the terrace, taking in the magnificent view of the sea. Right from the start of our stay in that beautiful villa I became — how should I put it? I wasn't exactly neglectful — I would never forget my mistake on the *Casparia,* the way I let myself ignore obvious dangers. But if Lidia and Francesca were the opposite poles, then I was letting myself become more like Francesca by the minute.

Only after sunset, when the sea was hidden by darkness, did I begin to grow anxious. Night has always been my time for worry. It was at night when Murray's ambitions would seem ridiculous. It was at night when I would let myself get drunk and Murray would get drunker.

That first night in our new villa I did not get drunk. I ate dinner alone after putting you boys to bed, and I stayed awake waiting for Murray to come home. I was reading *The Count of Monte Cristo* — I'd picked up the novel at an English bookstore in Florence — and I remember reading the chapter about Franz's hashish dream while I listened for the sound of Murray's motorcycle. Eventually I felt too tired to read, too anxious to sleep. I made tea and sat wrapped in a blanket out on the terrace. As the night wore on, the full moon seemed to shrink, the stars became brighter, the constellations more clearly defined, with Hercules stretching toward the west as though attempting to seize the jewel of Vega in his hand. A nightingale sang briefly but was silenced by a barking dog. Occasionally a car would rattle by on the Marciana road, and I would listen for the sound of it pulling up our dirt drive to deliver Murray, whose Lambretta might have broken down — one possibility out of many. I would try to compose myself, to disguise my worry with fatigue so I could greet him calmly, but the car would continue down the road, and I would go on waiting for my husband to come home.

This is what I reasoned that night: if Murray's motorcycle had broken down, he'd have to hitch a ride. If he didn't arrive by midnight it meant he was lost. He might have misplaced our address. Then he'd have to go to Lorenzo's house and find out where we'd gone. If he did this, then Lorenzo would surely give him a ride — which meant Murray should be back sooner. But Lorenzo might have offered him a drink. This would have delayed Murray's return for a couple of hours. We had no phone, so Murray had no way to contact me. He would assume that I'd gone to sleep. Lorenzo would open another bottle of wine and interrogate Murray about his plans. With the Rio and Calamita mines failing steadily, Elbans could only welcome investment. The Nardi family owned the lease to the land mined on Monte Calamita — what would they do when the mine closed down? What would anyone do? By the end of the decade there'd be no iron-ore mining on Elba at all, Lorenzo had already predicted for us, and he'd offer this prediction again as a wager, a five-hundred-lire bet, if Murray dared.

One thousand. Murray would always counter by upping the stakes. It was one of his certain habits, like always putting his right shoe on first.

Two A.M. Three A.M. The moon disappeared, and the sky brightened subtly to the hollow gray-blue that precedes dawn. I saw a shadow moving on the terrace. The dark body of an animal. A wild animal. A rat. A ferret. A cat — Meena.

I called to her, clicked my tongue, watched her freeze. She tipped her head, then decided to ignore me. Away she slunk, toward the sound of a barking dog.

A prowling cat. A barking dog. Hercules fading into dawn. Where was your father?

Morning came, and with it arrived Murray, his excuse cast as self-mocking explanation — he'd forgotten about the move, forgotten to head to Marciana after work, forgotten to put gas in his motorcycle, and on top of that he'd fallen asleep on the sofa of the other villa, slept straight through to 5 A.M., hadn't even taken off his shoes. Then he'd set off on his Lambretta, run out of gas, and ended up walking three miles into Marciana Marina, where he had to wait another hour for a gas station to open.

He needed a shave, a bath, breakfast. He looked awful, not just physically awful but dispirited. Yesterday's explorations must have disappointed him, I thought. His hopes for investment were ridiculous, and he'd already wasted too much money. It was all he could do to drag himself to the bedroom to change his clothes and get ready for another day of work.

But by the time he came to the table for breakfast he'd regained his optimism, so much so that he reminded me of Francis, giddy with denial. There was something he couldn't tell me. What? I'm not sure I wanted to know. I was grateful to have Murray home. He whistled while he cracked the shell of a soft-boiled egg with the edge of his spoon, *tap tap tapping* to the tune of "Home on the Range," until my worry turned to annoyance, and annoyance melted into amusement.

As I told you during our last dinner, Murray remained alone at Le Foci after Adriana had left. I believe this to be the truth, though it took many months for your father to explain.

OF THE THREE QUALITIES WHICH determine the market value of a gemstone — beauty, rarity, and durability — the last quality is the easiest to measure. Durability determines the rank of mineral specimens. Durability is a stone's defense against the wear of weather. Durability transforms certain stones into treasures and turns treasures into legends. If heroes were to find defunct paper bills instead of gold and gems when they unearthed a buried treasure, there wouldn't be much of a story to tell.

While rarity is a more elusive quality, the connection between rarity and worth is simple. If new sources increased the world's quantity of available diamonds tenfold, diamonds would lose value. If synthetic production of a particular type of gem rivals the natural process, miners lose their jobs.

Beauty is the quality most difficult to measure, as well as the most important. To some extent, a stone's beauty is contingent. One year garnets may be in fashion, the next year, pearls. But the intrinsic beauty of a gemstone is determined by one factor independent of human whim: light. Light creates luster, and luster is what gives a stone its character. Without luster, a diamond would be no more beautiful than quartz, and gold would be pyrite's equal. Without luster, topaz and ruby, amethyst and sapphire would be as dull as granite.

The greater the amount of light reflected instead of absorbed, the more lustrous the stone. The most remarkable version of this property is found in hexagonal crystals, such as diamonds, calcite, and tourmaline, which double an image by splitting the light.

Tourmaline's alkali tints range from black to transparent, rubellite to brown. Black schorl was the most common form of tourmaline found on Elba. Other specimens tended to be pink, yellow, and green, and frequently parti-colored. From the 1930s through the 1950s, the crystals were increasingly coveted. Pink and green watermelon crystals were highly valued, and blue tourmaline was the most valuable of all.

With the money his uncles finally sent, Murray purchased five hectares of terraced land on a wooded slope in the Mezza Luna zone between Sant'Andrea and Monte Giove. Stone walls hidden among the chestnuts suggested that centuries earlier this had been cultivated land. But when Murray purchased the title from a family that had owned the land for generations, only a footpath connected the property to the coastal road.

What Murray's land had, though, was tourmaline. Little black sticks of schorl, which Murray broke from the granite rock face when he was surveying the land. Because of tourmaline, our father agreed to buy the land for a price he knew was inflated.

In the mornings our parents would confer in low, growling voices outside, Claire still in her bathrobe and slippers, Murray already mounted on his motorcycle. They would discuss bills, loans, and their increasing expenses. Later in the morning Claire would take a taxi to the bank in Portoferraio in hopes of collecting the last of the loan Murray's uncles had promised to wire. Murray's uncles, however, were keeping Claire and Murray waiting, and Murray had to ask Lorenzo for a month's respite on the rent. Claire explained the situation to Lidia, who kept down costs by cooking her cacciucco with grouper instead of swordfish. Francesca was given the month of December off. And our mother began calling agents for information about ships heading back to New York.

The weather grew colder. The clouds overhead were dark gray with ragged edges, and rain would fall continuously for three or four days at a time. Patrick and Harry claimed that they were being bullied by the Elban boys at school, so Claire decided to keep them home for a while. She gave them reading lessons that amounted to an hour spent deciphering articles in a week-old *Herald Tribune,* worked with them briefly on math, and then she'd bundle us in raincoats and boots and send us outside.

I turned five in the middle of November. Patrick, who turned ten on the ninth of December, was responsible for the safety of the rest of us — which translated into tyranny. He was the king, we were his servants, and if he asked us to pick the spiny balls off a sandbur or collect dried-flower sacs from the sedge, we had to oblige.

After the disappointment of paltry gifts at our birthdays, we weren't looking forward to Christmas. Somehow, though, our parents managed to satisfy our greed. The presents were abundant on Christmas morning — toy soldiers and trucks, puzzles, model airplane kits, and even books in English. Lidia had the week off, so Claire mastered the oven and cooked potatoes and green beans and roasted a chicken, which she tried to fool us into believing was turkey.

After dinner we collapsed on the floor in front of the radio that provided only fuzzy reception on a single channel. We listened to a broadcast of a Christmas mass, not caring that we didn't understand a word of it. Claire was in the kitchen washing up; Francis Cape — who either had mistaken a casual comment for an invitation or else had somehow invited himself to dinner — lit his pipe, Murray lit a cigarette, and they settled in their chairs for a good long smoke.

They smoked in silence for a few minutes. Murray said something about work being done on the road to Marciana. Knowing Francis's resistance to all development on the island, he launched into a defense of the new roads, insisting that not only would they open up the island to tourists, they would ultimately save the Elbans time and labor, giving them the opportunity to concentrate on intensifying production on their farms as well as improving their dilapidated houses. He was describing a house he'd seen in San Piero when Francis interrupted him.

"That's all fine, Murray. But there's something important I want to discuss with you."

Murray's immediate thought was money: Francis wanted to borrow money from Murray or lend Murray money or else he knew of a secret source for money. But Francis had only to say the name "Adriana Nardi," and Murray felt a draining presentiment. What about the girl? Adriana had disappeared, Francis said. She'd left a note explaining only that she couldn't explain why she had to leave. She hadn't been seen or heard from for more than a month. At first her mother kept secret the fact of her disappearance. She made inquiries with friends in Bologna but failed to find any evidence that her daughter had been there at all. After a few weeks she contacted the local police. They questioned fishermen, sailors, and harbor workers. In the week before Christmas, the police told Signora Nardi that to the best of their knowledge Adriana had never left the island.

After Francis finished his account, the two men smoked in silence for a long minute. Murray considered what he couldn't say: Adriana had disappeared because of him. He knew this as surely as he knew that his land would never turn a profit, the knowledge as certain as it was untested, a theory born from common sense. Adriana had disappeared because of Murray. If she never returned, he would be held accountable.

"Well then, Francis, where is she?" Murray asked abruptly.

"Why, for God's sake, why should I know?" Francis could only sputter in outrage at the accusation implied in Murray's question.

"Why should you know. Of course you don't know. You don't have any idea where she's gone off to. Somewhere on the island. She's hiding out somewhere on the island." The possibility of this gave rise in Murray to a strange excitement — the scientist's excitement at the thought of proving his hypothesis. "Have they looked in the caves? The bunkers? Of course they have. Where else? She knew the secret places —" He stopped, blinked in surprise at himself for using the past tense. *Knows,* he thought. Say, *She knows . . .* He couldn't say it, not with Francis peering at him through the screen of pipe smoke. Knew. Knows. Was. Is.

In the living room Patrick shrieked, "Idiot!" Harry threw a wooden block that hit Patrick in the head. As Patrick lunged at him, he kneed Nat in the back by mistake.

"Dumbface!" Nat cried.

"Jerk!" Patrick yelled.

Murray was grateful for the uproar because it gave him the chance to get away from Francis. He attempted to mediate an elaborate truce among us. He wanted to hear Patrick's account of the fight, then Harry's. He invited Nat to add his own version. Yes, sharing should be encouraged, but on Christmas day a boy doesn't necessarily have to share his new toy backhoe.

"Let's talk about sharing," Murray said, his cigarette still clamped between his lips, the four of us watching in fascination as the long ash grew longer and still didn't crumble.

When he finally returned to the dining room to rejoin Francis, Claire was there and had already heard from Francis a good part of a longer version of the Adriana Nardi story. Had Claire ever met the Signora? Francis was asking as Murray settled into his seat.

"Never," Claire said.

"She's a retiring sort," Francis said, "not much interested in life, as far as I can tell."

Or else, Murray considered, Signora Nardi was inordinately interested in life and had found ways to watch without being seen. Perhaps she knew how to keep an eye on her daughter and hired someone to follow her. An absurd idea — yet it had the force of a startling memory. Murray pictured the living room of his Le Foci house. The moonlight on the floor. Adriana on the sofa beside him. Someone watching through the window, just like someone had watched him from a window of La Chiatta as he wheeled his Lambretta from the courtyard.

Murray had become a potential suspect in a potential crime —

or maybe not. Maybe no one had given him a second thought. He attempted to return to his earlier mood. The satisfaction of a smoke after a good dinner. A glass of cognac. Adriana just an annoyance.

At least the girl knew how to keep a secret — you could see this in her face, her pallor, her evasive sideways glances. She'd learned as a child to protect herself with secrecy, every word and gesture designed to deflect attention. But here was the paradox: her evasive manner invited attention, as though — no, not as though, in fact, she wanted to be seen, admired, exposed, to confess what she had been trained to hide.

Unless she were mad, her shattered mind held together by a dark obsession. I'm here, Signor Murdoch. Go away, Adriana. I don't want to go away. Go away.

A woman's voice. A rooster's crow.

He watched Francis and Claire talking, listened to the liquid, indecipherable murmur on the radio in the living room. He let himself drift, imagined a Saturday afternoon in his backyard in America. Screech of a blue jay, smell of fresh-cut grass, buzz of a chain saw in the neighbor's yard, and the sound of children's voices from the tree house — not so different from the sounds his children were making in the next room, reminding Murray of where he was, in a villa overlooking the Mediterranean, lured here by the simple promise of change.

He'd have admitted to being a ridiculous man with ridiculous ambitions, but he had committed no crime and had no reason to run away. He looked across the table at his wife for confirmation. She was chewing her thumbnail while she listened to Francis describing what he knew about Signora Nardi. Murray reached for the cognac and refilled Francis's glass and his own. Claire looked at Murray, and when their eyes met Murray was surprised to feel a different manner of scrutiny — the searching glance not of concern but of suspicion.

"You think I have something to do with this?" he said calmly, setting the bottle back on the table.

Claire flinched visibly but remained silent, and Francis watched them both with his lips pressed tight in what Murray read as a grin. The silence was unbearable. "I mean," Murray continued awkwardly, "the girl might have told me back when . . . she could have indicated . . . but she didn't, you know. She didn't admit it. If she was troubled. Or something."

Claire worked the dry skin of her cuticle. "Something," she muttered. The scorn implied by her echo ordinarily would have goaded Murray into an argument. Instead it stirred in him the same cool indignation he would have felt if he'd been holding a worthless hand of cards and Claire were threatening to call his bluff.

Guilt sounds like the crinkle of aluminum foil. The clank of a knife against the half-open lid of a tin can. A gas burner hissing without a flame. A cat clawing at a sofa's upholstery. Dry leaves blowing on pavement. Scotch tape being crumpled into a ball.

Claire heard guilt in Murray's voice, though not the guilt of a man who is pouring another glass of cognac when he's already drunk, which is the only kind of guilt she would have expected right then. When she looked at him suspiciously, it wasn't, as Murray had thought, in connection with Adriana Nardi. Fine to be concerned about Adriana, but at that moment Claire was more concerned about Murray's drinking, trying to decide how much was too much as she watched him refill his glass.

The sound of guilt is a man asking his wife if she thought he had something to do with a girl's disappearance. With this, Murray introduced to Claire a new kind of suspicion, causing her to wonder above all why his voice was unnaturally calm, and next, why he had to ask such a question at all.

Francis stayed past midnight. By then Murray was slurring his speech and bumping his knuckles against his glass. Claire took his drunkenness to be a retreat from the conversation he didn't want to have. The possibility that Murray had something to hide was more unsettling to Claire than drunkenness. Drunkenness was no more than a lapse. Claire decided to wait until the next day to talk with him.

But the days following filled up too quickly for her to pull Murray aside. He would set off early in the mornings, and in the evenings he'd bring home friends — Lorenzo, Mario and Pia Ginori, Francis. There was no time for Claire to have the kind of talk she wanted to have, a talk that would lead in a direction she didn't dare predict. She didn't even bother to tell Murray that for the time being she'd given up making arrangements to book our passage home.

Murray's uncles wired more money in early January, bolstering his confidence, and he was able to afford the rest of the down payment on the Mezza Luna property. He even sent photographs of the land to his uncles and promised to look for other potential acquisitions. His uncles wrote back to ask Murray what the hell he thought he was doing, buying land with the money they'd sent to help cover his expenses!

But Murray was undaunted. As the days passed, Claire felt less inclined to disturb his good humor, and she made an effort to convince herself of his innocence. Maybe the worst her husband could be accused of was to be trapped by someone else's affection. Sometimes, she reminded herself, we get entangled by accident.

At the end of January, during the quiet of siesta on an unusually warm day, Claire was reading on the terrace when someone knocked on the door. Directly overhead a gull glided lazily in circles, as silent as the words on the page —

The town, the churchyard, and the setting sun,
The clouds, the trees, the rounded hills all seem,
Though beautiful, cold — strange — as in a dream . . .

The sea rippled in the distance. The sunlight warmed Claire's face. And then came the rude interruption of the three brittle knocks.

A moment later Lidia came to the terrace to announce that Claire had a visitor. "Who?" Claire asked. Lidia turned around and went back inside without responding. Either she didn't hear or she pretended not to hear, leaving Claire to assume that the cook judged the visitor of too little importance to introduce.

No — the visitor was of great importance, and Lidia had already invited her into the living room and left to make coffee. When Claire approached, the woman extended her hand without bothering to rise from her chair. Claire smiled uneasily. She pretended to be pleased — pleased to make the acquaintance of . . . *it must be Signora Nardi,* she said gently, adding *Piacere,* which the Signora countered in her gravelly voice, "Thank you, Mrs. Murdoch."

She had bulging almond eyes, heavy lids, a long nose, and metal gray hair tied up in a bun. She wore a black wool dress that hung loosely on her small body, with a black shawl embroidered with delicate flowers. Claire thought of the woman on the *Casparia,* the woman who'd been dressed in black linen on a hot summer day, the one Claire had seen weeping at the rail. It occurred to her only now that she'd never seen the woman on the ship after that first day.

She was sorry to hear about Adriana — was this what she should say? Or this: She and her husband shared Signora Nardi's concern. But Claire sensed that the woman would appreciate directness.

"What news do you have of your daughter?"

"No news, Mrs. Murdoch. My daughter has disappeared like water into the air. You call it . . . what do you call it?"

"Evaporation, you mean?"

"I ask for your help, Mrs. Murdoch."

"We'll do anything we can."

"You are American."

"Yes."

"You have contacts."

Contacts — the word suggested a secret truth, as if Signora Nardi knew more about her than Claire knew about herself. "What do you mean, *contacts?*"

"In the government."

Her tone as much as her words suggested paranoia rather than reliable information. Perhaps, Claire thought with some relief, the Signora had read too many spy novels.

"The American government? We don't know anyone in the government, not personally. Not even a state senator! We'd very much like to help you, Signora Nardi, but we're not the kind of people who have important friends."

"You have money."

Claire had to stifle a laugh. "We're barely able to make ends meet!" She wanted to go on — they had no savings, and the Averils were losing patience. "But that's not the point. The point is, we want to help you if we can. Let me think. We could organize a search party. Do you know what that is — a search party?"

Lidia was back with the coffee tray. She handed a demitasse to Signora Nardi, offered her the sugar and a spoon. Claire watched the woman tip back her head and down the caffè like a man swallowing a shot of whiskey. When she spoke again, her rattling voice had turned into a growl.

"I do not need your parties. I need you to find for me the American *diavolo* who has stolen my daughter."

Guilt is the sound of a Lambretta carrying a man home shortly after dawn. Claire looked past her guest through the window and at the terrace beyond, where she'd stayed up waiting through the night back in November.

"What do you mean?"

Signora Nardi's laughter came abruptly. She started to explain, "He — " and then thought better of it. "I want to find the American who can tell me where my daughter is."

"There are other Americans on the island," Claire said stupidly. "I met an American in Porto Azzurro just last week. He asked me for directions. If we knew the name of his boat, we might be able to track him down."

"He was a man much older than my daughter — that is all I know for certain. Buonasera, Signora Murdoch. Arrivederla."

"Arrivederla, Signora Nardi. We will ask around, I promise."

It was a weak promise, Claire admitted to herself after Adriana's mother had left. A dismissive promise. She sipped her bitter caffè and told herself what she hadn't been willing to say to Signora Nardi. Asking around wasn't good enough; she could do better.

"Signora, please —" Claire caught up with her as she was getting into the taxi that had been idling in the drive. Signora Nardi waited, holding the door open.

"You suspect my husband, don't you?"

"I do not understand."

"*Suspect* . . . the word . . . to *suspect* someone is to —"

"I know what it means. But I do not understand why you think I suspect your husband."

"That's why you came here, isn't it? To share your suspicion?"

The woman drew in a deep breath, and Claire braced herself for the release of fury. But the Signora let the breath escape in a gentle sigh that suggested sympathy instead of anger. "Signora Murdoch. How should I say this? If I spoke in Italian. Never mind. Signora, at no time have I suspected your husband. I have met your husband. And I know what my daughter said. She said he was a good man. Molto vivace. A silly man also, she said. She trusted him, and I trust him." She paused, studied Claire's face, and asked abruptly, "Do you believe me?"

Startled by the woman's candor, Claire said, "Yes, I do, I do —" though she was thinking the opposite.

Patrick went twice into the Mezza Luna zone with Murray. The first time, the day after Christmas, Murray told him to look for colored stones amidst the dirty white quartz. When Patrick found a pinkish wedge lined with cracks, Murray identified it as feldspar. That was the extent of Patrick's first geology lesson.

The second time Patrick accompanied Murray was on a bright cold Saturday in early February, and Carlo was there, to Murray's surprise. He'd come to look for a knapsack he'd lost back in December and was sitting on a boulder beside a shallow, muddy pool of run-off water, finishing the wine in his flask, when Murray and Patrick arrived. Patrick spoke more Italian than Murray did by then, and he accepted Carlo's offer to accompany him on a walk around the site.

As they crossed a gulch Carlo found a forked twig about two feet long. He whittled the tip to a taper with his pocketknife and then showed Patrick how to grasp the stick with his clenched fingers held toward the sky. If Patrick happened to step upon a patch of ground over a vein of precious mineral, the twig would begin to turn and twist, Carlo explained, mimicking the motion with his hips. Then he led the way up the slope, stepping carefully between the brambles of rock roses.

The divining rod shook at ten different spots, Patrick told us later, and though he didn't find any gems, he did, with Carlo's help, find a geode, which he busted open on a flat rock, shattering one half, leaving the other circle of crystal intact.

We were awed by the crystal, especially after Patrick repeated to us what Carlo had told him — that it was a piece of a meteor from outer space. And if it came from outer space it must be magic, Patrick said.

"Magic how?" Nat asked.

"Magic like in being invisible?" Harry asked.

Magic like sawing a person in half? This was my question, though I kept it to myself.

"Magic like the kind that shows you the future," Patrick said, with a confidence that suggested expert knowledge. The problem, he went on to explain, was figuring out how to make the magic work. We pondered the geode half, stared at its crystal peaks and shards, but failed to decipher its code. And since potential magic becomes boring more quickly than real magic, we hid the geode in the bedroom closet and ran back outside.

That day we played a new game, invented by Patrick, who had

heard from Carlo about a tribe of giant ants living in the mountains of Elba. They were bigger than foxes, smaller than wolves, and when they dug tunnels in the sand they brought up nuggets of gold the size of raisins. We used pebbles for the gold and long green twigs for our antennae. Harry and I were ants. My job was to guard the horde of pebbles while Harry watched for intruders. Patrick and Nat would creep toward us from separate directions, taunting us with insults from their hiding places. Harry and I would throw handfuls of little pine cones at every moving shadow.

The game absorbed us. We played even when a misty rain started to fall. The gold made us greedy; competition made us violent. Harry scratched Patrick with a stick, Patrick pushed Harry to the ground, I hit Nat in the eye with a pine cone, Nat yanked a fistful of my hair. No one cried or threatened to go home. If our gold was depleted, we would reverse roles, and we, the giant ants of Monte Giove, would try to steal the gold back.

Death to the ants. The ants must die!
We have come to take back our gold.
The gold belongs to us now.
The gold belongs to us.
Vai, vai!
Scemi!

We smelled the needles carpeting the damp earth. We saw the black-and-white flash of a cuckoo against the dusky sky. We formed a circle and pissed into the opening of a burrow. Rain was as thick as syrup on our short hair. These are the memories I share with my brothers. But there are other details none of us can recall accurately. Was it Harry or Nat who climbed high into a pine tree and leaped to the branch of another tree? Was it Nat or me who tripped over an exposed root and knocked his head against the hard ground, blacking out for a few seconds? Who decided to band forces and collect more gold? We gathered striped granite gneiss, coarse gabbro, simple, brittle quartzite. Who found the greatest

treasure of all, a mica schist with two little tourmaline crystals pok-
ing up from the side? Patrick says he found the schist; Nat says
Harry found it. Harry doesn't remember.

Give me that!

It's mine and you're dead!

We didn't realize how dark it had become or how far we had
wandered up the mountain until we heard our father calling for us.
His voice was plaintive, without the tremor of impatience or the
promise of punishment — the voice of a guilty man who blames
himself for the disappearance of his sons. Which meant, if we
were interpreting the tone correctly, we were blameless and could
even add to our father's torment by hiding from him.

His flashlight beam was the searchlight of the giant ants, and
we were their prisoners of war. We would attempt a perilous escape.

Follow me, shhhh. We slid on our bellies down the side of a
gulch toward freedom.

Ouch!

Shut up.

You shut up.

Murray's flashlight beam swept over our heads, swung back,
and centered itself on Patrick's face.

"Patrick!"

"Hi, Dad."

"Where are . . . there . . . two . . . three . . . four, you're all here,
right? You're all okay, right?"

"Right, Dad."

Murray squinted through the rain and moved his lower jaw as
if to chew a tough piece of meat. "Now tell me what the fuck you
were doing."

"You said *fuck*."

"Get up here."

We'd misinterpreted Murray's tone of voice, underestimated
his capacity for anger. He was furious with us. This man who until

that night never had the rage or indignation to hit us raised his hand and boxed Patrick on the ear. We were stunned, all of us sharing with Patrick the shock of pain and, worse, humiliation. Murray reached for Harry to do the same, but Harry ran ahead down the path. Nat cowered on the slope of the gulch. I started to cry.

If Murray regretted hitting Patrick, he didn't admit it and instead kept grumbling curses at us as he followed Harry down the path. Nat and I flanked Patrick, who by virtue of his punishment had become our martyr. He was stoically silent. And with all that he'd had to endure, he was perceptive enough to realize that at my young age I couldn't manage the steep shale path in the dark without help. He held my hand.

Lamps were lit in all the rooms and in the mist the glow formed a yellow penumbra around the villa. When we arrived Harry was already in the kitchen in our mother's arms. She was clutching him and crying, and the scene made clear to the rest of us what trouble we'd caused by staying out so late. We'd been gone for hours. Our mother was sobbing for the children she thought she'd lost. We understood all too clearly that we were responsible for her distress. But we would never forgive Murray for hitting Patrick, smacking him like a dog, just like Lorenzo would slap his segugia bitch when it wouldn't stop barking.

If Murray hadn't been so cruel we would have thought our mother's reaction excessive and wondered if her grief had some other cause. Instead, we believed that we'd seen proof of an important set of truths. Our mother loved us; our father didn't.

Patrick still had the mica schist in his pocket, and later that night he hid it behind a bookshelf and swore us all to secrecy. We'd intended to give it to Murray. Not now. Our wicked father would never know that we had two perfect little towers of pink tourmaline — not the rarest kind, not nearly enough to make us rich, but enough to convince us that we should keep looking for more.

What are the limitations of sympathy? How much can we really understand about someone else? What qualities are genuine? To what extent is our perception of others inflected by imagination? What are the limitations of imagination? What are the risks of imagination? What are the rules of imagination? What does imagination have to do with sympathy? With suspicion? Why does a child run away from home? Why did it take so long for Claire to notice that it was past eight o'clock, dinner had grown cold, and her children were missing? Why did Claire blame Murray for this? Why did Murray blame Claire? Why didn't we answer them when they called into the darkness? Where had we gone? Where had all the children of Elba gone? Why did some come home and not others? When would carnivale begin? When would it end? Why were the children of Elba throwing fistfuls of flour? What was the meaning of flour? Why is celebration so similar to protest? What would happen to the children? Who will live a long full life and who will die in youth? Where was Adriana? How much did the mother know about her daughter? How much can any mother know? Claire, why didn't you ask Murray more questions if you continued to harbor suspicions? If your sense of foreboding was so strong, why didn't you say something to Murray later that night, after your children were safely in bed? Why did you avoid the subject? What didn't you want to know? What did you fear? Why were you so content during the day and so nervous at night? What were you thinking while you sat on the rocks and stared at the sea? What were you reading out on the terrace while we were wandering in the hills? What were you thinking when you had ten guests for dinner and everybody but you was talking at once? What is learned through conversation? What was to be gained by remaining on Elba? Why continue to invest in a worthless plot of land? What is the point of a gemstone? Why is a blue tourmaline, an indicolite, worth more than the red, rubellite variety? Why should Murray waste his time roaming the island of Elba when he could be back home drawing a salary? So what if tourmaline is vitreous, pleochroic, trigonal, and piezoelectric? Why go against sound advice? Why don't you just give up and go home, Murray? Why did you hit Patrick, Murray? Why wouldn't we forgive him? What was happening? Why was Murray becoming a stranger in his own house? Why didn't spring bring better weather? Why did it rain for twenty-seven days in a row in the month of March? Why did Claire stop giving Patrick and Harry their lessons? Who would loan us money? Why didn't Adriana come home?

The Undaunted

1 May 1814

What is my crime? No more than sharing with the people of France a fierce hatred of inequality. For this I was made emperor. For this I've been repudiated. For this I was forced to surrender to foreign commissioners. They say I am responsible for savage acts of violence. I say I am responsible for the freedom that my countrymen have come to consider their right. Three days ago I left Fréjus on what is supposed to be the final journey of my life. I insisted on appropriate honors. Captain Ussher refused. Colonel Campbell overruled him, and I walked alone up the gangway to the boom of a twenty-one-gun salute.

Did anyone stop to consider the name of the frigate? I am being taken to Elba on the Undaunted. *I boarded the* Undaunted *at night, the music of cannon fire announcing that a great man was being expelled from the country he had tried to save. To Captain Ussher and his crew I am pitiable. To Colonel Campbell I am —* *he understands the coincidence — undaunted. And so he does his best to placate me.*

I am a man who perspires profusely. I need no more than four hours of sleep a night. I am a great military strategist. And I recognize as well as anyone the Allies' stupidity at sending me to an island so near the coast.

I have only to bide my time and plan my course of action upon my return to France. Here on the Undaunted *I've been entertaining my hosts by answering any question they put to me. I've already explained to them that if Villeneuve hadn't gone off to Cádiz and joined Nelson, I'd have had my army in London within three days. If I'd conquered England, I would have made her the greatest power in the world. And yes, the Duchess of Bedford was a good dancer, but her mother was too fat.*

Francis Cape had arrived on the island in 1947, at a time when many Elbans felt the need to reinforce their isolation. And yet with the closing of the mines and a few years of poor harvest, they were beginning to weigh the benefits of tourism against the costs. Some Elbans made Francis feel welcome; others clearly considered him an intruder.

He stayed through the first winter at a small, spare pensione in Portoferraio, where he was the only guest for weeks at a time. His first inquiries about more permanent accommodations were met with shrugs. His early attempts to use his self-taught Italian and engage Elbans in conversation were met with condescending bafflement. Cos' ha detto? What did you say? On gloomy days in February he was almost ready to abandon his project and go back to England. But then he'd be walking along the beach at Bagnaia and the sun would pop out from behind the clouds, or he'd be wandering in the hills above Poggio and the bells of San Lorenzo would begin to ring. There was the young woman in the Café Medici in Portoferraio who would sprinkle cocoa on his cappuccino and with a toothpick carefully outline the shape of a heart on the foam. There was the old woman named Ninanina, who'd invite him into the rustic enoteca she ran with her husband and serve him a plate of grilled anchovies and a glass of wine for free.

And there was the extraordinary Nardi collection, unknown to most of the world. Francis paid his first visit to the Nardi villa in April of 1950. From that point on he lost his lingering inclination to leave the island. He found a small, serviceable flat in Portoferraio. He transferred his savings to a local bank. And he promised the Nardis, the signora and the signorina, that with his book on Napoleon Bonaparte he would do justice to their hospitality.

Adriana had turned fifteen years old in the spring of 1950. She was a reserved child, with a sweet but wary face that reminded Francis of the Madonna in Piero della Francesca's *Annunciation,* and Francis believed that she both craved attention and was filled with distrust. So he set out to win her trust. He brought her little figurines, porcelain kittens and mice purchased from the old woman who ran the enoteca in Portoferraio. Adriana accepted the gifts with a grim politeness that made Francis nervous. He decided that the figurines were too childish. He brought her colored pencils and paper but again felt from her cool acceptance that he'd made a mistake. He gave her a set of ivory coasters, which she understood to be a gift for her mother. He gave her a necklace of onyx beads but never saw her wearing it. He gave her a book of fairy tales in English.

The book was the first present that aroused any spontaneous response — a flash of a shy smile and a quick, probing glance, as if she were trying to find out how he knew what she most wanted. Though he'd conversed with her only in Italian, he'd assumed that, like her mother, she spoke some English and French — better French than English, as it turned out. But she wanted to learn English and told this to Francis by way of thanking him for the book, admitting her interest with a coyness that took him by surprise. She wanted to learn English. She said it once in Italian and repeated herself in English, embedding in the sentence a request: Would Francis teach her?

He began teaching her informally, stretching their ordinary conversations into lessons and reading with her through the book of fairy tales. She learned the words of a song sung by three heads floating in a well. She learned the words of a song sung by mermaids. She learned many useless things. But then Signora Nardi insisted on formalizing the instruction and paying Francis for one hour of lessons each day. He tried to refuse payment; Signora Nardi ignored him.

From the spring of 1950 through the next two years, Francis tutored Adriana in English. When he ran out of books he set her to work translating the letters in the archives and with her help deciphered passages he'd skipped or misread because of his limited Italian: a recipe sent to Napoleon's chef for a particular kind of fish soup the emperor had liked, an eighteenth-century account of unearthing the ruins of an Etruscan ironworks, and an exchange between Elisa Baciocchi, Princess of Piombino, and Antonio Buoncompagni about the bodies washing ashore at Gorgona after the sinking of the *Queen Charlotte.*

These were good, purposeful years for Francis. Besides tutoring Adriana he gathered voluminous notes for his book. He explored the island, befriended Elbans, and came to feel entirely at home, so much so that he began to resent the intrusion of tourists. In his opinion, Elba could do well enough without transforming itself into one big resort. He argued in favor of isolation, reminding the Elbans of their long history of self-sufficiency. When had they ever profited from affiliation? They could do no better than fish and tend their vines and keep their riches to themselves.

Adriana grew up, or at least older. In Francis's perception she remained a child — a stern, poised, mature child, but still a child — because only a child could continue to adore him as she did. She cast him as the father she had lost, and Francis accepted the role. He believed that she needed to adore him. He, in turn, was fond of her and took it upon himself to help her continue the education they'd begun together. Though he knew that Signora Nardi would disapprove, he secretly gave Adriana money to help make her life more comfortable when she went off to study in Bologna. And when she applied for the fellowship at St. Hilda's, he wrote a recommendation on her behalf to a relative, a second cousin who had some sort of function — Francis wasn't sure what, exactly — at a college in Oxford.

And then Murray Murdoch arrived on Elba, and Adriana decided that Francis Cape was useless. In the weeks before she disappeared she took to receiving him with an indifference that was humiliating. He had only to look at her averted eyes to see what she didn't want to see: a stupid, pretentious old man who could do nothing for her.

An old, old man, with rotting teeth, sour breath, rheumy eyes, gnarled fingers, and a disgusting habit of burping repeatedly into his fist all through a meal. He wanted to apologize to her for being so old. He wished she were old, as old as the gentlewoman who painted her face in the poem by George Turberville. A Hecuba rather than a Helen. He wanted to tell her all about his childhood to convince her that he was once young. She wouldn't have believed it. Francis Cape was never a child. He had been old long before Adriana was born. He had always been old.

Napoleon died at the age of fifty-two on St. Helena. Francis was seventy-three. If he had died at fifty-two he wouldn't have learned Italian, he wouldn't have come to Elba, he wouldn't have climbed to the top of Volterraio, and he never would have stood on the cliffs at Capo Vit at sunrise. But he also would have been spared knowing Adriana Nardi.

Until he'd met her, Francis had never experienced the problem of loving someone too much. He'd been a solid, decent English bachelor, his past sprinkled with solid, decent relationships. He could have married any number of good women but for one reason or another had remained single.

He wouldn't have loved Adriana too much if he hadn't become aware of how little he could do for her. He tried to please her and win back her adoration. He brought her books, he gave her money, he complimented her, he gave her more money.

He worked frantically on his history of Napoleon, felt simultaneously impassioned by his mission and ashamed of his inadequacies. Napoleon became the excuse to write about the magnificent beauty of Elba. Why would anyone want to leave? How could the little tyrant have been so foolish? On paper he ruled an island principality but in effect he was the emperor of paradise. Francis wanted to write a biography of the emperor of paradise. He didn't want to write about Napoleon's escape, but history obligated him to try. Every day he'd write another page or two. And every day he'd set aside the work he'd done and start over.

When my parents met Francis Cape they took him to be the respectable English bachelor that he was still pretending to be. Our mother felt a little sorry for him. Our father felt grateful for Francis's assistance. Francis had introduced him to Lorenzo, our padrone, and helped him to find a place to stay on Elba. He'd served as a translator for Murray and told him whom to trust. And he'd introduced Murray and Claire to Adriana Nardi.

At first Francis didn't mind Murray's friendship with Adriana, for he saw that it was making her a little perkier, a little more interested in life. Whenever Francis told Adriana that he was going to see the Murdochs, Adriana was keen on going along. But soon enough Francis began to notice Murray's inappropriate interest in the girl. What did he want from Adriana? He said he wanted to know whatever she could tell him about the island. Why did he care? What was at stake? Francis wondered if there was something he'd missed in the Nardi collection — not just a tantalizing fact about Napoleon but some sort of information that could have more material consequence. Something along the lines of a treasure map. Murray kept talking about the value of tourmaline. Had he found routes to ancient mines, perhaps? To intact veins of precious minerals?

But it was jealousy, plain and simple jealousy, that turned Francis's worry into deep resentment. Murray had come to steal Elba's most precious treasure — the treasure named Adriana Nardi. By then it was too late to help her. She liked the American, she told Francis. She liked best of all his airy hopes. Coming to an island to buy land that no one else wanted and hoping against hope to make money. She, too, would have liked to hope for something impossible, or at least to know that she had the luxury to be foolish. In a middle-aged American investor, Adriana had found a model fool.

Francis told Adriana that Murray had been seen digging in the yard behind his house with a teaspoon. He told her that the American was convinced he'd find gold. Gold! He told her that people with nothing better to do like to dig holes and then fill them up. But Adriana didn't have much to say in reply. She'd laugh and shrug and toss her hair back away from her eyes. And once she reminded Francis that chunks of Elban rubellite as big as melons were said to have been found by the Etruscans.

The secret treasure of love. A girl as lustrous as tourmaline. A man who wants the treasure for himself. The story made such sense that Francis came to believe he couldn't alter the plot. He thought of himself as no better than a spectator — or no worse.

On the occasions over the years when Francis had spoken at any length with Adriana's mother, they'd moved back and forth between English and Italian, with some French thrown in whenever the subject turned to island history. At first Francis had found the conversations awkward and could only follow the Signora's lead. But once he realized that he could be the one to choose the language, he grew to enjoy the shifts.

So he was discomforted by the Signora's decision to speak only in English with him. English had been the language Adriana had preferred to use with him once she'd become fluent. But with the

Signora, the exclusive use of English made him feel more awkward than ever in her presence.

He tried to offer consolation. No, the Signora didn't want consolation. Her daughter would be found, she said. You don't console the mother of a daughter who will be found.

"Forgive me, Signora. I only want to help."

"Everyone wants to help and no one is helping."

It was a clear day in late March after weeks of rain, the air over the island was spiced with the smell of bonfires in the fields, the sea was glittering, the vault of sky a magnetic blue. But in the dining room of the Nardi villa the only light was the sunlight shining through the slats of the shutters, turning the darkness a pale gray and the walls the greenish color of a gecko.

Francis had taken to visiting Signora Nardi regularly in the months since Adriana had been gone. He was served English tea at the dining-room table, with powdery scones baked by Luisa, the Nardis' cook. Francis would talk with the Signora about her daughter, praising the girl for her facility with English, her quick mind, her perfect pronunciation. The woman would listen with an expression that suggested boredom, but she wouldn't tell Francis to stop.

It was Francis who had persuaded the Signora to seek help from the local police. And it was from the police rather than Signora Nardi that Francis learned about the possible involvement of a foreigner. An American man who went by the name of Murray Murdoch? It was such an obvious identification that Francis didn't bother to point it out. Everyone on the island knew or knew about the investor from New York and his interest in Adriana Nardi. So why wasn't Murray asked some probing questions?

Apparently, Adriana had been seen by a taxi driver talking with an older man somewhere on the road — the driver couldn't say exactly where — between San Giovanni and Lacona. Is that so? Francis Cape was startled, but only for a moment. He wanted to point out that Le Foci was between San Giovanni and Lacona. But the Signora was explaining that the man had been old. A rich old white-haired straniero, most likely one of the millionaire yachters who docked in Porto Azzurro — this was the type of man Signora Nardi wanted to find.

Why didn't she allow herself to harbor suspicions about Murray Murdoch? Francis wanted to ask Signora Nardi this but couldn't. It was impossible to ask Signora Nardi anything. He couldn't ask her about the search for her daughter; he couldn't even ask her if she was well. Tutt'OK? This was one of his favorite greetings, and he called it out to his Elban friends when he passed them on the street. Tutt'OK? Everything was not OK with Signora Nardi, he already knew this, and anyway, he was expected to speak only in English.

He wanted to help. You can't help, Mr. Cape. He wanted to —

"To what?"

"To . . ."

"To what, Mr. Cape?"

He heard the chatter of sparrows out in the terrace garden, a garden as harsh as the Signora, with bramble roses and juniper thistles and gravel paths winding between meager olive trees. But on the Nardi property was also the beautiful garden in the ravine that Adriana had tended when she was home. Francis had been there many times since Adriana's disappearance. Already the lilies were blooming, and the ground was carpeted with purslane and chickweed. He didn't bother to pull the weeds; he wanted to see them grow, spread, choke the garden, destroy it. He hoped that Signora Nardi wouldn't send someone to weed the rock garden. He wanted to suggest this. He wanted to suggest —

"To what, Mr. Cape?"

"To suggest . . ."

"Yes?"

"The American investor. Shouldn't you find out more about him?"

"I know what I need to know."

"He is American." He'd been wanting to say this to her — Murray Murdoch is American! He wanted to startle her with his insinuation. But she just smiled coldly and danced her fingernails with a clatter across the table's mosaic tiles.

"He came here many times. Excuse me for reminding you of this. But I don't understand why you —"

"He is not an old man. Now do you understand, Mr. Cape?"

What could she possibly have said that would extend the meaning she conveyed with her eyes? Eyes with mud-colored irises, eyes telling him that there was nothing he could do or say in his own defense.

How slowly she moved when she reached for her tea. As though she were underwater, swimming away from Francis, out of his reach.

She was an agile woman — he hadn't realized how agile until that moment. Nor had he realized that her hostility was isolated, directed at him alone. He'd mistaken her dislike of him for natural reserve. But she wasn't a reserved woman, she wasn't even un-friendly. She simply despised Francis Cape. She'd despised him from the day they first met, and now she despised him for having something to do with the disappearance of her daughter.

Francis was an old man. A very old man. Yet he wasn't an American. Signora Nardi was looking for a wealthy American man, not an elderly librarian from London. He was confused. Francis Cape was an Englishman. So why should Signora Nardi despise him? He only wanted to help.

Not knowing what else to do, Francis added another lump of sugar to his tea. He stirred and stirred, but the sugar wouldn't dis-solve. Looking into his cup, he thought he might have dropped in a pebble by mistake. Then he discovered he could dig the edge of his spoon into the lump and crumble it.

Francis said he hoped the bad weather was over for the season. Signora Nardi hoped so too.

Soon it was time for Francis to leave. He stood. She offered to show him to the door. He declined.

"Arrivederla, Signora," he said, knowing full well that she'd hear this as an insult. "Buona giornata."

His knees were stiff, his jaw ached, and he needed to fart. How had he gotten so old? How old was he really? he asked himself as he stood outside the Nardi villa. He was surprised to realize that with his thoughts in such a swirl he could remember the year of his birth but not the day.

How old am I, Adriana? Tell me.

You are very very very very old, Mr. Francis Cape.

It would be easy to cast Signora Nardi as a type of woman familiar to readers of Victorian novels. She was stern, dusty, stuck in the past, repelled by the present, indifferent to the future. I find myself picturing her in a decrepit wedding dress with an ancient, cobwebbed feast laid out on the table. But my mother insists that Signora Nardi was a woman you would think you could know at a glance, and then you'd realize you didn't know at all.

Signora Nardi was not what she seemed. Not dusty. Not stern. And not loveless. She was no worse than solitary. She chose to stay alone in the villa day after day in order to be available. It was good for a daughter to know that her mother would always be at home. Signora Nardi wanted her daughter to be free to fill her life with experience, to find out what she could about the world, to travel and make friends, meet men, find love, and all the while to enjoy the certainty that she had a home and her mother was there. She could leave home. She could come back. Her mother was waiting.

Our mother often thought of Adriana's mother waiting in her lonely villa for her daughter to return. She imagined the Signora sitting inside her dark house, flinching at every unexpected sound. She imagined the Signora as a child, a little dark-haired beauty romping through the vineyards and olive groves, light-footed, light-hearted. Claire imagined being that child.

She'd only met Signora Nardi once, had thought afterward of Miss Havisham, and yet was surprised to feel at the same time the discomfort of recognition, the sense that in this strange, lonely Elban woman she was seeing a version of herself. The Signora had come to our home seeking help instead of revenge. She was prepared to trust Murray. The fact of this sank in slowly. Signora Nardi was not the kind of woman who would have been flagrant with trust. She was cautious. She had every right to be suspicious of Murray and instead believed he was innocent. Such confidence of judgment. Claire wanted the Signora to persuade her of her husband's innocence. As the days passed she kept thinking about her, kept returning to the memory of their brief conversation, kept trying to imagine the thoughts of the Signora, kept trying and failing to understand why she felt such a profound connection to this woman after her single visit, and eventually decided that the only way she could understand the Signora was to see her again.

Delayed by the rain and her own reluctance, Claire didn't visit the Nardi villa until the end of March. Coincidentally, she went the morning of the same day when Francis would pay his last visit.

Signora Nardi didn't have a phone, and since Claire didn't have the courage to write to her she arrived unannounced. The cook let her in and showed her to the library — a room lined with bookshelves from floor to ceiling, with shuttered French doors, closed and bolted, that would have opened to the garden. A grand piano filled one corner. The room was lit by a crystal chandelier that seemed to Claire too ornate for the setting. Arranged without any apparent order on some of the shelves at eye level were stone carvings, masks, iron arrowheads, and spear tips. Other objects in the collection, including the porcelain cup from which Murray had drunk his peppermint tea, were kept locked in a cabinet at the back of the room. On the walls were portraits, one of a man in a tasseled uniform, another of a woman in Victorian dress holding a lapdog, another of a gray-bearded man holding a pen.

Claire browsed through books while she waited. She pulled down a dusty copy of Marco Polo's *Travels,* but the pages were fragile so she carefully returned the book to the shelf. She was trying to make sense of the Italian in the prologue of Boccaccio's *Decameron* — "Umana cosa è aver compassione degli afflitti" — when she heard a door shut down the hall.

"Buongiorno, Signora."

"Signora Nardi, buongiorno. Sono, sono, mi dispiace . . ."

"Speak in English."

"I apologize. For arriving here without warning. I've been wanting to come see you again. You've heard nothing from Adriana?"

"Nothing. Come sit with me." Signora Nardi led her to the chairs on the far side of the glass cabinet. The cook appeared and transferred from her tray a little pewter coffeepot, hot milk and sugar, and a plate piled with meringues and chocolate biscuits.

What did they talk about? Even as soon as the afternoon of the same day, Claire wouldn't clearly remember the content of their conversation. They talked of Adriana — her education, her talents, her fellowship at Oxford. Signora Nardi had said something about Adriana's sullenness — what, exactly? Talk had turned to the island economy. The struggling iron mines on Elba. Local quarries. The inlaid serpentine on the library floor. What predictions had the Signora made about the island's future? Claire couldn't remember. What had she said about her own health? Claire couldn't remember.

Strange for Claire to remember their first encounter so vividly, the second with such difficulty. If she'd gone to the Nardi villa in search of understanding, she came away with no better sense of the Signora than before. But if, in fact, she'd gone for reassurance, somehow she'd received a fair dose. She'd left feeling comforted, though why or how she couldn't say. She felt certain that the Signora was more than just a good woman. She was a deserving woman. And she was powerful. And, as Claire had already sensed, she was potentially impetuous. Despite what others said about her, Signora Nardi hadn't finished with the world.

Spring on Elba that year was variable, with the sun rising behind storm clouds, burning through noon mist, and sinking from clear skies. It was hard to believe during a crystalline afternoon that we'd woken that morning to the sound of rain spilling from the roof. Single days were broken into pieces by the weather. My brothers never went back to school. Everything seemed mysterious to us. If a week might last a month, how could we make plans? We could only make up ways to occupy ourselves from hour to hour.

Only Murray made plans. He planned to buy more land in Cavoli, Chiessi, Pomonte. He'd heard about a grotto filled with tourmaline outside of San Piero. He roamed the area for days looking for the cave but never found it.

He considered purchasing an old farmhouse and the surrounding land in the plain between Marina di Campo and Portoferraio. He wired his mother for money, but she refused and again advised him to come home. He wrote to his uncles. They didn't bother to write back.

After finding shotgun shells on his land, he posted NO HUNTING signs. He decided to build a fence. He hired two men from Portoferraio to work for him and paid them the equivalent of fifty dollars each for a week's worth of doing nothing, since the wire fencing was never delivered. The next week he put them to work building a stone wall around the property. They worked slowly. Their siesta lasted three hours.

Murray ran his Lambretta off the road on his way home from the bank in Portoferraio one day. He was able to get the motorcycle started again, and he arrived spattered with mud but absorbed by anticipation of the next day's work. He was glad to find that Claire had waited for him instead of eating dinner with the rest of us. After changing his clothes, he opened a bottle of sparkling wine. Lidia had left them a plate of anchovies and a round of bread. A sip of the wine filled him with warmth, the white flesh of the anchovies melted like butter on his tongue, and when he blinked he found Claire looking at him from across the table without the sharp query of suspicion in her eyes.

A spring night on Elba. Claire and Murray, tousled, half dressed, bleary from the wine, made love on the sofa and fell asleep in each other's arms. Nat woke up late, went to the bathroom to pee, and then trudged sleepily into our parents' room, climbed onto the bed, and fell asleep between pillows that he mistook for our parents. Meena, inadvertently locked outside, yowled in the night, but no one heard her. When the rain began she took refuge beneath a board leaning against the garden shed. When the wind blew the board away, she scampered back to the villa and shivered in the doorway. And when the man emerged from the darkness, walking up the gravel path with the stiffness of a stilt-walker, and pounded weakly on the door, Meena didn't bother to move, for she knew what would happen in a minute or two if the man just kept knocking.

The door opened, and Meena scampered inside between Claire's feet. Claire suppressed an exclamation. Without a word she led Francis Cape into the front hall, where he stood dripping, trembling, his lips moving in soundless words.

Murray appeared, wearing only his trousers and undershirt. "Francis?" he asked. Could it really be Francis? Old Francis Cape gone out of his mind?

"It's me, all right. I'm here as a friend, you know."

Claire and Murray exchanged the familiar glance that people share when they believe themselves in the presence of insanity.

"I'm here to warn you."

"Come into the kitchen, Francis. Have a cup of tea. You need to calm down, collect your wits."

"It's you's the one in trouble." Startled by his own slurring speech, he shook his head, clenched his hands together to steady himself, and said, "I mean to say, I've just come from Uccello's, you remember it, the enoteca, we've been there, all of us, back when." He stopped abruptly, leaving Claire and Murray to fill in the rest of the sentence: back when Adriana was with us.

"Sit down, Francis. Sit and catch your breath, at least."

"I'm fine."

"You're soaked."

"The rain came in at the last minute. And there I was without my car."

"You didn't drive?"

"My car wouldn't start. I walked."

"You walked!"

"From Portoferraio? All the way from Portoferraio? My God, Francis!"

"I don't mind a good walk. I never mind a good walk. It's something I do quite well, you know. I walk. I can walk five miles at a stretch. And I know the roads. The moon was out only ten minutes ago. Then the downpour, all of a sudden. The rain this season. I've never seen anything like it. We've had wet springs, dry springs, but never such weather as this." He paused, looked first at Claire and then at Murray with an expression that both of them read as directly accusing.

"I was at Uccello's," he continued, "and the little woman there — you remember, the one called Ninanina. Ninanina, who is said to have the power of foresight. Did I ever tell you that? Ninanina pulled me aside, and she said to me, she said, Tell your American friend to take his family and get off the island. Tell him he must go home. She said it in Italian, of course, but I am giving you an accurate translation. Tell your American friend to pack up and go home. In my neighborhood, you, Murray Murdoch, are my American friend. And according to Ninanina, you and your whole family should leave the island as soon as possible. There is trouble brewing."

He was panting from the effort of speaking. Murray and Claire stood in silence. Ninanina — Murray tried to recollect — was the kind old woman who once had given him a second bottle of wine for free. Claire remembered her as the woman who offered her cheek to Francis when they'd walked into her enoteca.

"What trouble?" Murray finally asked.

"There are rumors. That's all I know. That's all I could gather."

"I don't understand," said Claire.

"Neither do I," said Murray.

"There are rumors," said Francis slowly, "concerning the disappearance of Adriana Nardi. And the involvement of the investor from the United States."

"That's ridiculous!" Murray spat with a fury that would seem courageous to Claire when she later recalled it.

"I am only the messenger." Francis's voice had become measured, even velvety. And his obvious consciousness of his effect was taken in by Claire, who in an instant decided once and for all that she abhorred the man. But at the same time she knew that the news he was bringing made them dependent on him.

Murray was only enraged. He circled the front hall sputtering, mumbling, protesting, pulling at his ears, kicking the wall. He'd replaced Francis in the role of the madman. Inadvertently, Claire met Francis's eyes and shared with him the same sympathetic glance she'd shared with Murray only minutes earlier.

There was no more talk of tea, and when Francis reached for the door, neither Claire nor Murray tried to stop him. Claire was already heading for the closet where we kept the luggage we'd purchased in Genoa. Murray was still walking in circles.

They argued in quiet, fierce voices. Claire wanted to leave the island the next day. Murray insisted on staying. He said he would not be driven away by rumors. He would not be the scapegoat of people who had no better way to entertain themselves than to turn on a foreigner. The islanders were provincial, uneducated, bigoted.

They doubled their prices as soon as Murray walked into the room. Their children were bullies. Their police were abusive. And don't forget — they shared a recent bloody history of collaboration with their mainland brothers. How easily guilt transforms into hate. They needed a stranger to hold responsible for their own negligence, and they found him in Murray, who, even if not entirely blameless, had done no one any real harm.

Claire and Murray didn't go to sleep until long after midnight. Their argument deteriorated into a cold standoff. Claire said she'd take the children and go to Paris and from there book a flight home. Murray said he'd leave when he was good and ready to leave.

But by the next morning Claire's resolve to return to America had weakened. The sky was clear, the morning clouds tinged with pink, the sea shimmering, the breeze fresh, the oranges sweet and bloody. The barking of dogs set the roosters crowing — or vice versa. The bells of San Lorenzo were ringing. Lidia was knocking on their bedroom door.

FROM ANCIENT ROMAN TIMES up through the 1920s, Italy derived most of its iron from the mines on Elba. But when we lived there, most of the mines had closed or were in the process of closing. Older men were unemployed, the deep wrinkles on their faces permanently stained a rusty yellow, and the young men who had survived the war and returned to the island were commuting to mainland jobs. New hotels were relatively small-scale. While there were tourists on the island, they usually arrived in yachts and didn't wander far outside the harbors of Portoferraio and Porto Azzurro.

To our young eyes, however, Elba was an abundant haven. We had no more awareness of the poverty on the island than we did of the battles being fought around the globe. What we saw were plates heaped with polpo lesso and scampi, grapevines sprouting new leaves, barley stalks trembling as they grew taller before our eyes. Harry remembers in particular the cap of cream on every cup of fresh milk. Patrick likes to describe the bowl in the kitchen that was stacked high with plums in summer, persimmons in winter. Every meal lasted for hours, and one meal followed so quickly after the last that we forgot what it was like to feel hungry. My older brothers didn't have to go to school or help with chores. I didn't have to take a bath every day. None of us had to be in bed by any particular time.

We didn't care that Claire and Murray were inattentive to us. Back in America we would have considered ourselves neglected and wondered what could be more important to our parents than seeing to the care and well-being of their children. But on Elba it seemed right and good that we were given the freedom to wander on our own.

In the morning Francesca would make us promise to stay within calling distance of the house, and then she'd go back to her room and fall asleep. She never knew how far we'd climb up the east side of Monte Giove. We played our game of Giant Ants, perfecting the rules as we went along. We decided that our ants would collect rubies and sapphires and tourmalines, along with gold; only green twigs could be used as antennae; when we were within sight of the ants' horde of gold we could approach it only by hopping on our right foot; if we were touched by an ant's antennae we had to spin three times and then fall to the ground; if we were dead, we had to stay dead until that round of the game was over. We called ourselves Jako One, Two, Three, and Four.

Qui, Jako Three!

Dove?

Guarda!

Io guarda la treasure.

Stai ferma!

You — io getta you!

We took over from our father the belief that we could find our fortune in the solid, integral stuff of the earth. Patrick showed us how to look for glassy beveled cubes with faces that sparkled when you tipped them to catch the sunlight, alloys speckled with yellow, black metallic rocks streaked with silver. He identified the pieces of pyrite, quartz, fluorite, and argentite in our collection and convinced us to discard chunks of marl and limestone. We didn't find another geode, but Harry found a smooth, hard puddle of tuff. We chipped away at it until we each had a handful of shards. We found frothy, shiny gray rocks that were probably obsidian. And once we found a trace of what must have been indicolite, the valuable blue form of tourmaline, tucked between points of white feldspar on a piece of granite too big to lift.

We used a flat-topped boulder for cleaving crystals and pounding smaller rocks into chalk. We argued about what to do with the chalk. Harry wanted to collect it in jars. Nat wanted to use it to paint our faces. Patrick wanted to scatter the chalk in the wind.

Jako Four, you're supposed to stai dead.

Shut up.

You shut up, you're dead. Jako Four is dead and la treasure's mio mio mio!

Mio!

Mio!

You lose, you bigga fat loser!

We came to know the terrain from different perspectives. The vista from the stone terraces midway up Monte Giove was always strange to us, Elba always in disguise. Which way was Portoferraio? Was that Corsica or the mainland we were seeing? We weren't sure. Patrick and Harry disagreed about the island to the north. Harry said it was Capraia, Patrick said it was Gorgona.

But when we were scrambling up and down and across the slopes, the land seemed as familiar as the four of us were to each other. We knew everything that could be known about the earth. We knew the weight of a rock before we picked it up. We knew its hardness and cleavage. We knew what was valuable.

Lascia me!

Guarda, it's, it's . . .

Jako Three.

What did you find?

Io found la treasure. Follow me.

Who among us first noticed? And what did he notice, exactly? None of us can explain. I wonder if together we noted some change in the air, perhaps an odd shape in the clouds or a glory's rainbow diffraction when the sun shone through the misting rain. How quiet it was. So quiet we could hear a snake wriggling in the grass. *Jako One, come in. Are you scaredia? If you're scaredia, close your eyes and sing. What are the songs you know by heart? Ascolta* — four boys singing without making a sound. *Can you*

*hear me, Harry? Io can hear you. Nat? Sì? Oliver? Sì? Patrick?
Donta mova there, donta speak. Now talk con me. You're talking
ma not talking. Think con me. We hear thinking!*

None of us is sure what happened on Elba, but my brothers
and I all remember the sensation of finding ourselves suddenly
capable of miraculous power — the power to speak to each other
without talking aloud. Nat's explanation was that the mountain itself was magic. Patrick reminded us of the crystal he kept under
his bed. Harry wanted to know whether what we were experiencing was good magic or bad magic.

Whatever had happened, Patrick insisted that we must keep it
secret. The rest of us agreed. The need for secrecy was so clear that
we didn't even bother to seal our pact with blood and spit.

We cut our game short and went home early that day. As soon
as we reached the place where the path intersected with the dirt
road heading toward Poggio, we turned back into four ordinary
young boys babbling together so loudly that we scared a whole
flock of starlings from a telephone wire. They rose in a smoky
mass. We shouted and threw rocks that fell far short of their mark.
We picked up more rocks and threw them into the air.

The disappointment we felt at not bringing down a single bird
grew out of proportion. None of us had ever hit a bird with a rock,
but now we thought ourselves ridiculous for having failed. Even
stronger than our disappointment was our sense of shame. Four
boys against a flock of starlings, and we didn't have a single trophy
to show for it. Forgetting what had happened to us on Monte
Giove, we talked of nothing but the birds — how close they were
to us, how poorly we'd aimed — as we trudged up the stairs into our
house. We didn't speak to Lidia when we passed her in the kitchen,
and we didn't bother to wake Francesca to tell her we were home.

We gathered in the living room and waited in sulky silence for
our dinner. Neither of our parents was at home. We didn't care.
Lidia served us bowls of green gurguglione, which we ate for the
first time without complaining. Francesca and Lidia joined us for

supper. Francesca asked us what was wrong, but we were too tired to speak, and soon Francesca and Lidia were engaged in a stormy conversation we didn't even try to follow. We put ourselves to bed. I didn't want to be alone so Nat let me share his bed.

I lay close enough to Nat to feel his warmth without touching him. I felt better, the foggy, inexplicable sensation of shame was dispersing, and in my dopey state I remembered our game of the ants of Monte Giove. I looked forward to tomorrow.

When we weren't in the woods, our language was as coarse and plain as ever, but we wondered if our magic had left some visible trace on us. At home we would study the adults for signs that they'd noticed a change. As far as we could tell, they didn't notice anything. Lidia and Francesca had taken to whispering between themselves, and our parents spent much of their time away from the house. That Claire and Murray were absorbed in problems of great magnitude might have worried us if we had known, but no one bothered to tell us.

Money was one problem. No one, not even Francesca, who often shared gossip with us, told us that our father's mother had stopped sending money, and the uncles wanted Murray to justify the money he'd already spent. Lidia needed money to buy our food. Lorenzo gave our parents another month's grace on the rent, but when the month passed he began charging interest.

Murray, biding time, trying to make work for himself, put in a bid for more land in the San Piero zone but couldn't raise the money to meet the deadline for a down payment. He waited for other land to come on the market. Every farmer he met talked about someone else who was selling his land. But no one wanted to sell to the investor from America.

We had no idea what trouble our parents were in. We would go off each day to a different world and leave the bland, real world of adults behind. They could have their real world. We didn't want it.

A world worth only the value of its resale, a world without magic. That's what we'd been taught to think; no one ever bothered to correct us.

So we didn't know about the dreams. Everyone else on Elba seemed to know about them, but not us. Everyone was talking about the dreams, about the peste di sogni spreading across the island.

It was a fisherman in Porto Azzurro who had the first dream. He dreamt that he was in the crypt of the Parrocchiale, keeping guard at an open tomb. Inside, a girl was sleeping on a marble pallet. He recognized her as the Nardi girl. He felt no need to wake her. When a man, a stranger, came along with a bucket of wet concrete, the fisherman put his finger to his lips to signal him to be quiet. The man nodded. He set down the bucket and began mixing the concrete with a huge wooden spoon, stirring it like a thick pot of minestrone. Then he began stacking bricks across the entrance to the tomb and slathering them with the concrete. The fisherman tried to stop him but discovered that he couldn't move or speak.

Who was the man? his friends wanted to know after the fisherman had recounted the dream. The fisherman couldn't say. Was the man a stranger? Yes. Was he American? Yes, he must have been American because he was wearing the helmet worn by U.S. troops — a detail that had great weight among the listeners, since most of them remembered the American soldiers who came to Elba in '44, and they remembered their helmets.

At first, though, the fisherman's dream seemed no more than a fanciful concoction, and while the friends talked at length about it, they didn't presume the dream to have an importance worthy of sharing with others beyond their circle. But when one of the fisherman's friends happened to hear his sister-in-law's cousin talking about her own dream after mass two days later and the cousin said the name *Nardi,* the fisherman's friend exclaimed aloud at the coincidence.

The second dream, the one dreamt by the cousin, a seamstress from the tiny village of Lacona, involved fire. The seamstress had dreamt that she'd seen the glow of a fire on little Isola della Stella, and she'd swum all the way across the strait to investigate. By the time she reached the island the fire had burned out. She climbed over the rocks and found the charred body of a girl lying amidst smoldering embers. The girl was still alive, barely, but burned beyond recognition. The cousin asked her name, and she said, *Nardi.* Then she fell silent, and her eyes rolled back in death. The cousin started to run. She tripped over the outstretched legs of a man. He was sitting on the ground across from the bier, smoking a cigarette. The cousin begged him for help, but he looked at her with the blank look of a foreigner who doesn't speak or understand the language.

Two dreams became three. At Ninanina's enoteca in Portoferraio, one of the men who had worked briefly for Murray listened to the fisherman's friend finishing the story of the cousin's dream, and then he told about his own dream. He had dreamt that he'd been helping the American signore test explosives on a hill above Rio nell'Elba when he'd seen the Nardi girl wandering across the slope. He called to her but it was too late. There was the pop of dynamite, and thick smoke filled the air.

Someone else described a dream that he'd heard from the maid of Signora Claudia Patresi, a wealthy, ancient, bedridden woman who'd come to the island from La Spezia five years earlier to die in the company of her niece. She was dying slowly. In Claudia Patresi's dream, she'd been ice-skating on a long, deserted river — she hadn't been ice-skating since she'd visited Vienna in 1892! — and she'd skated up to a man who was fishing just as he was pulling a fish from the hole. But it wasn't a fish. It was a girl. The Nardi girl, her face the color of clay, her cheeks swollen by the grip of the hook.

Three dreams became four. Four became eight. But what are dreams? people asked. Dreams are hopes that have gone rotten. Dreams are your punishment for drinking too much wine. Dreams are the stories the devil whispers in your ear while you are sleeping.

Eight dreams became ten, twelve, sixteen. In Poggio, in Capoliveri, in Zanca, Procchio, Carpani, people gathered to tell their
dreams. Those who forgot their dreams upon waking drank black-
berry tea to help them remember. People did not only dream of the
Nardi girl. They dreamt that the sea was so thickly covered with
dead fish that they could walk all the way to Corsica. They dreamt
that Volterraio erupted. They dreamt of talking dogs and moving
statues and church bells that wouldn't ring.

What are dreams? How can you tell a true dream from a false
dream? Who's to say that everyone, from the fisherman to old
Claudia Patresi, wasn't lying? Why would they lie? Why wouldn't
they lie? And why not blame everything on the power of suggestion?

Twenty dreams. Twenty-one, twenty-two. The roar of argument in the bars grew louder. What about life? Truth? Here, this, a
hand in front of your face! What are dreams? Add a hundred of
them together and you get nothing.

Francis Cape stood at the counter in Ninanina's enoteca and
sipped his wine. He didn't say much, but he listened carefully. He
couldn't believe what he was hearing. He'd admit this to Ninanina
when she was refilling his glass, and she'd flash a dark look and
say, "You know what dreams can tell us, Francesco, sì?" But when
he said no, he didn't, she'd only shake her head.

What can dreams tell us? The people of Elba were divided.
Most were skeptical at first, wary of confusing dreams and reality. A few of the most fervent believers were prepared to accept
the dreams as revelations. Local clergy had nothing to say about the
matter. The editor of Portoferraio's local newspaper attributed
the dreams to xenophobia, but he couldn't publish an editorial
about what amounted to no more than hearsay.

What can dreams tell us? Francis Cape, himself capable of the
wildest, most impure, unspeakable dreams, had always thought
dreams were no better than ridiculous. He was shocked to see his

Elban neighbors treating their dreams with increasing solemnity. They might have been a religious people, but their priests were adept at keeping superstition in check.

Whoever heard of dreams being responsible for turning hundreds of people against an innocent man? This was the gist of what Francis Cape wondered as he listened to the Elbans. And this was the question our mother asked our father after she finally went to see Francis Cape at his home and asked him exactly what he'd meant by his warning.

"Salem, Massachusetts," Murray said in reply to Claire, standing behind her with a tumbler of scotch in his hand, watching her reflection in the mirror. Her face was covered with her hands; her hair fell in a curtain. "Salem in the sixteen hundreds."

"Oh, Murray, come off it."

"They say that colorful dreams come from abstinence. Maybe that's the problem with these people. They're not getting enough."

"It's not funny, Murray."

"Dreams are funny. They are hilarious. Nightmares are the funniest kind. Harry dreaming last month he cut off Ollie's winky by mistake. Remember? And then there was Nat's dream about gentilissima Lidia cooking the cat!"

"Murray . . ."

"I love you, Claire."

"What's this about?"

"I'm telling you I love you."

"This is serious, Murray."

"Nothing more serious."

"Stop it."

"I haven't had a dream in . . . I can't remember how long it's been, it's been so long."

"Murray."

"You want me to stop?"

"Yes."

"Whoever heard of dreams turning people against an innocent man? You're right, Claire. It can't happen."

"We need to leave Elba. You need to stop this."

"Stop this?"

"Murray . . ."

"You want me to stop?"

"Yes."

"You really want me to stop?"

"Yes. No."

"You don't want me to stop?"

"No."

"It feels good?"

"Yes."

"You sure? I can stop if you want me to."

"No."

"You sure?"

"Yes."

"You do want me to stop?"

"No."

"You don't?"

"Don't stop, Murray. OK?"

"OK."

What are dreams? They are stories we tell ourselves when we are alone.

Then the body decides to return us to reality — the reality of stomach cramps, sore throats, swollen glands. The fact of pain. The necessity of food, oxygen, and water. The fact of fever.

It was Meena the cat who got sick first, though our parents hardly noticed. We noticed, but we couldn't do anything but watch her ribs pulse beneath her fur and her tongue twitch as she panted. She lay on Nat's bed for three days without eating or drinking. Her nose was hot. The insides of her velvety ears were hot. And then on the fourth day she dragged herself to her water bowl and drank until the bowl was empty. By the fifth day she was as sly and quick and aloof as ever.

Harry was the next one to fall ill. He complained of a headache, and when Francesca felt his forehead her hand jerked away from the shock of heat. She put him to bed and sent a neighbor, Marco Scozzi, to fetch our parents, who had gone into Portoferraio to have lunch.

Our mother came home with Marco; she left Murray in Portoferraio to shop for presents for Harry, whose birthday was the following Wednesday. She gave Harry half an aspirin, coaxed him to take a few sips of water, and let him sleep for the rest of the day. In the evening she put cotton balls soaked in warm olive oil in his ears. If he wasn't better in a couple of days, she told herself, she'd check with the pharmacist. If he took a turn for the worse, she'd call a doctor.

Patrick woke up with a fever the next morning. He and Harry stayed in their bedroom with the shutters closed because the light hurt their eyes. They weren't even interested in the comic books Murray brought them. Nat mixed dish soap with water and blew bubbles in the room, but Patrick mumbled for him to stop, and when he didn't, Harry called him an idiot. Nat left the room crying.

The first cause for alarm was Harry's complaint that the back of his neck hurt. Claire immediately called Lorenzo, who gave her the name of a local doctor. The doctor was in Pisa for the day, but his wife booked a home visit for the following afternoon.

By the evening I was sick. This was not like any kind of sickness I had ever known. My gut ached, my head ached, my ears throbbed with pain, I couldn't swallow or speak, and I didn't have the strength to squeeze my fingers into a fist.

In our Marciana house I shared a room with Nat. When I fell ill my parents moved a cot into Harry and Patrick's room for me —

"the sick room" it was called, Nat announced. He wasn't sick — hahah! He didn't have to stay in bed — hahah! His voice hurt my ears. Someday, I knew, Patrick would beat him up for this.

Damp washcloths were draped over my forehead. Warm cotton plugged my ears. I heard my mother's voice but I couldn't understand what she was saying. I wondered if there was ever a time in my life when I hadn't been sick.

In the afternoon someone unbuttoned my pajama top and I felt the cold of what must have been a stethoscope against my skin. Then a lizard started to crawl across my chest and up my neck, along my jaw, beneath my ears. I heard a man's voice, a voice inflected with Italian, calling my name. I didn't understand why he needed to call me when I was lying right there in front of him, whoever he was. I wanted to tell him to leave me alone. I wanted to sleep. I did sleep, but not for long. I was woken by a huge black glossy ant, so huge it could hardly squeeze through the doorway. I screamed, and my mother rushed into the room. As she approached me the ant faded and disappeared. But it had been there long enough for my mother to see it, so I didn't bother to explain my terror.

Through the next period all I perceived besides the pain were odors, each of them distinct: honey, olive oil, ammonia and vinegar and candied cherries and the perfumed residue of shampoo in my mother's hair. When I smelled her beside me I was angry — why wouldn't she quit bothering me and let me sleep? When I didn't smell her I was angry — why wasn't she with me, making the pain go away?

At some point I revived enough to know that I wanted to tell my mother she was stupid, I wanted to tell my brothers they were ugly, I wanted a sip of water, I didn't want a sip of water, I wanted to sleep but I didn't want to sleep because I was afraid the giant ant would come back. I didn't understand why no one was helping me. It wasn't fair. I was five years old, and I was supposed to get a glass of water when I wanted it. But there was water only when I didn't want it. Didn't anyone know that everything inside me was hurting? Where was everyone? I looked across the room and saw Patrick sleeping on his stomach, his covers tossed to his ankles, one arm dangling off the side of the bed. The sight reassured me. Patrick was here. Patrick would take care of me. Patrick, wake up! But he wouldn't wake up. Whenever Patrick wouldn't let me wake him up I knew he was just pretending to sleep. Patrick was stupid! Everyone was stupid and ugly, except my mother, who poured warm olive oil into my ears and made them feel better. I did feel better. The room was filled with light, Patrick was sitting up in bed reading a book, Harry was sleeping, and there was a bowl of orange Jell-O beside my bed. Jell-O!

We all improved abruptly. One day we'd been stiff with pain, the next day we were complaining because we couldn't run around outside in our bare feet.

Then it was Nat's turn. He'd spent the week feeling alternately proud of his good health and bored without the company of his brothers. Our parents were useless. Even Meena the cat wouldn't play with him. He told Francesca he wanted to be sick. She ignored him. He pretended to be too sick to get out of bed, and for a moment he had Claire fooled. He was pleased to see how angry he'd made her. The next day he really did feel sick, and he was surprised when Claire wouldn't rush to his bedside.

By the time Nat fell ill, Claire had a clear sense of the fever's trajectory — its abrupt climb and steady high plateau over a course of five days. We'd all had the same symptoms and been sick for the same amount of time.

We had to put off celebrating Harry's birthday, which upset the rest of us but not Nat, who was too sick to care. We all felt the justice of his illness. It was his punishment for taunting us. He deserved to suffer as we'd suffered. Hahaha, Nat. Look at you now. Poverino.

I'm not sure how we realized that Nat's sickness was taking a different shape. The light hurt his eyes just as it had hurt ours.

He'd ask for water then push it away when it was brought to him, just as we'd done. He was terribly sick. We'd been terribly sick. Poverino Nat. We taunted him. He didn't have the strength to do more than gesture with his hand for us to go away. We went away — but we'll be back, Poverino, we said.

We hadn't realized that Claire had been staying up with us and then with Nat through the night, snatching an hour here and there during the day to rest. Even when she went to lie down she couldn't sleep. Or she'd drift toward sleep and after a minute wake with a start. Once she woke to find a ladybug sitting on her hand. She'd stayed still for a long while, watching the bug, and then had sent it with a puff out the window.

Claire was so exhausted that at first she attributed her anxiety about Nat to her own fatigue. Day three of the fever. Day four still to go, she told herself. Day five he would be sitting up and eating Jell-O.

The doctor had prescribed a liquid antibiotic, but as far as Claire could tell it hadn't helped the rest of us. Still, she gave it to Nat in the proper doses, tilting his head back in her hand and pouring a teaspoonful into his mouth. Once she bumped her arm against the table and spilled the medicine across Nat's pillow. She blotted it dry but didn't bother to change the case, and when I came into the room I mistook the stain for blood pouring from Nat's ear.

The fourth day came and went and then the fifth, and Nat showed no signs of improvement. He huddled beneath the sheet, and when I touched the lumpy outline of his body, he'd shudder. Claire continued with the routine of his care. The doctor came for a second visit and prescribed a stronger antibiotic. Claire asked if they should take him to the hospital in Livorno and realized only by hearing herself ask the question that she was scared, as scared as she'd been when the engineer had dangled Nat over the *Casparia*'s rail. When the comparison came to mind, she could only stare at the doctor, stunned.

He said he didn't want Nat moved. Which meant he was telling her that her son was too sick to go to the hospital.

She collapsed in Murray's arms after the doctor left, and Murray was grateful for the chance to offer her comfort. He reassured her, promised her that Nat would be fine, promised to bring in another doctor, reminded her of the time Harry contracted pneumonia, what a scare they'd had, but he'd recovered, hadn't he?

Claire realized as she clung to Murray that they'd taken to escaping from their troubles into each other. The natural ease of their love had been weakened by suspicion. Lately, suspicion had been replaced by a narrow, consuming need for each other's company. They'd been neglecting their children. They'd been horrible parents. She was a horrible mother.

And even now, Murray's presence was enough to subdue Claire's rising guilt. He convinced her she needed to sleep. She was mistaking guilt for exhaustion. Of course she was exhausted. All right, she'd sleep and let Murray take care of Nat for a while. He helped her to bed and was going to help her slip under the covers, but she sent him back to Nat's room.

When she woke she couldn't tell whether it was morning or afternoon. Wandering through the quiet house, she felt like she did when she woke in the middle of the night, though daylight lit up the windows. In Nat's room she found Murray asleep on the edge of Nat's bed, but Nat was awake, and when he saw her he smiled weakly. She smoothed his wet bangs to the side of his forehead. His skin was cool to her touch — or at least cooler than it had been for seven days, and his eyes had lost their milkiness. Claire wanted to cry. She disguised her emotion with a little gulp of laughter that woke Murray. They spoke in low, calm, efficient voices about what would be best for Nat — orange juice or orange Jell-O.

It took Nat another three days to recover strength enough to stand up, and he remained disoriented in some ways. But he ate heartily, laughed when we made faces at him, threw comic books and spoons and even a full cup of water across the room at us when we teased him. He ate a big piece of the chocolate cake Claire baked for Harry's birthday party. He worked on puzzles. He played with Harry's new troop of toy soldiers. He called Patrick a dumbhead and me a snotface. And when he was finally allowed to go outside and play with us one beautiful June day, when for the first time in weeks we were able to roam in our pack of four away from the house and up the slope of Monte Giove, Nat resumed his place in our game of ants. *Jako Three, come in, it's Jako One here.*

Maybe the game kept us from recognizing that Nat had changed. When we were playing, scrambling toward and away from the secret horde of gold, the four of us were as close to being a single self as we would ever come. We didn't need speech to understand each other. In retrospect, though, we can point to signs that Nat was having trouble. At home when someone spoke to him we'd see a strange expression on his face, new furrows in his forehead suggesting deep confusion. He'd have to look directly at us, he'd ask *what,* we'd repeat ourselves, he'd ask *what* again, we'd repeat ourselves again, and when he still looked at us, confused, we would resort to pointing, or else we'd just give up.

He hadn't gone deaf, not exactly. What happened to Nat was stranger than deafness. The fever had left him with hearing that was fragile, like a long-distance line at the mercy of the weather. Sounds would be coming to him with a clarity that was almost painful, then they'd fade out, and for an interval lasting at least a few minutes and sometimes as long as an hour he wouldn't be able to hear anything at all.

Like the rest of us would have done in his place, Nat decided to keep his condition a secret. And he was good at deception. If he wanted to know what he'd missed, he'd wait until we'd forgotten that we'd already repeated ourselves. He'd fall asleep in front of the radio. He'd fall asleep on Murray's lap. He'd decipher Lidia's meaning from the expression on her face. He'd shrug when Francesca asked him a question. He was clever in so many ways that none of us caught on.

OLLIE, I'M LOSING TRACK. There's nearly fifty years of life between then and now, almost fifty years to clutter my mind. I don't remember the doctor prescribing a second antibiotic for Nat. I asked Nat about this and he says he doesn't remember either. Where are you getting your information? How do you know so much? That last exchange between Francis Cape and Signora Nardi, for instance. How did you know about that? I don't recall telling you, and you say you weren't able to find anyone during your last visit to Elba who remembered the Nardi family. But you're right — the Signora did give Francis reason to feel accused. I found out about this later from our cook, Lidia, who was friendly with Signora Nardi's cook.

The more I talk about Elba, the murkier my memory becomes. Did it really rain so much that spring? Did I roast a chicken for Christmas? You say we had a radio. I don't remember any radio. And did I tell you I was reading Keats? Not only have I forgotten what I did four and a half decades ago, but I've forgotten what I said to you when you were last here.

What do you know, and what are you making up as you go along? I can't discern the difference anymore.

You've told me you want to write something that's true. A true history of fact. You make me wonder. Are you running from your own life into the past, and from the past into a fairy tale? What you're writing about my life doesn't match my collection of memories. What do I remember? I'm not sure. What do I know? What do you know? Do you really know, Ollie, that Signora Claudia Patresi dreamed about ice-skating? Where did you hear this?

I don't remember knowing about you boys playing secret

games in the mountains. But I do remember wondering what you were up to. All the whispering you did. You took to talking in a peculiar concoction of Italian and English. Do you really remember it? I remember. You boys talking amongst yourselves in your own stew of a language. Not just an Italian phrase thrown in here and there. What I heard was an incomprehensible mix of sounds. Could it be that what you're remembering is not a magical means of communication but nonsense that you could only pretend to understand?

What do you know for sure? I've gone back to old journals and sometimes I can't even read my handwriting! But as far as I can tell I never mention anyone named Ninanina. I remember the tiny woman who ran the enoteca in Portoferraio. Her name was Ninanina? This rings a bell. But how did you find this out, Ollie?

We've had a full week of clear skies, but it's been so cold the snow hasn't even started to melt. The white snow, the white sun . . . and did I tell you that for the first year ever, the swans are wintering here? Every morning I see them drifting back and forth across the inlet. I've tried to feed them, but they're too vain to eat. They want to be admired, that's all. Lloyd Hunter next door tried to scare them off with a shotgun. He's worried they'll freeze. But the swans have decided to stay and that's that. A pop of a gun isn't going to change their minds. I told this to Emily, who told this to her father, who told Emily to tell me that if the swans freeze to death, it's my fault. Even if they don't eat the bread I leave for them, I'm the one responsible for deceiving them into thinking they could survive our winter — so says Lloyd Hunter. I told Emily to tell her father if he shoots that gun once more, I'm going to call the police. Lloyd told Emily to tell me that's it, I can find someone else to shovel my walk. Which is a peculiar thing to say, since Lloyd Hunter hasn't offered to shovel snow for me for years.

Now what do I really remember? I let my thoughts drift like those swans across the dark water, and I remember the hollow sounds of voices coming through the fog in Portoferraio. I remember the gritty black sand on the beach at Padulella. Looking out from the darkness of the stone chapel on Volterraio to the sea. Watching you boys running after Meena into the vineyard. Nat's tired smile after he'd been sick, the smile of a little boy who thinks he's just played a splendid joke. I remember watching Lidia squeeze a lemon over a plate of anchovies. I remember walking out of the Chiesa della Misericordia into the rain. The pink-tinged sky at twilight. Harry calling us to come see the dead mouse floating in a pail of muddy water. Patrick calling us to come outside on the first cold day of autumn to see our breath make clouds. I remember everything I did routinely as if I'd done it only once — drinking my morning caffé, walking to Marciana Marina, floating on my back in that salty sea.

I am an old woman, ten years older than old Francis Cape had been in 1957. Do you want to hear what your old mother remembers about making love? I'm not going to tell you. But when you discuss your parents' absorption in each other, you might consider the complexities of love. You might think about how passion can become cruel when it is defensive.

What else do I remember? Looking for a gold earring I lost on the street in Porto Azzurro. Watching six fishermen in a row pass along a single wooden match to light their six cigarettes.

Do I really remember any of this? The more I read about my life on Elba, the more I forget. Alzheimer's. Little Emily Hunter keeps asking me if I have Alzheimer's yet. No, not yet, Emily, but soon.

You invited me to go back to Elba with you this spring. I declined. But I wish your father were still alive to accompany you. It would have done him good to return. And you can imagine all he'd tell you. By the time we left Elba, Murray knew that island better than he knew any other place else in the world. He knew it inside and out. He'd have plenty to add to this story.

Imagine Murray and me trying to sort through our memories to come up with a single version of our past. Remembering together what happened, what didn't happen, what almost and might have happened. I often find myself anticipating Murray's objections. Claire, the black sand beach was at Topinetti. And the earring I lost was pearl, not gold — a present to me from Murray's mother.

I remember looking for diamonds on Volterraio. I remember Harry cupping a lizard in his hands. I remember Nat's sharp reply when I asked him if he was having trouble hearing. He could hear just fine, he said, and I believed him. I remember you, Ollie, running toward the end of the pier in Marciana Marina while I yelled at you to stop. I remember the fisherman who caught you and carried you back to us.

I don't remember ever threatening again to take you boys and leave Elba. I was ready to stay with Murray as long as he wanted to stay. Only guilty men run from suspicion, he insisted, and though I didn't entirely agree, I was afraid that if he did leave the island the police would concoct a formal charge against Murray in order to bring him back. We couldn't leave, no more than we could have unlocked a padlock without the key. There were days when I thought we'd never go home.

I close my eyes and remember the winter wind against my face. The summer wind. The warm green water of the Terranera sulfur baths. The smell of fishing nets drying in the sun in Porto Azzurro. The fresh schiacciata from the bakery in Poggio. The gift of goat cheese from our neighbor. The bundles of fresh thyme and rosemary and mint brought to us by Lidia's niece. The red poppies in the meadows. Dust rising as we trudged along the path to the beach at Lacona. Riding on the back of Murray's motorcycle at night after we'd finished off a bottle of wine at a restaurant in Capoliveri. Standing in a doorway, watching you boys fill a box with the toys you wanted to take back to America.

THE TRUTH, FRANCIS CAPE would have said, is a sequence of names and dates arranged as verifiable facts. The truth is a fingerprint left behind by a thief or a document signed by a king. The truth is something you see with your own eyes and remember forever.

The truth, Francis knew, was that Adriana went to visit our father in Le Foci one autumn night in 1956. She hadn't stayed long with him — just long enough to let him have his way with her. Wasn't that so, Adriana? No! Oh yes it was! Francis had been able to tell at a glance that Adriana's denial was a lie. By coincidence, he'd been out walking near our Le Foci villa that same night . . . except it hadn't been a coincidence at all. He'd gone to La Chiatta first, but after learning that Adriana was out for the evening, he'd wandered over to Le Foci, though not necessarily with the expectation of finding Adriana there. Really, he hoped he wouldn't find her there. No one was supposed to be at Le Foci. Hadn't our family already moved to another residence? Then why was Murray Murdoch's Lambretta parked in the drive? Francis Cape waited outside, waited for ten minutes, twenty, a lifetime, long enough for Murray and Adriana to enjoy their liaison, and when Adriana left the house and rushed toward the road, Francis hurried to meet her. Out of sight of the house, he'd grabbed her, said what he needed to say, kissed her, and slapped her when she tried to resist, and she'd fled.

Of course she'd fled. He was an old man and she a young woman in love with someone else. She wanted him to leave her alone. That's what she'd told him. Leave me alone, Francis Cape! How could he leave her alone after he'd loved her for years? She was like a daughter to him. She'd grown up as he'd grown old. He wanted her to be his wife — was this such a terrible desire?

He disgusted her. He offended her. He'd been the reason she left Elba early the next morning. He was a very very very old man and if he was lucky he'd die in his sleep before the week had ended. But he didn't die. Instead, he kept moving forward in time, away from the unalterable past. He hadn't meant to do anything wrong. He was as innocent as any sinner. The devil made him do it. No, worse. You can always find a woman to blame. Remember, Francis, where Plato writes that the worst punishment for a sinful man is to be reborn as a woman? Blame women. Especially young women. Especially young women who make themselves available through the poise of courtesy and then will have nothing to do with you when you need them most.

He blamed himself for causing Adriana to go away, but he blamed Murray for cheating him of the girl's affection. The American investor had taken advantage of Adriana. He deserved to be punished. Still, Francis was amazed by the plague of dreams. The Elbans were dreaming of Murray's guilt. How did they know he was guilty? Where were their dreams coming from?

Francis had dreams, too. He dreamed that he was rich, capricious, charismatic, virile, and Adriana Nardi was his willing partner. He dreamed he was Napoleon, and Adriana was his mistress. He was the emperor of paradise, in no hurry to leave his island. The girl would do anything with him, to him, for him. She loved him. He loved her. Why should he go back to France and resume the war when life on Elba was so splendid?

Night after night, Francis Cape fell happily asleep. In his dreams he was youthful but not stupid, handsome but not arrogant, carefree, unburdened by ambition. He was the great Napoleon, and he needed nothing more than a girl in his bed and a flask of wine to share with her.

Then to wake each morning to the reality of his life: there were no frescoes on his crumbling plaster walls, no gold-braided uniforms in his closet, no canopy over his bed, no young girl tucked against him. From bliss to sodden consciousness. He was learning to hate his life. It didn't help to blame Adriana in her absence, especially as time went on. It felt much better to blame the American investor. So he sought out our father and worked on him the way a doctor will work on a patient he loathes.

Soothing him —

"Rumors, that's all! They have no hard evidence."

Reassuring him —

"Stick it out, Murray. You'll be absolved sooner or later."

Pondering —

"They won't find any evidence against you if there's no evidence to be found. Unless they make it up. And why would they do that?"

Suggesting to him —

"I'll be the first to agree that this island is more beautiful than any other place on Earth. But is beauty worth such trouble? Don't you think you'd have been better off if you'd stayed at home? Aren't there other ways to get rich? I had hopes for you, Murray, I must say. Shall we open another bottle? Are you all right, Murray? You look a touch bleary. I've always found it helpful to imagine how it could be worse. In this case it would be something along the lines of a public accusation. Let yourself imagine it, Murray. You'll feel better if you imagine it. But then remind yourself that you're innocent. There can't be actual evidence against you. You weren't anywhere near the girl on the night she disappeared."

"What difference would that make? I mean, if I were —"

"Were what, Murray?"

"Were . . . I don't know . . . if I'd seen her. Just seen her at a distance. Caught a glimpse of her that last night."

"If you'd seen Adriana the night she disappeared? Now that's a different matter. If you'd seen the girl that night, you'd have some explaining to do. Did you see her, Murray? Did you go to her house?"

"No!"

"So you didn't see her. When was the last time you saw her?"

"I don't remember."

"One of our dinners, perhaps?"

"Yes, dinner. Some dinner in October. The last time you brought her along to dinner — when was that?"

"Oh, I don't recall exactly. A few weeks before she disappeared, to be sure. You didn't see her afterward? You didn't go to take another look at one of those old maps in the family's collection? Tell me, Murray: what was it you were looking for? Buried treasure? Montecristo's just down the road, you know. You Americans and your optimism. More? Later we'll try the grappa, sì? Now tell me, how are the boys? They feeling better? Are you all in good health? That's what counts, remember. Forget about suspicion. You and your family have your health. At my age, I know what it means to be healthy. I walk five miles a day. Every morning I walk out to the Rada lighthouse and watch the sky brighten with dawn. I haven't had to call for a doctor since I came to the island. A decade of good health. This following a decade during which I gave up hope of surviving. That's the way it was. Those grim days in London when we all thought the world was ending. And then to come here and sit for long hours listening to the little silver leaves of the olive trees crinkling in the breeze. It's a glorious place, isn't it? Not a place where you'd expect trouble. I'm told the island hasn't had a murder since the nineteenth century. To be sure, there have been casualties of war. Our Allied friends came to Portoferraio in '44 and blew apart a few stout vessels in the German fleet, I'm proud to say. And still I feel welcome here. If only I could press on with my book. First, though, I want to help you find a way out of this fix you're in. Tell me what I can do for you, my friend. I'd like to help, you know. I'd like to find a way to convince the Elbans that you are innocent. If only Adriana would come back. Where do you think she's gone off to? Why did she go away?"

Francis probed Murray, roused and reassured him. He offered more wine, grappa, gin. He kept Murray out late. As long as Francis was with Murray, Claire stayed away. She couldn't stand Francis Cape. She didn't trust him. But it was Francis who had come to warn them about the dreams, and for this reason alone Murray felt indebted to him. Besides, Francis knew the Elbans and could provide Murray with a daily report on their gossip.

Claire was scared. The fever had scared her. The darkness scared her. The soft, dry scirocco scared her when it puffed the curtains at night. She would have preferred Murray to stay at home in the evening and told him so, but he felt an increasing need to meet with Francis and hear what was being said about him. And in the midst of summer, they could enjoy a degree of anonymity. There were more tourists on Elba than ever before. Two new hotels had opened up in Portoferraio. Builders from Piombino came by boat each day to put up more concrete bungalows. With all the strangers on the island, Francis and Murray could sit together in a café in Porto Azzurro, and no one would recognize them.

Sometimes Murray would only half listen to what Francis was saying. Sometimes he wouldn't listen at all. Instead, he'd look around at the group of German tourists and wonder what they'd been doing during the war. Francis Cape had been hiding in a basement in London. Murray had been playing football on Elba. What were you doing? Murray wanted to ask the Germans around him. You, sir. Where were you?

Only a little more than a decade had passed since the end of the war, and already the nations of western Europe had united in an economic partnership. If a world war could be forgotten after a decade, Murray's involvement with Adriana Nardi could be forgotten after a year. She had been missing for nine months. When would her absence be explained?

What Murray feared most: Adriana had left his house that night back in November, walked to the cliffs above Cavo, and thrown herself off.

What Claire feared most: there was something crucial Murray hadn't told her.

What Francis Cape feared most: Adriana would come home without warning.

"If you don't know for certain why she went away, can you make an educated guess, Murray?"

"Francis, you're a friend, yes? I can trust you, yes? What if I told you that I did see Adriana that night? What if I told you that? What would you do?"

"Why, I'd only wonder what else you had to say."

"What if I told you that I was alone in our first house, you remember, that property of Lorenzo's, the one near Le Foci."

"Of course I remember."

"The day we moved, I went back to Le Foci instead of to Marciana. I wasn't thinking. I went home at the end of the day to an empty house. And I stayed there for a while. A long while. And Adriana came over."

"Good lord, Murray. Why didn't you admit this before?"

"Francis . . ."

"I don't understand why you've kept this to yourself. Unless there's more to understand. Unless you're hiding something, Murray."

"I didn't mean to . . . I don't know."

"You didn't mean to what? You didn't mean to hurt her?"

"No."

"What did you do to her? Murray, answer me. What did you do to that girl? You —"

"I am."

"You —"

"I . . ."

"You did!"

"No —"

"You did!"

"Wait! You've misunderstood me. I didn't do anything! Damn you, Francis, come back!"

This was on a summer night, the warm air perfumed with roses.

Francis left Murray sitting by himself under the pergola at the café, and he went home. He reviewed the conversation with Murray as he drove. He hadn't intended their dialogue to go in that direction and would have attempted to redirect it if he'd seen what was coming. Murray had forced him into the position of accuser. It wasn't Francis's fault that Murray had confessed. Confessed to what? Murray was confused. It wasn't Francis's fault that Murray was confused. And you couldn't blame Francis for the fact that Elbans across the island were dreaming about Adriana Nardi and Murray Murdoch. Francis hadn't actively incited suspicion. He really hadn't done much more than ask a few questions and offer to help.

What would be done to him? Murray asked himself. What had he done? Played with a girl's affections, then jilted her. Mr. Murray Murdoch, are you there? Yes I am, though as far as you're concerned, Adriana, no I'm not. Go away. She went away, threw herself off a cliff, and her body was sucked into greedy Neptune's surf — all because of Murray.

Ridiculous!

Really?

It's possible, isn't it? It's possible that Elbans believed the American signore was capable of murder. He, the father of four young boys. The Elbans were suspicious of him. Suspicion being the action of accusation held in suspense.

When you're suspicious you need a distraction. A wife suspicious of her husband will renounce suspicion when neighbors begin to grow hostile. A community suspicious of a foreigner could use the distraction of some great national calamity. Short of a war, a drought would be of some use. A forest fire. A flood. Anything to draw attention away from Murray Murdoch.

They'd be coming after him soon. If they didn't lynch him, they'd lock him in a cell and torture him until he admitted to a murder he hadn't committed. How are confessions drawn from innocent people? With cattle prongs, electric wires, water drops, pliers, knives, bottles, hoods, forks, acid. The extravagant art of pain. But can anyone say for sure that the dead won't return to take revenge?

The only other customers left in the café besides Murray were two German couples. Next year there would be more Germans on Elba. And French, Slavs, Swedes, British. And Americans. More and more each successive year. Proving that a nation can't blast its way to imperial rule — ownership must be bought, paid for with hard cash. Money money money. Murray no longer had hopes of making a profit or even paying the loan back to his uncles. All he wanted to do was go home and start his life over again. Yes, of course, and civilization wanted to start the century over again.

He wanted to be with Claire, to be alone with her. He didn't want to have to share her with the rest of us. He didn't want the responsibility of children anymore. Four sons were too much to handle. They wandered off into the hills after dark. They were rude. They bumped into people. They broke things. They spilled things. They got sick, and when they got better they wanted nothing to do with their father and didn't even speak the same language.

Who did speak Murray's language? Not the people around him. Even Francis, an Englishman, had misunderstood him to mean that he'd done actual physical harm to the Nardi girl. Only Claire spoke the same language. Mrs. Claire Murdoch. She needed to know what Murray had done — and what he hadn't done. He would tell her about Adriana's appearance that night in the empty house in Le Foci. He would ask Claire to forgive him.

He left, forgetting about the bill. He felt an unexpected, unfamiliar wave of relief as he melted into the shadows beyond the café lights. Darkness belongs to fugitives. He could almost taste it on his tongue. Though the alcohol in his blood made him lurch, he perceived his steps to be smooth, stealthy, buoyant. As long as he was still free, he would find a way to remain free.

"Signore!"

But if he were caught —

"Signore, per favore!"

If he were apprehended —

"Signor Americano!"

If he were chased by a young Italian man, a waiter who wanted nothing more than payment for the bill but who in Murray's mind became the leader of a mob, if he were chased and apprehended, he would be torn to pieces. So he must run. Run fast, Signor Americano! He must run from his accusers. A girl was missing. Suspicion was growing. Run, Murray! He ran, stumbled, and somehow, even in his drunken state, managed to stay on his feet and keep running. He ran along the flatlands road leading toward Portoferraio. At one point the wind was behind him, then, a moment later, against him. Eventually — he had no idea how far he'd gone — he heard only the echo of his own footsteps slapping the paved road. With a great wheezing breath, he slowed to a walk. He tried to pretend that he was just an ordinary man returning home from a drink with a friend. A leaden fatigue came over him. He had no idea what time it was. He expected to be startled at any moment by the beam of a flashlight on his face. We've found you, Signor Americano! But no one found him. He didn't know where to go next. He told himself that he shouldn't go back to the villa. He mustn't go back. But he wanted to go back. And so he did.

Of suspicion, accusations, confessions, and missing girls, my brothers and I knew nothing. We did not hear our father return home late that night, nor were we woken by our parents' fierce whispers. It was the night Murray told our mother that he was responsible for Adriana's disappearance, but we slept soundly, and when we woke the next morning, Elba seemed as fresh and promising as ever. The rooster crowed; the goats complained; the motorcycles and milk trucks passed noisily up on the road toward Poggio.

Of the four of us, Nat was the most tranquil — and the one

most indifferent to our parents' troubles. He was often the first to wake, and he'd go outside alone and watch the chickens scratching in the yard. He'd collect the eggs for Lidia, cupping each one between his hands to feel its warmth, and if the rest of us still hadn't woken, he'd walk down the road to the Scozzi farm and watch Marco Scozzi milking the goats. Sometimes he'd return with a round of pecorino, a jar of plum jam, a bag of peaches. Marco Scozzi called him Cherubino, and when Nat looked at him, confused, Marco pointed at the swallows swooping across the sky. There you are, Marco had said. And so Nat went away understanding that he was a little bird and someday would be able to fly above the clouds.

I am a bird. Nat would repeat this to himself. *I am a bird, a bird, a bird* — and this served as a ready explanation for the intervals of silence. Nat had become a bird. You don't have to die to become a bird. You just have to get very sick and then get better. And when you're better you will be able to see everything with such clarity that you won't need words anymore. You won't need much of anything besides a little bit of cheese and bread and jam and water, and maybe one of Marco's fresh peaches still warm from the sun. You won't even need parents. And though you won't have much use for your brothers, you'll tolerate them because without them you'd be bored.

Without any active insurrection, Nat usurped Patrick's place as the leader of our group. Little Nat, who was just six years old. We found ourselves following his orders before we'd even admitted to ourselves that he was in charge. With Nat as our captain, we all felt within us an increased sense of individual purpose. We were whatever we were supposed to be. Nat filled his role with the confidence of an experienced actor playing a part for the hundredth time. Harry was adept at finding pieces of transparent quartz we could use as diamonds. Patrick, the most knowledgeable, provided solutions to all mysteries. And I was the lookout, the one to warn of intruders and other dangers when we were playing.

After the night our father broke down and told Claire about his involvement with the Nardi girl, that regrettable embrace when she came to the house at Le Foci, both our parents stayed at home. Through the rest of the month, neither left the house, not even to sit outside on the terrace. It was beautiful weather — bright blue summer skies, with a soft, cooling breeze blowing off the sea, which we enjoyed after scrambling over rocks up the mountain. But Claire and Murray stayed inside, received no visitors, and ate their meals separately from us, behavior we interpreted as the expression of uselessness. Most adults had to pretend to have a purpose. Our parents had stopped pretending, and their indifference was affecting Lidia and Francesca. Francesca was growing fat; Lidia was growing careless and twice had dropped glasses on the hard tile floor of the kitchen.

We had enough sympathy to feel sorry for the adults in our household but not enough to want to help them. We took our cues from Nat, who led us farther and farther from the villa each day. He could run in bare feet up the rocky slope of Monte Giove as if he were flying, he could leap down steep inclines, and he could stand on a precipice and flap his arms and make the sunlight glitter.

Guarda! Look at me!

Look at him!

I'm a bird!

Birds can volare. Volare, Jako Three. Let's guarda you!

How deep was our confusion? Sometimes I wonder if the quartz crystals we found on Elba were really diamonds, the pyrite gold, and all the colorful feldspar blooming with tourmaline. The whole island was the treasure chest our father had promised it would be, and we'd opened it with a magical key. We could have done anything if we'd let ourselves believe completely in the power of our wishes.

Guarda! Jakos, guarda!

He's doing it, he's really doing it!

No!

Sì!

This is something I think I remember: blinking rapidly against the blinding sun, then staring wide-eyed as my brother Nat, just a dark silhouette bounded by light, flapped his arms wildly, then rose about six inches and hovered for a few long seconds in the air above the granite crag.

He did! Jakos, he really did volare!

He didn't. I was guarding and he didn't.

Did I? Did I really do it?

You did!

He didn't!

He vero did!

IN LA CHIATTA, HER VILLA sandwiched between olive groves and the sea, directly across the bay from Portoferraio, Signora Nardi waited for her daughter to come home. She waited with a calm that many considered unnatural, tending to the business of the Calamita leases with her characteristic placidness. From time to time she'd swing open the shutter above the table where she worked and look toward the meadow where Lorenzo's cows were pegged out to graze. She would glide her hand along the table's inlaid mosaic, smoothing the tiles. She would listen to her cook, Luisa, running water from the hose into the courtyard's stone trough.

There were some who wondered how a mother could be so calm in the face of her daughter's disappearance, and some who suggested that the Signora had never really loved her adopted daughter. Others scoffed at such contemptuous speculation and said that the Signora was only pretending to be calm for the sake of dignity. Was she as calm as she appeared? No one dared to ask her, for they accepted the family's privacy as a right earned by centuries of nobility. Elbans liked to think that they would have fought to protect the Nardi family, not because of the Nardis' wealth but because three hundred years of the island's past was preserved in the name.

The islanders, though, had failed to protect the daughter. For this they blamed the American. Of course they blamed the American. There'd been talk about others involved in the girl's life — romances she'd kept hidden even from her mother. There'd been talk that the girl was wild and desperate and would give herself to any straniero who flattered her. There'd been talk about the girl and Signor Americano even before she'd disappeared.

She'd been gone for many months. The police had long since

stopped searching for evidence. The people of Elba dreamed their dreams and whispered about our father. My brothers and I played our games. Signora Nardi went on waiting.

Her closest friends spoke of her with a sternness that suggested disappointment. They loved Signora Nardi and would prove their love with a lifetime of loyalty, but they couldn't understand why she didn't wail and cry to the Blessed Virgin for help and solace, why instead she chose to wait as calmly as a mother will wait for her daughter to return from a dance. Signora, her friends wanted to say, there was no dance. Your daughter has gone away and no one can say when she will come back.

Would she come back? Could she, Adriana Nardi, taken in like dirty wash when she was a young child, have no sense of gratitude? Her beauty was coarse — was it this that made her vulnerable to men who otherwise would have respected the family name? Or was it that the girl, raised to be a lady and educated to take her place in the world beyond the island, had been born to be a whore?

Vado via perchè devo andare via, she wrote in the note she left behind. She had gone away deliberately and just as deliberately she would return. Whatever faults she had, whatever confusions drove her from home, the girl wouldn't disappear forever.

Signora Nardi had taken every logical action to find her daughter and had contacted everyone who might have had news of her. But there was no news. There were plenty of rumors. There were strange dreams and gossip and suspicion. But there was no reliable news, and Signora Nardi could do no more than wait for the sun to cross the sky, the olives to darken on their branches, the rain to start and to stop again, the mail to arrive.

Only Luisa, the Nardis' cook for more than thirty years, understood that the Signora's calm hid a busy mind, and at any waking moment, whether she was alone or with company, silent or involved in conversation, she was engaged in recovering what she could from the past, sifting through memories of her daughter, looking for clues.

Absence asks for the return of memory. With Luisa's help,

Signora Nardi tried to remember any action or comment that might have revealed traces of whatever secret had caused Adriana to run away. The girl had said one day last fall that she wanted to visit the prison at Pianosa. What did it matter that she'd said this? Luisa wondered. And then Luisa remembered that Adriana had said she wanted to learn to ski. Why suddenly did she want to learn to ski? And why didn't the summer sun brown her this year as it had done in past years? Luisa wanted to know. No Elban girl should be so white! Was this evidence of something? Everything was evidence, as far as Adriana's mother was concerned. Adriana's hand bumping her forehead as she went to tuck a curl behind her ear — this was evidence. The distracted look in her eyes — this, too. And the faint rise at the corners of her lips as she smiled to herself, the hesitations in her voice, and the way she'd taken to drinking water in big, furious gulps.

And there was the pleasant, droning ronzio — the sound of humming. In the months before she'd disappeared, Adriana had taken to humming, barely audibly but almost constantly through her waking hours. Hadn't Luisa heard the humming? Adriana's old, sweet habit of humming?

Sì, sì, certo, Luisa had heard her bimba humming again, though she had to admit that she'd thought nothing of it. It was not unusual for girls of a certain age to make a habit of humming. But the Signora pointed out that she hadn't heard her daughter humming for many, many years. Didn't Luisa remember how when Adriana was a young girl she seemed to breathe music, the sound like the whirring of wings following her everywhere? Didn't Luisa remember how she used to hum herself to sleep and hum herself awake, how she hummed as she read and as she listened to stories? Remember, Luisa: she hummed the day the Germans bombed Elba in September, 1943, and she hummed through the night nine months later when the Allies attacked. Didn't Luisa remember that night?

Of course Luisa remembered. It was the night when Mario Tonietti, the widower of Signora Nardi's sister, who had died of cancer in 1935, ran all the way from Portoferraio to Magazzini in his bare feet to tell them to hide. Luisa recalled how the oil lamp had flickered and gone out when Mario Tonietti entered the parlor. She remembered the high pitch of his voice, like the voice of a boy, rising to be heard above the sound of sirens and distant explosions.

What wild stories people could tell about that night. Even as it was happening and windows lit up with the fires across the harbor, the stories were being told and retold. The story of a pregnant woman crushed by falling rubble as she ran from her home. The story of a man bubbling at the mouth with blood the color of blackberries. The story of a child shot in the back on the steps of Via del Paradiso.

The night of June 17, 1944, when the Allies attacked Elba, and the French, the Germans, the Africans, the Italians shot at anything that moved. And not just shot. They had dogs, people would say afterward, real dogs that breathed fire like dragons. And poison arrows that melted men into puddles. And little grenades the size of peas that they'd force down the throats of old women.

By the time Mario Tonietti arrived at La Chiatta, Massimo Volbiani and his wife were already dead. Irene Cartino was dead. Allegra Venuti was dead. Federico the grocer was dead. Cosimo the butcher was dead. They were all dead, killed for the crime of being alive. But there wasn't time to mourn — Mario Tonietti, bless him, had come to lead the way to a cave below Volterraio, where they could wait out the night in safety.

But Mario Tonietti's stories had taken too long, and by the time he'd finished what he thought Signora Nardi needed to know, there were already voices in the fields and the nearby scattershot of gunfire. It was too late to run from the house, too late to do anything but hide the child in the cabinet under the kitchen sink and wait, frozen with awareness of their helplessness, for the fighting to end.

What happened that night on Elba? No one could say for sure, not even the people who lived through it. No one could name the

men who grabbed fourteen-year-old Sofia Canuti, took turns rap-
ing her, and cut her throat. No one saw it happen. No one would
ever know for sure whether to believe crazy old Stefano Grigi, a
fisherman from Marciana Marina, when he said that he'd helped
bury the bones of a prisoner who'd been killed, cooked, and eaten
by a band of soldiers. Which soldiers, Stefano? He had to admit he
wasn't sure. No one knew what to believe. The shroud of darkness
made it impossible to distinguish between enemy and friend. The
best you could do was try to save your family.

For many years afterward, people came to Ninanina's enoteca
to trade the stories that had already been told many times. It was
here that Luisa came to help her cousin prepare food. She would
listen to the stories, and when she was tired of listening she would
tell what she remembered.

She remembered that Adriana had been a good girl that night
and had followed her mother's directions, huddling in the cabinet
in absolute silence even after Signora Nardi closed the doors. How
about that for courage! A child of ten spending the night in a dark
cabinet and not making a sound. At one point Luisa had heard the
distant shriek of what she'd thought was a woman but later
learned was one of Lorenzo's pigs that had been shot in the snout.
She and the Signora and Mario Tonietti sat around the kitchen
table, not daring even to whisper, waiting for the soldiers to burst
through the door. But the soldiers never came to La Chiatta. By
morning the sky was empty, the fields quiet, and when Luisa and
the Signora opened the cabinet under the sink and brave Adriana
tumbled out, they devoured her with kisses.

Elbans who lived through that night would spend the rest
of their lives remembering. There was so much to remember that
Luisa forgot about how afterward she didn't hear Adriana humming. Not for twelve years did she hear the girl humming. And
then, all of a sudden, she'd started humming again.

What did it mean, the humming? Ninanina asked. Luisa could
only shrug. Girls of a certain age make a habit of humming. It

probably meant nothing. But with Adriana gone Luisa shared Signora Nardi's regret that she hadn't listened more closely.

When she comes home, Luisa told Ninanina with a pride that struck witnesses as defensive, she will ask her bimba to sing for her. She wanted to hear the girl sing a whole song, clear as a bell, start to finish.

In the same house where she had waited with her daughter and cook and brother-in-law through the night of the Liberation, Signora Nardi waited for her daughter to come home. She knew how to wait. Through winter, spring, and summer, she waited patiently, deep in thought, though she was prepared to welcome most visitors, Claire among them, and would speak of her daughter as if she were expected home any minute.

Adriana was safe — Signora Nardi believed this not just because she wanted to believe it but because in her absence she had begun to piece together the nature of her secret. She didn't speak of this to anyone, not even to Luisa. Let the dreams continue and suspicion build against an innocent man. Signora Nardi had long ago concluded that Signor Americano was too foolish to be guilty of doing any serious harm. And perhaps a dose of suspicion wouldn't hurt him. It might even do him some good. Malcolm Murdoch, the father of four boys, the man who had dragged his family to the island of exile — he could learn something about himself in the process of deflecting accusations. At the very least, he could learn the value of caution.

Signora Nardi was an insightful woman. But insight didn't save her from the occasional misjudgment. She believed her Elban neighbors had a powerful sense of justice and would never do more than trade stories about their dreams. In this sense our father was safe. Any action taken against him would have to be legal, and Signora Nardi would ensure that it didn't progress to conviction. Murray had a protector in Adriana's mother, a good fairy who would swish her wand and rescue him from peril at the last moment. No one would hurt him. Signora Nardi might as well have locked him in a secret vault and dropped the key into the sea.

But as the engineer from Ohio had said at the first dinner on the *Casparia,* the most dangerous thing you can do is get out of bed in the morning. Signora Nardi, noble as her intentions might have been, confident as she was of the general goodwill of the Elban people and her daughter's imminent return, couldn't keep our father from getting out of bed.

The moon over Elba is whiter than elsewhere, and the sea breeze is saltier. The soapstone is as soft as goose down. Obsidian tastes of licorice. Wells are lined with melted gold. The bladders of gulls are filled with nuggets of jargoon. A goat born on the eve of Ascension Day has hooves made of tin-stone. Beryls grow on persimmon trees. If you crack open a chestnut during an eclipse, you'll find a fire-opal. If you wear clogs carved of peridot, you'll add ten years to your life. The eyes of feral cats are amethyst. The eyes of wild dogs are citrine. Inside every hailstone there is a piece of sapphire the size of a pinhead. The shells of gull eggs are made of thin alexandrite. The shells of hummingbird eggs are made of hiddenite. Cut open the bladder of a dying petrel and you'll find schorl. Cut open the beating heart of a pigeon and you'll find rubellite. Catch a falling star and it will turn to blue tourmaline in your hands. This is true.

If my father were here, I'd ask for clarification. What is true, Dad? He'd say, everything I tell you. He knew about falling stars turning into tourmaline because he saw it happen.

What else happened? I'd want to ask him. Is there anything that hasn't happened on the island of Elba? What is possible, and what will never be more than the mind's concoction? Where do people go on an island when they want to go away?

The rest, my father would say, I'd have to figure out on my own.

The Life of a Rock

BORN MALCOLM AVERIL MURDOCH INTO A FAMILY CLINGING TO its shrinking fortune, educated in private schools, contemptuous of his aristocratic friends but himself cursed with a prospector's greed. Destined to crave the freedom to mess up his life. Malcolm Averil Murdoch, called Murray. Six foot one inch, weighing 190 pounds, brown-haired, green-eyed, an awkward dancer, inept at cards, good at checkers, a modern prospector who would be remembered in family history as the guy who lost a fortune on Elba. Elba! An island known to the rest of the world as a place from which exiled emperors escape. Soot Island.

I'll show you what can happen on Elba.

He went ahead and left his job, borrowed money, and led us across the ocean.

Here we are! How did we get here? Onboard the *Casparia* from Genoa, from Genoa to Florence, from Florence by bus to Piombino, and then the ferry. But we must have made a wrong turn somewhere. This wasn't the island Murray had envisioned. There must have been some mistake. One mistake leading to a whole series of miscalculations. Claire, what went wrong? Claire, can we go home?

She held him. They made love, moving together. . . . How would Claire have described it? Energetically? Lustily? With a hint of ferocity in their antics? Afterward, Murray felt ashamed, as if he'd hurt her. He had hurt her. Disgraced her. Forced her to bear the weight of suspicion that cast him as the man responsible for the death of a young woman. You'll answer for your crime, Signor Americano.

Just as lapidary involves shaping a gemstone to reflect light, suspicion involves shaping the recent past into a probable story. The effort of bringing something to light. You, Malcolm Averil Murdoch, where were you on the night Adriana disappeared? Were you sealing her inside a tomb? Were you burning her on a pyre? What were you doing? Tell us.

I was just fooling around.

Coward.

Yes.

All she'd wanted was to talk with you. Just talk. You answered her with the pretense of understanding. She ran from you, ran to the cliffs above Cavo and threw herself off. Is that what happened, Murray?

Maybe. Probably. Suspicion feeding on probability. Suspicion growing against you. Suspicion growing inside you. Stop looking at me like that! Elbans all over the island waking up from dreams about the investor from America, telling their dreams to their friends, shaping the dreams into evidence.

Everywhere he went, people were whispering. That's him, that's the one. Signor Americano. Pss, ssss, wind in the pineta, surf against the rocks. Suspicion generated by the need to tell the perfect story. Testimony rendered secondary by the powerful shock of logic. The truth brought to light. It couldn't have happened any other way, of course. Of course.

And did you see the way Lidia looked at him? Why did she bother to keep working for his family? Because she needed the money. Why did Francesca smile so sweetly? Because she was afraid of Murray. The investor from America was a monster. Everybody knew what he'd done.

Psss, over there. That's him.

Signor Americano, wait! No, he wouldn't wait. He would run. If he kept running maybe they'd tire of the chase and give up.

Did you do it, Murray? Tell the truth. What is the truth? Like everyone else, he wouldn't know until Adriana had been found.

The contagion of dreams passed from neighbor to neighbor until finally, inevitably, it reached the Murdoch's villa. Murray Murdoch watched his wife toss and turn in her sleep. He heard her moan and grind her teeth. He caught her when she sat bolt upright.

"It was just a dream, Claire." Never say *just,* Murray. You should know better.

He didn't ask, and she didn't offer to tell him, what the dream was about. They both only pretended to go back to sleep. They lay awake, side by side, until dawn brightened the room and Lidia arrived with the coffee and frothy warm milk. Claire read a book as she sipped her coffee. Murray read last week's *Herald Tribune* only up to the second page, where there was an article about an explosion in Palermo. A car loaded with dynamite. Three bystanders killed, including a young boy.

Signor Americano needed a drink. He drank wine at lunch, but by late afternoon he wanted a tall bourbon on ice. Another one, prego. Another one.

"Murray, you're drinking too much."

"You always say that, Claire."

"I haven't said it since we left New York."

"You haven't needed to say it. You've thought it. I can always tell when you're thinking it."

"Does it bother you to hear it said aloud? You're drinking too much."

"So I'm drinking too much. What else? Smoking too much. Spending too much money. What else?"

"That's enough, Murray."

"Messing around with young girls. Is that what you were dreaming about last night, Claire? Me doing it with the Nardi girl?"

"I don't want to have this conversation."

"Why not? Because you don't want to know what really happened?"

"I already know what happened."

"Maybe there's more to tell."

"Like what?"

"Like about how I strangled the Nardi girl with my belt. And carried her body all the way to Cavo in a potato sack tied to my bike. And threw her off the cliff there."

"Nope. You hadn't mentioned that. Murray, if I were you I'd make that drink my last and go to bed. I'm going to bed. Goodnight, my dear. Don't stay up late. You could use a good night's rest."

Murray Murdoch loved his wife. And he loved his boys, he really did. He could prove his love by leaving them, sparing them humiliation. And at the same time he could make up for his earlier cowardice, offering himself as sacrifice. He imagined closing the door behind him and standing with his back to the villa, facing the angry mob. I'm the one you want. At least he'd die with the knowledge of his heroism. Instead, he had nothing better to do than finish the bourbon and try to keep his mind from wandering.

Focus, Murray. It might help to stand, stretch, look at yourself in the mirror. Notice how your reflection is just as distant from the mirror on the farther side as you are distant on this side.

But what about . . .

Don't think it, Murray.

Claire's dream last night?

Consider, Murray, how when light passes through a surface, rays are refracted at different angles of incidence, depending upon the medium.

What did Claire dream?

Think about light, Murray. The fact of an image. These are your own hands you're holding in front of you. The hands of Malcolm Averil Murdoch — lacking the luminosity of gemstones, lacking the beauty of tourmaline.

What happened to Adriana?

Think about something else, Murray.

He could use a drink, but the bottle was empty. Wine, then. There was no wine. Then he'd finish the grappa. Go ahead. Just a swallow left. Not enough to keep him focused, but enough to un-balance him. He teetered, rocked back on his heels, forward on his toes, and would have fallen against the glass if Nat hadn't appeared in the corner of the mirror holding an empty cup.

"Water," he said.

Murray put one hand on a chair back to balance himself. He went into the kitchen and poured Nat a glass of water from a pitcher. Murray let Nat sit on his lap while he sipped the water. They sat a long time together. Nat smelled the odors of Murray's skin, his sugary aftershave, his liquor. Eventually Nat finished the water in a gulp, and Murray carried him back to bed.

But Nat wondered why his father had been staring into the mirror in the living room. What was so interesting about a mirror? Nat went to see for himself. Murray was already stretched on the sofa again, his eyes closed. Nat positioned himself in front of the mirror and stared at his reflection. Bored with what he saw, he stretched his lips wide with his fingers and stuck out his tongue. That was better. He curled his upper eyelids inside out. There — that was even better. He made a fish face. He pushed up his nose to make a pig snout.

With the mirror on the wall adjacent to the entrance hall and the sofa against the perpendicular wall, Murray was not within the mirror's range, so Nat couldn't see him.

"Nat, go to bed. Nat! Nat, cut it out. I'm telling you to go to bed. Nat, I'm gonna be mad soon. Very soon. Nat! Nat?"

Nat the aardvark. Nat the platypus. Nat the vampire. Nat the wooden soldier. March in place, soldier! March march march march.

"Nat, honey, can't you hear me?"

If Nat opened his mouth very wide, maybe he could see all the way to his stomach. He tried. What was that hanging from the roof of his mouth? It was a tiny baby bat!

"I'm talking to you, Nathaniel. Nat, goddamn it!"

Understanding came to our father neither as a blast of awareness nor in increments. It came to him as subdued recognition, as though he'd already known what he was realizing for the first time. His son couldn't hear him. With everything else in Murray's life held in suspension, this was something irrefutable. Nathaniel couldn't hear. Of course he couldn't hear. Murray already knew this, had known without knowing that he knew it. Nat was deaf. Murray's son had been ill, and now he was deaf.

"Nat." Murray had crossed the room and was about to touch his shoulder when Nat whirled around.

"I'm not sleepy."

Murray turned his head so his son wouldn't be able to see his face. "How old are you, Nat?"

"I don't want to go to bed."

"Knock-knock. I said, knock-knock. Say *who's there.* Nat, it's your turn."

"What?"

"Forget it. Go to bed."

"What?"

"It's the middle of the night. Go to bed."

"What?"

"Bed. Go. To. Bed. Vai!"

You thought you could keep it a secret, Nat. Well, your old dad has found you out. You can't hear, can you? Can you? Nat!

"Nat!" He watched Nat shuffle down the hall in Harry's old pajamas, the pants long enough to drape over his toes. "Why didn't you tell us, Nat? We could have helped." Without answering, Nat turned the corner into his bedroom. Murray stared down the empty hall in hopes that Nat would pop out from the room and say, Fooled ya!

Nat, you little imp.

But Nat had already gone back to bed.

Murray took one last look in the mirror, tightened his tie, and left the villa through the front door. He considered only as an afterthought how the left hand becomes the right hand in a mirror reflection.

Signor Americano set out walking. There were no stars out, and the cloud bed was smoky gray and swallowed the top of the mountains. The breeze carried the puckering fragrance of grapes. A quick rainstorm had passed through an hour earlier, and the ground, dry for months, was springy.

Signor Americano was going away. Somewhere. Nowhere. Direction contingent upon absence. Our father had no particular route in mind. He just wanted to get away. Go on, Dad, we won't mind. Just be back by morning, okay? But how could he go back to the mess he'd left behind? A man decides to walk away from his family — one step after the other. His value contingent upon nothing, scarcity being the measure of worth. Signor Americano would make himself scarce for his family's sake. And go where? Home? Home was bankruptcy — money increasing in worth with rarity. Home was the Averils and humiliation. Home was the past, the absence of the here and now.

If not home, then . . .

Croaking and chirping of frogs from the marsh below the verge. Accordion music of a cuckoo. Signor Americano could sing as loud as he pleased and no one would hear him. In this sense Nat's deafness was inconsequential. A change in the weather . . . The value of song contingent upon the absence of an audience . . . A change of heart . . .

He wasn't crazy. He was just drunk. Not so drunk that he was seeing pink elephants, but drunk enough to believe he was doing the right thing by going away. He imagined running his finger lightly over the slope of Claire's nose, kissing her on the cheek, soothing her when she woke with a start. It's okay, Claire. I just wanted to tell you I'm leaving for a while. I'll be home in a few days. Don't worry about me. Take care of yourself and the boys. Good-bye. I love you. Love contingent upon absence. He kept forgetting how much he did love her. And now, remembering. His innocence and stupidity. Not unlike Orson Welles in *The Lady from Shanghai*. It's easy. You just pull the trigger.

He continued down the road toward Marciana Marina and from there picked up the coastal road. Outside of Procchio a truck full of fishermen rattled past, and one of the fishermen called, "Salve, Signore!" He waved back to show that he wasn't afraid. The truck slowed, stopped, moved in reverse. He remembered only then that he'd forgotten his hat. The fishermen offered him a lift to Portoferraio. He accepted and climbed up into the bed of the truck. He rode in silence while the fishermen sang melancholy songs.

In Portoferraio he wandered through the streets that were brightening with dawn and finally found the lane leading up the east slope of the hill toward Fort Stella. He was tired. He was still drunk and wanted to be drunker. And he could think of nothing better to do than to go and find someone who considered him a scoundrel, pound on his door until he answered, and stumble into the hovel of a flat shouting, "Tell me something! Anything! Tell me about Napoleon!"

Francis Cape, dressed in a tattered blue-and-white-striped

nightshirt, his white hair almost fluorescent in the dim light, held the door open. Murray stood in the center of the room. Francis asked him to leave. Wait — Murray wanted to hear about Napoleon. Was it true that during the year he was king of Elba, Napoleon passed a law to make his birthday a public holiday?

"You're intoxicated."

Signor Americano wasn't intoxicated enough.

"Won't you offer me refreshment?"

"I'm showing you the door."

"Yes. A door. That's a door. I know what a door is. This is a floor. That's a ceiling. What else do you want to show me?"

"Get out of here."

Francis might have been an old man, but he wasn't old enough to be exempt from human courtesy. Malcolm Murdoch would teach him a lesson. You're showing me a door. I'm showing you a man, Mr. Cape. Murray sat in the only chair in the room, an armchair with maroon upholstery as tattered as Francis's nightshirt, and folded his arms. I'm showing you human dignity. I'm showing you persistence. Resistance. Revolution. And you're showing me a . . . what is that, Mr. Cape? A butter knife?

"Leave now."

"Golly, Francis. I mean . . ." I'm showing you the reflection of yourself, Francis Cape. Light bouncing off the emotion of hatred to form an image at equal distance from the surface. Francis Cape and Signor Americano being, at that moment, equally ridiculous.

Neither meant to do what he did next: Francis swiping that ridiculous little knife in front of Murray's face, Murray leaping up, throwing a punch aimed at Francis's arm, successfully knocking the knife from his hand and sending it clattering across the floor, then continuing the motion, his fist cutting upward at an angle to bang against Francis's sternum. The old man so feeble that the thump sent him stumbling, and he tripped over his feet and fell, landing splat on his backside, where he sat with his legs stretched out in front of him, his white knobby knees bare below the hem of his nightshirt, the look on his face so comical that Murray couldn't help but laugh.

Francis looked up at Murray in confusion. Murray tried to shake away hilarity.

"Christ, I'm sorry, Francis. I shouldn't laugh."

Francis looked from Murray to the open doorway, from the open doorway to the ceiling, from the ceiling back to Murray. His expression hardened into accusation.

"Are you hurt? Here, let me help you up."

Francis used the fringed arm of the chair to pull himself up. The white pallor of his face had darkened to a sickly gray. He moved backward a step, wobbled, but remained standing. With stoical control that had a vaguely fatigued quality to it, as if he'd rehearsed the scene too many times, he rested his hand on his chest and said, "Get out of here."

"You're not hurt, are you?"

"Get out of here at once. Leave, I tell you, and don't come back."

An elderly scholar with an aching chest. An American investor in the middle of his life. As Murray rushed down the dark cement stairs of the building, he said to himself what he would have liked to say aloud: Francis Cape, you don't know how lucky you are.

Murray headed back the way he had come beneath a sky that was the color of Francis Cape's face. On the outskirts of Portoferraio, he boarded an empty bus. As far as he could tell, the bus was traveling south from Portoferraio. Somewhere in the hills between Portoferraio and Marina di Campo, he got off the bus and wandered up an unpaved cart road. He followed this past a shuttered farmhouse and continued along a footpath that cut through a barley field. The path ended, but he kept walking. In case anyone was watching, he walked in big bold strides, crushing the flower clusters beneath his shoes to suggest an urgent purpose.

He came to a gully and followed the edge to the bottom of a hill. He climbed through an olive grove, up the hill, and picked a single unripe olive. He gnawed it and spit out the bitter flesh and continued to suck on the pit. He saw a donkey standing in the dappled light beneath the branches of the biggest olive tree in the grove, its hide shivering over its barreled ribs, its ears scissoring angrily against a swarm of gnats. When Murray clucked, the donkey trotted farther away. Murray cupped his hands together as though cradling oats, and the donkey took a few lazy steps toward him and sniffed the air. Murray approached slowly. The donkey waited for him and nudged Murray's hands apart with its nose. But the animal had no reaction to the deception. It stood patiently while Murray climbed onto its back. Murray gave a good kick, and the donkey squealed, flared its nostrils, but wouldn't budge. "Yah, yah, andiamo!" The donkey flicked its ears angrily, took a step forward, and then paused to drop a little pile of manure.

Was that really you, Dad? Our father, Signor Americano. See what he did when he found himself in a pickle? He mounted an ass! The action relieving him, temporarily, of the awareness of his difficulties. Combine a donkey, mist, the smell of wild mint and thyme, maybe add the chime of a monastery's bells in the distance, and you'll have an experience that doesn't match up with reality as you thought you knew it.

But the donkey wouldn't take another step in any direction, so Murray climbed off. He slapped the beast's rump, sending it at a trot down the hill. Murray followed the grass path in the other direction, zigzagging across the terraces uphill toward Orello and Barbatoia, up into the region hidden by the mist, where the cultivated land gave way to barren outcrops, to eroded lava flows, to buttes and cones and ancient volcanic plugs. A region where a prospector belongs, the place where Malcolm Murdoch should have headed long ago.

There's no logic to the distribution of minerals, is there, Murray? The "perplexing irregularity in the outer crust of the earth" is how one geologist has described it. The best a prospector can do is to begin looking in an area where the rugged surface is bare of soil, the heart of rock exposed. Look, Murray. Keep your eyes open. As you walk along up into the mountains of Elba, look down at the ground for the shine of a lustrous surface, the glint of color.

He wasn't drunk anymore; he was crazy. Not so crazy that his imagination completely controlled his perception but crazy enough to make the deliberate choice to ignore the facts of his situation. He was hungry. He wanted meat. A good bloody piece of Angus covered with A.1 sauce. A baked potato smothered in sour cream. Green-bean casserole, the kind Claire made using frozen beans and canned onions.

He needed a bath. His head ached. He owned a worthless plot of land. He was a thirty-eight-year-old Caucasian American man who'd taken his four young children and his wife on an extended vacation. He was a brother. He was a cousin, a son, an heir. He was, unfairly, the object of suspicion. But he could no longer pretend that he hadn't done anything wrong.

He climbed further into the mountains, scraping the heels of his palms on the steep craggy slopes. He climbed to the plateau where the gods were sleeping after one of their long nights of carousing. He climbed past their marble temple. He climbed through the clouds. And there it was, high up on the mountainside close to the summit: a door cut into a scar of bare rock and a stony gallery leading deep into the heart of the earth.

Signor Americano leaned back against an outcrop of limestone and lit a cigarette. He told himself he didn't have to rush into the cave. He could take his time about it. He needed to collect his thoughts, make a plan. Hesitation uncharacteristic for this impulsive man. But he was on the brink of something big, wasn't he?

The earth inviting him to come under the surface and have a look around, at no expense.

He smoked slowly, thoughtfully. Hesitation the perfect state for him right now. Holding himself in suspense in front of the mouth of the cave. Discovery ready to swallow him up.

Javan, the son of Japheth, stubbing his toe against a lump of Cyprus copper. The glint of silver in a campfire in El Rosario. Gold in the sand on Douglas Island. Vanadium in the asphalt of Peru. The history of discovery a history of fortunate coincidences — and failures. "Because the goldesmithes and goldefyners of London and many other namyd counynge menn had made many prooffes of the ewer and could fynde noe whitt of goold therein." Frobisher, with his *Meta Incognita.* You know what they say: the chieftain was covered with mud and then dusted with powdered gold blown through tubes. The gilded king. Where is he? Somewhere in the mysterious wilderness, floating on a golden raft across a sacred lake. And suddenly his wife appears.

Hello, Claire.

Murray, look at you!

Do you like me this way?

You're . . . you're . . .

Yes?

Amazing! Beautiful! I can't believe it! Like she'd really say this. Claire always the one anchoring him to responsibility. Don't touch me, not until you take a bath, Murray.

Seriously. Let's back up, Dad. Tell us about Claire when you first met her. Following her from a party, watching her walking along Central Park West in the rain in her bare feet, holding in one hand high-heeled shoes that belonged to a friend and were too small for her. Claire, your boss's secretary. Shall I carry you? The way curiosity flares into hope, is dimmed by restraint, is relit, is confirmed. Married in City Hall to avoid the Averils. Time measured by the establishment of new routines — Friday's dinner, the weekend ahead, Sunday morning in the apartment, sunlight, sheets bunched at the foot of the mattress, haphazard toss of pillows, pulp of fresh orange juice, a paragraph from a newspaper article read aloud. The two of you. Then three, four, five, six plus a cat.

And then, on a lark, the island of Elba. What went wrong? The simple act of leaving home creating the possibility of leaving the past behind.

Up and down and quick, up again, and "I see stars," as the expression goes. But they don't look like stars. They look like fragments of diamonds drifting in clear liquid around my head. My back to the darkness of the cave. In front of me, the mountains making a bowl filled with daylight, the mist lifting, dispersing like steam from soup. Did I really ride a donkey this morning? Why? Why do I do anything?

I was a boy once, too. Hard to believe, eh? Your dad in pinstriped shorts held up by suspenders, sneaking off to school with a live mouse in his pocket! Four cats against a little mouse outside the 89th Street stable. Some images survive time completely intact: that little mouse cowering against the doorjamb and four scrawny cats pawing and pacing with devilish languor, stretching out the torment for as long as they could. Sorry to disappoint you, kitties. I caught the mouse by its tail. Monsieur Petit, I called him, with some pretension, for I was learning French. Turned out Monsieur was a Madame, and three days later my mother found seven little pink worms in my sweater drawer. The only time I ever heard her shriek.

My mother. My father. My wife. My children. The pronoun a convenient reduction of personal history. Your father. Your husband. Your son. Oh to have been in Bisbee in January of 1881, receiving a short option of one million dollars for the Copper Queen Mine. Our family suffering from what an uncle on the Murdoch side called congenital greed. Sires training their offspring to want what had been missed, overlooked, and lost, generation after generation. You'll see how it happens. First you laugh at your parents. Their ridiculous habits and hopes. Then you learn to want what they had. Then you learn to want what they wanted and didn't have. And then, after a series of misunderstandings, you leave the island and go home.

I am Malcolm Averil Murdoch. Did you know I am naturally left-handed but was forced to use my right hand in early grades? What else would you like to know about me? Here I sit, my back to a cave, my face to the sun, having reached the peak of indecision. What next? Trapped by an impressive record of misjudgments. Oh for the ease of Catholic absolution. Or the carefreeness of the Epicureans. But remember where Dante puts Epicure! I'd rather be —

Myself as I'd planned to be when I was a young boy looking forward. Instead I'm the ass riding the ass. Deterioration provoked by stupidity. The way the lungs turn black and calcareous, like the inside of a cave, from cigarette smoke.

What had he done? Excluding the last six hours or so, he hadn't done much. Misty island of misty dreams. What happened? Signor Americano couldn't say exactly. So why did he hit a feeble old man? Good question.

It wasn't an accident, was it, Dad?

No.

Your one decisive action since we left America. You went to see Francis Cape with the intention of hurting him.

Yes.

Why?

Consider the life of a rock.

Cut it out, Dad.

Sediment compressed to form sedimentary rock. Sedimentary rock heated to form liquid magma. Magma blown to the earth's surface, cooling to form igneous rocks. Igneous intrusion causing contact metamorphism. Igneous and metamorphic rocks eroded into sediment. Buried sediment compressed into rock. I'd put myself at the igneous / metamorphic stage. More igneous than metamorphic. A crusty, coarse-grained piece of gabbro.

Say what you mean, Dad.

Compare minerals to rocks. It's not their luster, their rarity, their hardness that makes them desirable. It's their chemical composition. They are what they are, unlike most everything else in the world. Why is a diamond the most valuable gem? Because it has the simplest chemical composition. Diamond equals C. Not much in the world is as simple. And now you can see my fundamental mistake. I thought tourmaline would prove my worth. What's tourmaline? Tourmaline is a mix of boric oxide, silica, water, iron, etcetera, etcetera. The chemical composition of tourmaline is longer than the alphabet. What's tourmaline? Everything and nothing. Tourmaline is what a man looks for when he doesn't know what he's looking for.

In fact, you didn't think any of this, did you, Dad? And you never got further than the mouth of the cave. For all I know, there was no cave. What you found might have been no more than a shallow gouge in the limestone outcrop. You didn't even bother to look around your feet for the broken shards of tourmaline that would have indicated a rich vein nearby.

You smoked a cigarette. Maybe you smoked another cigarette. You watched the day grow brighter. You fell asleep and slept for a few hours. You slept so soundly you didn't feel the gecko scuttle across the back of your hand on its way to a patch of sun-warmed rock.

Our dad, Signor Americano. Moses on the mountain. Jeremiah in the wilderness. Your one opportunity for discovery, and you slept through it.

When he woke the sun was already in the west, the air was dry, and he had to piss. He pissed into the mouth of the cave, and he headed down the mountain, intending to go right home.

But you didn't come right home — remember?

The walk was long, so he stopped in La Pila for a bite to eat and a glass of wine, and he got to talking with the barista, who didn't speak a lick of English. In his own poor Italian, Murray introduced himself, watching the man carefully to see what effect his name had. The barista had never heard of our father. Was that possible? He returned Murray's stare with frank curiosity. Murray told him he owned land in the Mezza Luna region. The man had never heard of Mezza Luna. Murray began to explain. The man interrupted, rattling something Murray didn't understand, and motioned to the kitchen. He disappeared for a moment and returned with a liter of wine. They drank together for a few hours.

Anonymity as unexpected as it was welcome. Murray had finally found his refuge in a little bar in La Pila. He asked the barista if he knew of a pensione nearby, and the man offered him the back room of the bar, a little room with a single cot, a curtained window looking out into a dark pantry, crates filled with onions and potatoes stacked against the wall.

So that's where you were.

Drinking some. Sleeping. Smoking. At Murray's insistence, the owner and his wife put him to work in the afternoon chopping vegetables. They ate all their meals together. They took great delight in watching our father drink. Ancora, ancora. There was no malice in them. What they saw was the gradual animation of a dreary Americano. He drank steadily from pranzo on. His host and hostess drank, too, both of them, not just wine but Amora and grappa and even rum. Yet as far as Murray could tell, they didn't suffer any effects from the liquor.

He slept deeply, but only for a few hours at a time. He'd wake, confused, in the middle of the night. The room absolutely lightless. Yet somehow he'd managed to continue to lie quietly in his bed.

Tick tock tick. Signor Americano was alone. He'd never really been alone before. Oh, he'd been by himself, but not alone like this. Discovery no longer an attraction. Only trying to subdue panic. Using thought to try not to think. Then your hand happens to brush against the velvet skin of a peach that your host offered you after dinner. A little orange peach you left on a saucer. And the next thing you know you are remembering the tiny velvet bear your oldest son kept on his bedside table when he was younger and you were still in the apartment on East 74th. A little brown bear, with nose and eyes and eyebrows inked in black. Patrick's glasses cradling the water glass. Harry still in a crib. The smell of a baby's scalp. Another son. As many as possible. This was back in the days when fathers would chew on unlit cigars in the hospital lounge while waiting for their children to be born. Your own father dead from heart failure when you were six. Buried in the cemetery in Queens. You don't even remember the funeral.

Darkness itself the cramping factor. You'd rather be sleeping than thinking, but oh the way the mind works. Thinking about what happens when you stop thinking.

Which of your sons started crying in the middle of the night because he was afraid of dying? Barely able to put words into a whole sentence, and he was fretting about metaphysics. Whatever. Nothing to say other than offering the hypothesis of Father, Son, and Holy Ghost. Let's consider the proposition of divinity. Who is God, Daddy? How should I know?

The proposition of heaven and hell. Life directed toward judgment. Don't you believe it. Hell no more than hatred of the dead. That's your punishment, in varying degrees. Devils stoking the fires of memory. What you did. And what you didn't do. You being the sort who always meant well. Claire knew it, didn't she? She knew you better than you knew you. Our father the prospector. You wanted to give us a future. A father's effort to secure a place in the paradise of memory. A life judged by its life in the memories of others. The salvation of eulogy. The dishonest pabulum of respect.

He wanted needed loved his wife and children. So why at every turn did he succeed in messing up their lives? The stupidity of ambition. There's gold in them thar hills! Come on, boys. Claire, I promise, you won't regret it. Me. Your willingness. The warmth of your body returning life to me in the dark hours of the night. How can anybody ever sleep alone? I am scared, Claire. What good does it do to think it? Or even to say it aloud. I am scared. Don't even remember my own father's funeral. If a tree falls in the forest. Failure written in stone. Destined to end with my pockets full of gabbro. Not a glimmer of tourmaline in sight.

We went to look for buried treasure. Our father's script for success a mishmash of fantasy and jest and showmanship. The prospector's doomed effort to prove the validity of his wild guess. One version among many of ambition. Bolstered by his family. The prop of us. Following one little crack in the foundation, the slow collapse. Not even a chance of finding what he was looking for. Scripted failure. Marked by destiny to be a man whose most useful function would be as a contrary example — a warning to others. Look what happened to Murray Murdoch, who hauled us all to Elba for no good reason.

Where is Elba?

I told you I don't know!

Darkness like the darkness of an unlit room seen at noon from across a street, across a yard, across a piazza. Darkness like the bottom of a well. Darkness flattened by distance. A dark so dark that it had no dimension. This was the dark in which our father lay, thinking.

Musty, earthy smell of potatoes. Velvet skin of a peach. I am underground. Hello! Can't anyone hear me? Enormous pressure developed gradually on the hanging wall. Surviving pillars gave way. Sudden propulsion of air shaking the whole tunnel. Excavated to a maximum depth of 200 feet. I am alone. He is alone. My brother. My mother. My wife. My sons. He couldn't even remember his father's funeral, though the many funerals he'd attended since then all felt like repetitions.

My turn. His turn. How do I want you to remember me? How do you want us to remember you? Monsieur Petit in your pocket. Your hat cocked at an angle. Clocking our sprints with the second hand of your wristwatch. Napping on the couch on Saturday afternoon. Mowing the lawn. Riding a motorcycle. Our father, Signor Americano. Too late. You are what you were, and now you're stuck in a little room in a little village on a little island, it's the middle of the night, and no one can hear you calling for help.

He fell asleep at last, woke at dawn, slept some more, and woke again shortly before noon. He ate bread soaked in olive oil, he chopped vegetables, drank wine, played cards with the owner and his wife. How could they possibly make a living from this bar with so few customers? our father began to wonder. And then on Friday afternoon the bar filled with men — young men smoking hand-rolled cigarettes, old men playing rapid hands of a kind of poker Murray had never seen before.

The owner introduced him as Signor Murdee. Signor Americano, sono io. Not a single man in the crowd of two dozen knew him or recognized his name. "Sono Malcolm Murdoch." Shrugs of "Piacere." He was the most infamous man on Elba, and they knew nothing about him. How was it possible?

Anything's possible on this island of dreams. When Napoleon wandered the island, he was sometimes mistaken for a common soldier. Now Signor Americano was being mistaken for an ordinary tourist. Possibly, he'd found a hamlet so isolated that the people here hadn't heard the rumors. Or possibly — time to consider this, Murray — there were no more rumors to hear.

Non ho capito.

Suspicion rises like steam from water as the air cools at night. And then disperses. Without evidence, suspicion always disperses. Murray, those dreams Francis Cape was telling you about — he wasn't making them up. Those dreams were being dreamt, told and retold, measured and compared. But for weeks, new dreams had been dreamt, dreams that had nothing to do with either you or the missing Nardi girl, dreams that weren't worth retelling. You were being forgotten.

There were grapes that needed to be picked. Figs, oranges, apples, lemons, pomegranates. Let's taste the Sangiovese, peel the chestnuts, fry the squid. Ciao, Alberto, come stai? Did you hear? Elena, the one who played the girl at this summer's festival in Capoliveri — why, she's marrying Marco, who played Barbarossa. Elena e Barbarossa si sposano!

Music, laughter, a machine spitting caffè. Wait — sono Signor Murdoch. I'm the one people are talking about. Cosa? You know — the American who can tell you what happened to the Nardi girl.

They didn't care what he wanted to tell them. But if he was willing to stake cento lire on the first game, he was welcome to play.

He ate spaghetti with them. He played cards. He laughed when they laughed, though he understood next to nothing of their jokes. He was the stranger, the foreigner, as exotic as the dollar bill he passed around. He'd come all the way from New York to play cards with them, and they were grateful.

He lost the dollar, along with the rest of his money, within three hands. He borrowed money from the barista. He played another hand and won — a sign that his luck was changing. Here he was, no longer a presence provoking whispers. His innocence accepted as a fact. His past a story too dull to tell.

He'd play one more hand and go home. But they didn't want him to go. Look at the rain, Signor Murdee. A deluge. Guarda. They opened the door to show him the rain spilling in a beaded curtain from the overhang.

All right, he'd stay. Bravissimo!

They sang, smoked, played cards. More men arrived. They stamped their feet dry on the boards, shook water from their hats. Antonio! Leopoldo! Massimo! Arnoldo! Tell us, who had the foresight to begin picking in time to finish before the storm? Who will make the best Aleatico this year? Who has a vat to loan Roberto?

They all had to crowd in the doorway to see Paolo's new motorcycle. And then they needed the warmth of grappa, more conversation, volley of jokes, and news of the world, courtesy of a
one-legged, gray-haired man named Ricardo, who hobbled into the
bar on his crutch just as some of the men were preparing to leave.

Come va, Riccardo? Clatter of talk, clatter of nonsense. The
men who had put on their coats took them off again to trade news
about weather, thefts, accidents. Murray gave up trying to understand what was being said and didn't hear Riccardo report that an
old Englishman had been found dead in his room in Portoferraio.
Apparently he'd been dead for a few days.

An Englishman. Molto vecchio. Did Signor Murdee know of
him?

What?

Antonio rattled a version of what Roberto had reported. There
were only a few words that Murray understood, words such as
inglese, professore, solitario, vecchio, and morto. But they were
enough to draw a nod of dumb comprehension that continued
even while the other men genuflected for all the anonymous dead
of the world and then pressed on through other news — the price
of tuna going up, the price of swordfish going down, and a new
hotel being built in the hills above Procchio.

Spodumene, iolite, benitoite. Euclase, phenakite, enstatite. Oh give
me some sphene, Gene. A little dioptase in your coffee? How about
some fibrolite on your scapolite, Willemite?

It is evidently desirable that you should be able to resist the
chemical actions of everyday life. Having failed to. You demantoid,
you. Mister Malcolm Averil Murdokite, specific gravity 3.10,
strongly dichroic. What do you have to say for yourself?

Um. Did I ever tell you about the time I was walking along East
29th in Manhattan and a woman ran up to me, thrust a package
into my hands, and ran on? A man in a dirty apron ran after her,

past me. The package. Raw sirloin inside the wax paper. Me and
Claire cooked and ate it for dinner. And the time Patrick, just learn-
ing to talk, called a man on a bus a boll weevil. C-A-T spells cat.
Where did you learn boll weevil, kiddo?

Make like a frog, Granma. Why? Because Daddy says when you
croak we'll go to Florida. Ain't he a darlin'? Claire, will you watch the
kids for a while? I'm going to mine for tourmaline. I guess I forgot to
mention that I've always wanted to try my hand at mining. That and
earn enough money so I have plenty to give away. None of which.

Unknown to the world at large, the industrial manufacture of
precious stones. Man's restless efforts to bridle nature. Unrigh-
teous products of alchemists. Murray Murdokite should have been
an alchemist. He and Faust. Homemade sapphires. There's no limit
to delight, ladies and gentlemen, with the purchase of my little
machine here.

In 1837, Gaudin produced a few flakes of crystallized corundum. In 1877, Fremy and Feil lined a crucible with homemade
flakes of ruby. In 1904, Verneuil and his blowpipe. Oxygen admitted at C, passing through the tube, E, E terminating at D. *Tap tap
tap* goes the hammer, A, onto disc B. Coal gas plus oxygen in a
blowpipe equals a beautiful pear-shaped crystalline alumina. If
only you'd gambled on manufacturing instead of nature, Murray.
Now look at you. The reflection your inversion.

Never caring that he never had a chance to:

1) Wade through high water at night in Venice. The challenge
   of figuring out where the flooded street ended and the canal
   began.
2) Run for office.
3) Witness the birth of a child.
4) Witness the slaughter of a lamb.
5) Talk with us. To us. You never really talked to us, Dad. Other
   fathers. Oh, forget it.

Here I sit, imagining you as you were before I remember you.
The melting of sedimentary rock into magma. Once a man looking

forward. Afterward, a man looking back. Every investment a mistake. Every casual gesture a provocation. Your habit of looking for friends in the wrong places. One thing leading to another, and the next thing you know a girl is missing, your son is deaf, and il professore è morto, flattened by a punch meant to deflect a butter knife. Then and then.

A nun inside her cloister for seventy years. Bliss of faith. Compare her to, say, Nietzsche, and his ascetic ideal derived from a degenerating life. What's the point of thought? Dad wondered, walking along a road in the rain at night. And for that matter who decided for us that cut stones are more beautiful than stones broken through some convulsion in the earth's crust, roughened by attrition, carved by solvents?

There he goes, walking away from La Pila toward wherever. Drunk again. Geez. Don't you know when to stop!

How dare you.

I'm just pretending, Dad. A little game I'm playing here on the page. My review, having watched the video of your life. The night we almost lost you forever. At last, having reached the place you'd been heading toward and having found what you were looking for. The transformation complete.

You have no idea, Ollie.

No more than scraps of possibilities. It's possible, Dad, that the thought of Nietzsche crossed your mind when you were heading away from La Pila after learning about the death of Francis Cape. It's also possible that you were exercising your mind, trying to remember a long sequence of numbers, moving backward from the end. Flexing your corrugator supercilii. Or maybe you were thinking about Giorgione's *Three Ages of Man*.

You will never know.

And so I am forced to make an educated guess, Dad. You. He. Thinking about that sweet little natal cleft between his wife's buttocks.

Stop it, Ollie.

Walking at night through the rain. Like any man upon realizing that he will never be innocent. Programmed to generate the events that would result in this state of mind. Setting off for Elba in order to become what you became. Our father, Signor Americano. Walking. Releasing himself to madness. Howl, spit, eek, suffamoaninacheron. Who out there wants to go mad with me?

Voices.

I wasn't hearing voices, Ollie.

Skin pricked by the nibs of invisible quills.

Not that, either. I walked. That's all. No thunder, no lightning.

Just walking along. The rain letting up. The rising moon glowing behind a silky mist. He was just walking along. A little more than a year after arriving on the island. Shrug. Nothing much to say about it. Shrug. Doesn't it feel good to shrug? A gentle tightening of the trapezius. Oh, there was that thing with the Nardi girl. Didn't amount to much. Shrug. Some money he owed — shrug. That bout of fever. His son having trouble hearing. They'd take him to the doctor tomorrow. Shrug. And the old man they'd known — Francis Cape. Heard he'd passed away a few days ago. Rest in peace. Shrug. That's all. A short history of Nietzsche's sickened soul.

Listen to the gods. Their catcalls.

That's me whistling. Shrug.

As though nothing had happened.

Nothing out of the ordinary scheme of things.

You being an ordinary man who once upon a time wanted to be more than you were. The prompt of your ambition. Before Elba, you were the one who rounded us up and ordered us to live, live well! Show me what you're made of! On your mark, get set, go!

You see, it's not my fault I use too many exclamation points. My tendency for exaggeration a gift from my father. He was like so many others — men and women who, in resigning themselves to their fate, must forfeit their spirited ingenuity and become ordinary. Not even madness to enliven their story. They are the ones left out of history, the explorers, inventors, artists, teachers, doctors, electricians, ophthalmologists, chimney sweeps and plumbers, bus drivers and farmers and lab assistants, etcetera, etcetera, who set out to accomplish something extraordinary, and after a series of setbacks just gave up.

You can write whatever you please, Ollie. But if you publish it, I'll —

Our father, Signor Americano.

You'll never know what happened to me that night.

Holding yourself responsible for everything else. And now for the death of an old man.

Do this, Ollie. Cup your hands over your ears. Close your eyes. Imagine a girl's muffled sob.

I did. And then a car backfired on the street below, and I blinked and saw a flock of pigeons rise and curl, silver swirl tilting into a white arc around a tree.

Always the interruption of the world. Proof that no matter how hard you try, you will never be able to imagine your way into my mind.

Night. Fog. And out of nowhere, the snuffle of a girl. A girl crying softly to herself. Hidden amidst the stalks of barley. In the gorge. Behind an empty military redoubt. Behind the crumbling stone wall. Between two rocks. Her face bruised, her lips bloody. Signorina, where are you? Where? Sweet child. I'll find you. Are you there? Where? A wayward girl is easy to charm, to use, to beat and leave for dead. That old tale. If only you'd cry out, I could find you. The gray darkness of a misty midnight on the island of Elba, and somewhere in the mud, an injured girl. I'll find you. In the grass. Beneath a bush. If you're not over here, then you're over there. Where? What girl? On a night like this. I must be mistaken. But how could I mistake the unmistakable sound of a girl crying softly in the dark? Me, a father, a husband, a soldier afraid of war. You must be cold, Signorina. Hungry. What good does it do to cry?

Don't cry, Signorina. I'll find you, if you're there to be found. If you're not. But I heard you, I'm sure I heard you. A sound without equivalent. Puff snuffle of a cry. A girl in the night, unable to sustain herself without help. I'll help you. First I have to find you, then I'll help you.

What in the name of God am I —

I'm looking for a girl.

What girl?

How can I answer that until I find her? Signorina, where are you?

And when I find her?

I'll take her home.

Where's home?

Puff snuffle. Come on, Signorina. You're here somewhere, I know it. I can feel you in my bones. On my hands and knees in the mud, looking for a girl. A night like this. Sting of nettles. Clothes soaked through. I'll do some good yet. Where are you, Signorina? If the Averils could see me now.

Stop it!

Dad?

Stop it this instant.

Geez, Dad, I'm sorry.

The boundless foolishness of your imagination, Oliver.

That's exactly what I was hoping you'd say.

As if I'd lost my mind.

I'm way off, aren't I? You weren't crawling around on your hands through the mud that night and through the next day looking for an injured girl. Of course you weren't. But what were you doing? What happened? Something happened. I'm trying to understand but am hampered by the boundless foolishness of my imagination. My penchant for exaggeration. The distortions. Unreality a temptation for those of us used to fiction. At least tell me what you were intending, Dad. Tell me the truth. If you tell me, I promise I won't write it down.

Josephine loved Napoleon and was beloved. She pleaded with him, "Dearest, do not forsake me. Recall my skillful conduct during your Egyptian expedition." Still, he divorced her in December of 1809 and a few weeks later asked for the hand of the archduchess of Austria, Marie-Louise.

He met his betrothed on the road to Soissons and introduced himself. Her immediate emotion was plain relief.

"Why, Herr Napoleon, you don't look at all like your portraits!"

He was there at her side while she groaned her way through the difficult birth of their son.

"Emperor," asked the accoucheur, "which life should be sacrificed, in the event such action must be taken?"

"Why, save the mother, of course," said Napoleon. Not because he loved his wife but because he considered it her right to live.

And then the son: voilà, the king of Rome.

And then banishment.

The dust rose behind the wheels of his carriage. Seven hundred infantry and one hundred and fifty cavalry of the imperial guard volunteered to accompany the emperor into exile, along with a ten-man band and fourteen drummers. But where were his wife and son?

Tub-dum, tub-dum. In exchange for his empire, he was given an island. Long live the king of Elba!

The great grand king of Elba. "We will live because it is our right to live, my people! I bid you welcome. Your beautiful island is mine to share, and I will reign justly."

Turning a map of the island on its side so the west coast was at the top, he saw in it the silhouetted bust of a hatless man. Capo Sant'Andrea the brow. Punta del Nasuto — why, the nose, obviously! The long cravat extended between Marmi *and Acquabona. And the bulk of the pedestal between Capo della Vita and Punta dei Ripalti. The bust of a king. The land a shadow of himself. His dukedom in a poor isle, and all of us ourselves.*

To the captain of the ship that had brought him here he gave a snuff-box with his portrait set in diamonds. To the crew he sent wine and money. He wandered the island, and in three weeks he knew every foot of it. He fortified the garrison at Longone, strengthened watchtowers, disbanded the coast guard and replaced them with his own soldiers.

Meanwhile, the Allies, seeking a comprehensive settlement, gathered in Vienna. Among the group were two emperors, four kings, one queen, two hereditary princes, three grand duchesses, and more than two hundred heads of ducal houses. Balls and banquets were given nightly. There were pantomimes and balloon ascents and a performance of Fidelio *conducted by Beethoven himself.*

The last great party of the crowned heads of Europe, and Napoleon missed it. He could do no better than build a wooden ballroom in the Piazza d'Armi and entertain the Elbans with fireworks.

The grand king of Elba. This cell's my court. A compact man, impeccably turned out, with nothing much to do.

What time is it?

What time is it now?

Able was I ere I saw Elba. From a hill above Portoferraio, looking up at the peaks of Capanne and Giove, north to the sea, east toward Volterraio, he is reported to have said: "It must be confessed that my island is very small."

Or else, Francis Cape had considered on more than one occasion, he could begin with a description of the Palazzina dei Mulini, with its pinkish-white plaster facade, green shutters, and the long wing extending on the seaward side toward the cliff edge. Napoleon had lived in the cramped, dark rooms on the ground floor and slept on a collapsible bed. Upstairs, prepared for his wife and son should they ever join him, were the brighter, grander apartments, with gilded canopied beds ringed with carved swans and faded drapes bunched with golden tassels.

Or else Francis could begin with the end — Napoleon on his bed at St. Helena, groaning "tête d'armée," his last words before swooning into death.

It must have been then, at his last conscious moment, that Napoleon had recognized the mistake he'd made by leaving Elba. Francis Cape would never leave Elba. He didn't even have the inclination to leave this room he called his home. There was a time when he'd hoped, upon finishing his book, to reward himself by building a modest house of his own, a villetta with a drive flanked with limes and stone pines and a courtyard leading to a garage, behind which would have been the rabbit hutch and a small garden, where he could plant a few vines and olive trees. And keep a tortoise. A villetta with a garden, a garden with a tortoise. That had been his vision of completeness.

But the knowledge that he'd reached the end of his life without either finishing his book on Napoleon or building his house was by no means unendurable. He'd found happiness on Elba. He'd discovered pleasure.

There was one afternoon in particular. Was it April of '52 or '53? Bored with his work, he'd gone to visit Adriana, though they didn't have a lesson scheduled that day. Still, she seemed delighted to see him. Lorenzo had invited Adriana and her mother to come taste his Sangiovese. Signora Nardi had declined. Adriana suggested to Francis that he accompany her in her mother's place.

On a warm spring day in the dusty light in Lorenzo's cantina, he'd watched Lorenzo expertly flick the oil from the top of a demijohn filled with red wine. Six months from vine to glass, six months to the day, Lorenzo insisted, makes for a wine that sings of Earth and Sun.

Salute!

Adriana, her cheeks flushed from the wine, her long dark lashes lowering as she took another sip. The simple, correct pleasure contained in Francis's respectful love. He hadn't wanted anything more than to admire the child and watch her as she grew up.

Just as a father will admire his own daughter, watching from the distance of propriety the slow transformation of the body. Nothing wrong with that, is there?

It hadn't been wrong until Murray Murdoch came along. Americans have a special talent for turning paradise into a wasteland. They drill and pound and blast, ransacking the earth, and then they go away without bothering to clean up the mess. Like Murray had gone away after giving Francis Cape a good whack in the chest.

That was . . . when? Francis had lost track of time. No matter, now that time had lost track of him. Nor did it matter that he hadn't completed his book. Or married. He was, at long last, without regret. It was as if Murray had beaten out the demons that had been assaulting him of late. Francis was at peace. Looking back, he could say with confidence that in the last decade of his life he'd finally learned how to live.

And if everything wasn't as perfect as it had been, eventually it would be. Francis had only to be patient. Napoleon's great fault, it could be said, was not ambition but impatience. Desire lit by the *ticktock* of a pocketwatch. Whatever the king wanted he wanted right away. Not even a year had passed and he set sail on the *Inconstant* for Corsica, the island of his birth, and from there to France and Fontainebleau. And the next thing you know:

The English front in a concave line of columns four deep, pouring forth a ceaseless storm of musketry. The desperate cry of "Sauve qui peut!" drowned out by the explosions. And all the while a little man with a spyglass watching from the heights of La Belle Alliance.

The answer, as Francis Cape could have told Monsieur Bonaparte, was to stay put once you've found paradise. Don't move. Don't even get up out of your seat. With all the contingencies within and without, you don't want to take any chances.

After Murray had left, Francis sank back in his chair, and that's where he stayed. With the chair positioned at an angle so the right arm was adjacent with one edge of the single small table, Francis had only to turn his head slightly to see out the window. Luckily, he'd left one of the shutters open to let in the night breeze, giving him a view of the brightening sky. Unluckily, he hadn't bothered to put up the netting, so a mosquito — one of the wicked Mediterranean zanzare that are impossible to trap and kill — flew in and proceeded to torment him by buzzing relentlessly around his ears.

The place on his chest where he'd been hit no longer hurt him. Nothing hurt him anymore. The pink sky, the aroma of caffè drifting up from the bar across the street, the traffic noise increasing as the hours passed — it was all so pleasant. Only the zanzara's zanzaring — *zanzanzanzan* — to bother him. It was the kind of annoyance he'd totally forget once it had passed. *Zanzanzan.* But he could still relish the tranquillity of soul and setting. A kind of nirvana inflected by pride. He was proud of his patience. *Zanzanzanzanzan.* No matter. He could wait. He could wait forever.

Breakfast at ten, dinner at eight. I am a man of plain tastes. I prefer fresh water to coffee, unsalted bread, sauceless meat, boiled peas with no more than a sprinkling of chopped mint. I drink two glasses of Chambertin in the evening. Look at me. I am the general who walked on foot by the side of the sick as we crossed the fierce hot sands from Jaffa to Cairo. And I am the willing sacrifice to the hatred of the enemies of France. May they prove sincere in their declarations and only have aimed at me!

The day, it appeared, would be overcast; the pink was dulling to a creamy gray. But the wind was gentle, the sea calm for the fishermen. Francis Cape went on waiting. After a while he began to ask himself what he was waiting for. Or whom. He would have admitted, if pressed, that he'd grown tired of seeking out others. The company he kept was always the company he earned with the exhausting effort of courtesy. Fortunately he'd made plenty of friends on Elba, and he knew how to make himself useful. It was Francis, remember, who introduced Murray Murdoch to Lorenzo. Wasn't he the one who bridged the divide between locals and *stranieri*? With a foot in both camps, he kept communication open. And when Adriana Nardi had come to him wanting to learn English, he hadn't turned her away.

Good Francis Cape. *Zanzanzanzanzan.* He sensed that his manners were considered by the locals to be old-fashioned. In contrast to most foreigners, he was gracious, respectful, and, above all, patient.

Just look at him. He could wait and wait and wait without complaining. Doing no more than offering to the world the opportunity to come and visit him. Francis Cape was a gentleman. There weren't many gentlemen left. The kind of wars that must be fought in this century had reduced the numbers. In modern war, all actions taken had to be as quick as they were cowardly. But back in the days of Waterloo, battlefields were, on the whole, open and fair, and it paid to be patient. Had Napoleon successfully learned how to be patient, he might have triumphed. Instead it was brave old Blucher, who, after having his horse shot under him, was able to get up, brush himself off, and lead his regiment in such a skillful retreat that Napoleon did not know until noon the next day which way he had taken.

Who were the gentlemen left in the world? Recently, Francis had read in the *Tribune* about a man named David Strangeways. Mr. Strangeways had been in charge of Deception Operations in northern Europe during the war. As one of the leading military strategists in England, he was appointed to command the task force overseeing the nuclear tests at Christmas Island. The good man, absolutely opposed to the bomb, was forced to weigh his conscience against his duty. He refused the appointment, quit the military, and went off to take Holy Orders.

There's a gentleman for you. An oddity, certainly. The appropriately named Mr. Strangeways.

Francis recognized that he himself had been less than a gentleman in recent months. Suspicion does not allow for much gentility. Suspicious of Adriana's involvement with Murray, Francis had been forced to act in ways that could only be described as cowardly.

Yet from this tranquil vantage point, looking back over his life, he could say with confidence that though he'd made mistakes of a moral nature, he'd never done anything terribly wrong. Not like Napoleon, who would have improved his state of mind, along with his eternal prospects, if he'd asked to be forgiven —

For the murder of the youthful d'Enghien: convicted of capital crimes against the Republic, he asked for nothing more than an interview with me. I refused and ordered the prisoner immediately remanded, led to a ditch outside the castle, and shot by a party of elite gendarmes standing on the parapet above him. His body was thrown into a grave without a funeral.

For the murder of the humble Palm, bookseller of Naumburg, convicted of libel after publishing an inciting pamphlet and shot immediately.

For the murder of Stabbs, son of a clergyman. The officers of Pavia. And all the male inhabitants massacred at Lugo.

Even for the murder of the twenty bystanders in the Rue St-Nicaise, who were blown up in my place.

Napoleon, it must be admitted, was a confused man. Had his army been defeated early on, he would have lived to be a gentleman. That's what he'd aspired to when he was a youth on Corsica. But for a powerful man, tyranny will always be easier than gentility.

Francis Cape had never been in a position where he was burdened with great power. At best, he could be described as distinguished. His Elban neighbors called him il professore. He liked the title, even if it wasn't accurate. The only teaching he ever did was of elemental English to a young Italian girl. And really, it must be said that she ended up teaching him far more than he had taught her, though what she'd taught him could not be put into words. What he'd learned — *zanzanzanzanzan.* What he'd come to understand. Now that he was in a position to reflect upon the wisdom he'd gained from experience, he couldn't begin and didn't want to try to describe it. And he in no way minded being at a loss for words. This new serenity — it was most welcome, after the past year. He understood without really understanding what it was he understood. Murky certainty was good enough for him. Knowledge that exceeds the capacity of the language to articulate it should be respected. This was similar to but not the equivalent of faith. God being the mysterious subject of faith, knowledge being the definite content of a subject.

Silence was a form of respect. Patient silence. Francis's happiness was contingent upon his ability to experience pleasure without giving in to desire — a formula easily mastered. If he spaced his meals as Napoleon did — breakfast at ten, dinner at eight — if he ate heartily but simply, he could avoid the pangs of hunger. Similarly, he could love without needing to possess the object of his love, simply by enjoying the feeling of respectful, patient admiration.

Deprived of my pension, I had to cut the number of my servants by one-third and pay half of each salary with promissory notes. I've even replaced my Chambertin with a coarse local wine. I am forced to do almost everything for myself — soon I will be going to the market and cooking. If I plead poverty, it is out of justified concern.

Francis was beginning to feel mildly hungry. Though he would have preferred a panino made by Ninanina, he heated himself a can of soup on his gas bombola and, after eating, resumed his position in the chair and continued to wait.

Sooner or later, someone would have to come visit him. The postman, if no one else. On days when the postman didn't find him enjoying the sunlight from a bench on Piazza Repubblica, he'd come find Francis at home.

The clamor of the town had quieted with siesta. Francis went on waiting. The coo of pigeons outside his window returned to him as the sound of his happiness — the purr of a contented man.

It amused him to think of Napoleon reduced to shopping at the market, arguing with fishmongers over the cost of octopus.

Murat, where are you? Soult and Bernadotte? Where has everybody gone? Marie-Louise? My incomparable Josephine?

This foolish little king who was destroyed by his own ambition. Had they been included in some artist's scheme of heaven and hell, Francis would have been floating on a puffy cloud, looking down, and Napoleon would have been impaled on fiery prongs, looking up.

Taking whatever I could gain by force or art. The fullness of my presumption, some would say.

Napoleon had learned next to nothing from life. Francis Cape had learned enough to rise above life. Having spent the past year wrenched by emotions he shouldn't have allowed himself to feel, and having reached the peak of these emotions this very morning, Francis Cape was left drained. And with emptiness came invulnerability. He no longer could feel any kind of pain. He'd feel only what he wanted to feel. Pleasure. A serene anticipation. Pride.

It was amazingly easy to conjure happiness. He wanted to be happy; therefore he was happy. He was happy just sitting there. He was happy thinking about what he'd done with his life. He was happy knowing he needn't be burdened with regrets.

Hurry up, let's go, while Campbell is away!

Zanzanzanzanzan. This mild irritation the only threat to his happiness. Just when everything's right in the world, along comes a mosquito. *Zanzanzanzan.* Senza la zanzara, everything would be perfect. If only he'd remembered to put up the netting. He could close the shutters, at least. How did it get so late? Already dusk was dulling the evening light. Soon it would be time for supper, and Francis had forgotten to go out and get some bread. No matter. He had biscuits in the cupboard, along with spaghetti and sauce. That would do. He could even offer a portion to a visitor, if anyone came to see him. Why hadn't the postman come? Was it a holiday? What saint was martyred on this day?

No matter. In truth, Francis didn't really want a visitor. A single mosquito was bad enough. *Zanzanzan.* How irritating. How irritating? Hardly irritating at all. Francis was on the verge of being beyond rousing. Unlike Napoleon . . . yes, he was unlike Napoleon in every way. The king of Elba had never stopped wanting to possess whatever he desired; the professor of Portoferraio could desire with complete passivity.

Happy, happy Francis. He pictured in his mind twelve monks in Villeneuve L'Archeveque, dancing in the darkness around an olive tree, stopping only for a moment to watch the lawful king of Elba gallop by, alone, in the direction of Fontainebleau.

Nothing could shake his belief that he was yet in time . . .

The bells tolling vespers. *Huzza, huzza* for the fallen king. He wants his throne back. You can't have it, Monsieur. He wants his pension. In contrast, Francis Cape, content with his one simple chair, wants for nothing.

What could I say? My stomach filled with tumor, my spirit melancholy, my strength rapidly declining. I was and always had been, it must be admitted, unequal to the effort life requires.

Not Francis, whose mildness was turning out to be its own reward. Nothing remaining of last year's turmoil but a single mosquito buzzing around his head — *zanzanzanzan.* If he could only swat the bug and kill it, he'd be utterly free to enjoy his happiness.

Any intrusion unwanted, now and forever. Please do not disturb. After Murray had left, Francis had waited patiently all day long for someone to come see him. No one came. No matter. He no longer wanted company. He preferred to be alone. An old man sitting in a room above the dark streets of Portoferraio, wanting noth-ing more than to be left alone. *Zanzanzan. Knock knock. Zanzan. Knock knock.*

Who's there? Francis, you're supposed to ask who's out there. Or just go ahead and open the door.

Was there really someone knocking? If someone was knocking at this time of night, who could it be? It could only be Murray Murdoch — *zanzanzan* — the mosquito in Francis Cape's life. Francis thought he'd gone away. But he'd come back. Why had he come back? To torment him some more. Signor Americano, like Napoleon, always wanting more than he would ever have. Francis Cape floating in heaven above them both.

Knock knock. Answer the door, Francis.

What? And let that devil back into his home? No, thank you.

Rattle of knuckles against wood. Buzz of a wicked zanzara. Demons clawing at the floorboards. Francis Cape was at peace with himself, unlike everyone else in the world. And in order to stay at peace, he must not open the door.

But someone is knocking, Francis.

Zanzanzan.

His favorite toy, they say, was a miniature brass cannon. And his favorite place to play was a seaside grotto about a mile from the Corsican village of Ajaccio, where he used to gather mussels and crack them open and eat them there on the spot.

Everyone else is burdened with conflicting emotions. Not Francis Cape. Everyone else is trying in some way to conquer the world. Not Francis Cape. You'd do him a great favor if you left him alone.

Knock knock. Hello in there. *KNOCK KNOCK!*

"Go away!"

What did he say? Did he say, go away? That's exactly what he said. Go away. And you thought he was a gentleman.

"Francis, it's me, Adriana."

It must have been about half past eight by then. The sky, still overcast, couldn't hold the glow of the setting sun. But as often happens late on a damp day, the smells were magnified, and up from the streets of Portoferraio drifted the aromas of fish: of trash cans filled with fish heads and fish scales, fish stock simmering over a low flame, fish fillets baking beneath a blanket of tomatoes. Fish, fish, fish. Though Francis had closed his shutters, he'd left his windows open, and now, though he hadn't eaten fish all day, his room smelled like a pescheria. Everywhere, the smell of fish. In the streets. In his room. In the hall, where Adriana Nardi was standing, waiting to be let in.

Francis had told whoever was knocking at his door to go away. Having identified herself, Adriana waited for a different kind of reply. She listened for the rattling sounds of an old man trying to put his disorderly home in order while he called to her, Just one moment, I'll be right there, vengo subito. She waited for the door to open wide. She being the kind of girl who, Francis knew, wouldn't wait for long.

He wanted to match his actions to her expectations, he really did. He wanted to get up and throw open the door. *Zanzanzan.* And say, My God, I wasn't expecting you. Why are you here? Why have you come to see me?

Giving her the chance to respond, I've come to apologize.

You, apologize? But it is I who should —

But I —

No, I —

Unless she greeted him with an expression so stony in its aspect that he felt the coldness of stone inside him.

Go away. That's what he'd said. He wanted to take it back. But you can't erase what has already been heard. Go away. Don't go away, Adriana. *Zanzanzan.* He desperately wanted to open the door and greet her — *zanzanzan.* He wanted to push himself up out of the chair and was just at the point of mustering what was left of his strength, anticipating — *zanzanzan* — the shock of what he was about to see — *zanzanzan* — the awful, wonderful shock — *zanzan* — her skin the creamy color of a peeled chestnut, her black hair, her lips, her hands too thin, her fingers gangly, that tiny mole above her right eyebrow, the collar of her maroon blouse cut in a high V, no necklace, her torso always seeming to teeter slightly, her waist too high, her legs too long, her nose too sharp, her eyebrows too thick, her teeth too small, her smile never wide enough, her eyes always mischievous, always full of spirit, full of life, little rubies in her ears reflecting the lamplight from his room, blinding Francis, so at the instant prior to the encounter that would have been, he believed, too momentous to survive, he couldn't —

Paolina? Maria? Josephine? Marie-Louise?

"Francis, it's me, Adriana." Did he even care? What did he care about? He cared about making others care about what he cared about, most importantly, a little man in a black cocked hat and Hessian boots who was said to enjoy picnics.

We can picture him resting under a lentisk tree. From a distance, he looks entirely approachable.

Why not, then, take advantage of the situation and confirm once and for all that Napoleon is indeed the author of the following sentence: "In the final analysis everything that is human has its limits."

And why, sir, did you want your regiment of young scouts to ride horses that only had their front hooves shod?

A man who has a strictly logical mind is a man to admire. Still, it occurred to Francis that, taken as a whole, the character made no sense.

The sky was weighted with rain clouds. Bicycle wheels rattled over cobblestone. Doves cooed. Men argued in the street.

Hai detto che —

Cosa?

If in doubt, advance to meet the enemy. Keep a cool head. Receive impressions of what is happening and never fret or be amazed or intoxicated by good news or bad.

History, it could be said, is the story of logic colliding against itself.

All persons who have committed excesses, and stirred up rebellion, either by setting up any rallying signal for the crowd, or by exciting it against the French, or the government, must be brought before a military tribunal and instantly shot.

First there were the Ligurians. Then the Etruscans. Then the Romans, the Pisans, the Genoese, the Medici, the Spanish. Then at the Treaty of Amiens the island came under French rule.

There was a lot that could be said.

One might consider the impact of the Turkish threat. One might consider many things. Sitting in the Chiesa della Misericordia, one might consider whether the king of Elba would really want a mass said annually for his soul. The same man who, faithful to his oath, declared that he would descend from the throne and quit France.

He agreed to exile, don't forget. He could have fought to the end. Instead he stepped down from his throne and left France without much of a fuss. Twice. But wherever he was, he always accepted visitors.

Which reminded Francis that he should have told Adriana to try the door. It wasn't locked. It wasn't ever locked.

Ricordate: He'd relinquished his title. He'd quit France and even offered to quit life, if such an action would have served the good of his subjects.

In another mood he might have begun, *C'era una volta un piccolo re.*

He knew himself to be a good man. It was as simple as that. The kind of man who sat in the shade of a lentisk tree. And who wouldn't even raise a hand to kill the mosquito buzzing around his head. *Zanzan.* The kind of man who wouldn't swim in the sea because he was sure that the outgoing tide would pull him in exact proportion to the force of his will to return to shore, and he would get nowhere.

He'd declared that he was ready to descend from his throne —
against his own best judgment. And quit France. Good riddance.
Zan. They hooted as his carriage rolled away from Fontainebleau.
They called him the great proud.

Go away, he'd said. The stupidest thing he'd ever said. *Zzzz.* Go
away. What he'd meant to say was that he was ready to give up
everything for the good of others and thus, with a few simple
words, to secure his place in heaven.

He didn't bother to get out of his chair because he was sure
that gravity would push him down in exact proportion to the force
of his will to rise to his feet. Instead, he felt like closing his eyes for
a while. At the same hour when our father was helping the barista
in La Pila finish a bottle of wine, Francis Cape closed his eyes. Leaving Adriana to return home in a rage because bruttissimo Francis
Cape had refused, if you can believe it, even to open the door!

NAPOLEON BONAPARTE, KING OF Elba. Francis Cape, scholar of Napoleon. Malcolm Murdoch, Signor Americano. Is it my turn again, Ollie? You say you want to know what I believe really happened on Elba. I was a young mother then. I am an old woman now. Have forty-five years passed? This is the part of the story I find most difficult to believe. The simple fact of passing time. Someone we love is here in time and then not. Not. Your father, my husband. Was that him peeling potatoes at a bar in La Pila? Was that him walking along a deserted road in a drizzle on an autumn night in 1957?

You know, instead of fretting about the mysteries of death, we should try to understand what we lose by staying alive. We lose someone we love, and we lose with him a good chunk of experience. We need the mingling of minds in order to know what is real. A story becomes true with recognition. The joy of recognition. The surprise of it. Someone else to recognize what you remember.

I want my husband to remember with me that first morning in Florence when we were woken at seven by the bells. The murky darkness of the shuttered hotel room. Our bodies sharing the damp heat of that warm morning in the summer of 1956. One of us to recognize what the other recollects. If he didn't remember the bells, he'd remember the heat. He'd remember the feather mattresses in our Le Foci house. Stopping to watch an old man in a doorway weave a basket. Drinking the new olive oil by the spoonful. Lines of sunlight falling across the papers on the desk when the windows were closed and the shutters opened. I remember. Murray would recognize these memories, even if he didn't share the details of them.

The memories that you children share. The memories I share

with you and you with me. All the memories I've lost because Murray isn't here to remind me. All that we'll never know for sure.

Dear Ollie, you say you want to know what I believe. What I remember. What I know for a fact.

Fact: we embarked in July of 1956 for Genoa.

Fact: we accumulated a debt of over 10,000 dollars during our fifteen months on Elba.

Fact: Francis Cape is buried in Livorno.

Fact: your father spent two nights, not three, at the bar in La Pila.

Fact: for four days I did not contact the police to report your father missing. I was afraid his absence would be interpreted as evidence of terrible guilt, so I did not contact anyone. I waited. I thought I'd learned how to wait from Signora Nardi's example.

Fact: Adriana Nardi came home the day before your father left us, as I told you. But I didn't tell you that when she went to see Francis Cape, she was not alone. Her mother was with her. Signora Nardi intended to surprise Francis when he opened the door.

Fact: I cannot account for the third full night your father spent away from home. You boys went looking for him on the fourth night.

Fact: Even Meena the cat was lost for a few days. But you all returned safe and sound — or, as it seemed to me then, you were returned, the way possessions are returned by the kind of thieves who only intend to borrow. We even got Meena back. Meena, along with those four kittens, all of them odd little flat-faced, long-haired creatures. Do you remember? The night Patrick insisted on keeping one in bed with him and then rolled over and crushed it in his sleep. Do you remember? Does Patrick remember? Have you asked him?

Elba, 1956–1957. Sixteen months in the life of an island. We were home by Christmas. We would have come home much sooner if your father had never met Adriana Nardi. But whether we remained on Elba during her long absence because your father needed to clear his name or because he needed to satisfy a secret longing in his heart, I'll never know for sure. If there's more to the story you've been writing, Ollie, if there were encounters your father kept hidden from me for the rest of his life, if, in fact, he did love Adriana, I can only believe that it must have been a destructive, frivolous love, prompted by his search for a haven where he couldn't disappoint the people he loved most.

Signora Nardi, having recovered her daughter, came and sat with me while the police searched the hills for you. I didn't want her there. I didn't want anyone besides my husband and children. She forced me to talk to her. I remember hearing myself admit, against my will, that I was afraid of my husband. And then, seeing her confusion, I explained that I wasn't afraid of what he'd do to others but what he would do to himself. It was some comfort to consider my children's self-protective instinct. But my husband was a self-destructive man. What would he do? She wanted to hear more, but I'd already said enough.

If I wouldn't talk, then she expected me to listen. I didn't want to listen and was about to say so, but she spoke rapidly, swearing me to secrecy before I could beg her to leave me alone. Of course I didn't want to be alone. I wanted her to sit beside me and stroke my hair and tell me something significant enough that it would require a promise from me never to repeat it to anyone. I gave her my promise, Ollie. Now, these many years later, I am breaking this promise for the first time with much regret.

The story Signora Nardi told me that night was the story of her daughter. And this is the story you deserve to hear. The true story of Adriana Nardi. She was not the coy young girl I'd taken her to be. She was not in love with Murray. Nor was she afraid of Francis Cape. She was a lonely girl bouncing from one heartbreak to another when your father first saw her in the Nardi garden. Yet she was far more capable than any of us realized.

As I told you months ago, Adriana had dropped her university studies and come home shortly before we arrived on the island. As many people who knew her guessed, she'd been involved — to the point of being secretly engaged — with a young professor there. He'd broken the engagement off abruptly; she came home to Elba, where, in a naive effort to reclaim her life, she threw herself into a brief affair with a brutal young man who worked at the prison on Pianosa. All of this Adriana hid from her mother while it was happening. And by the time the early symptoms of pregnancy had begun and the prison guard had deserted her, Adriana was too ashamed to go to her mother for help.

Imagine her that night at our villa in Le Foci. Honestly, I don't think she expected to find Murray alone. I don't know why she was there. Maybe she'd come to talk to me, just like her mother came to me, both of them mistaking our presence on the island as evidence of our influence. Maybe she just wanted to unburden herself. Maybe she wanted to test Murray's capacity for sympathy. She wasn't there, you can be sure, to test her powers of seduction. Murray misunderstood. And then, after leaving Murray, she'd met Francis Cape. Il professore. He wanted to keep Adriana to himself — a justified want, he'd thought, since it was inspired by love. He wanted to marry her. He wanted to kill her.

Il professore, the same pathetic man who tried to stab Murray with a butter knife. He could have done better than a butter knife. He could have wielded a good sharp knife with a five-inch blade. I'm sure he wished he'd had a better weapon ready when Murray came to see him. And I suspect he'd regretted not bringing a knife along when he followed Adriana to Le Foci.

Do you understand what I'm telling you, Ollie? Francis Cape wanted to marry Adriana, and when she refused him, he wanted to kill her. He would have killed her if he'd had the means. Instead he tried to slap sense into her so she would recognize that he was serious. Francis Cape was always serious. Francis Cape only ever told the truth. And all Adriana could do was laugh at him.

A life held in balance. Think of all the outcomes that are possible at any one moment. Adriana could have been killed by Francis

Cape that night. But he was an old man and she a swift girl. She fled down the road before Francis could stop her.

Adriana was seven weeks pregnant when she left Elba. She made her way to Paris and there had the pregnancy terminated. Not an easy thing to do back in 1956. The ordeal could have destroyed her. Instead, it enhanced in her the same ferocity her mother was known for. She struggled, survived, prospered. And while I don't know for certain what's become of her over the years, I expect she'd say now, so many years later, that Malcolm Murdoch and Francis Cape both played only smart parts in her complicated life.

But you want facts, you say. Facts, like the banded ironstone we found on Volterraio. The flint and sandstone and chalk. All the coarse, worthless breccia.

Facts as certain as the warmth of my husband's body in my arms. Nothing I could say to persuade him that he hadn't done anyone any real harm.

Facts, such as the stupidity of a drunk.

Patrick, have you seen your father? Lidia, mio marito — dov'è andato? Has anyone seen Murray? Did he leave a note? Is he back yet? No, grazie, Lidia, niente. Aspetto per Murray. What time is it? Has he called? No, Harry, stay here. I don't want you boys going out this afternoon. Un po' di minestra, sì, that would be fine, Lidia. You know, Murray, I can't fall asleep without you beside me. Where are you? Is it too late to find you? Did you come to this island to do whatever it is you've already done? It is over? Has it happened?

My husband. And then my cat. And then my four young sons. Ten o'clock at night, and my sons were missing, and Murray wasn't there to go out in search of them.

You know what I did then? I felt my head grow unbelievably heavy, my eyes blur, my mouth go dry, my pulse slow, and I fell asleep. Amazingly, I fell asleep. I'd hardly slept for three days and nights. My sons were missing. My husband was gone. And I fell asleep. And dreamt, of all people, about the engineer from Ohio, the one who'd thrown himself off the *Casparia*. I dreamt only of seeing him leaning on the ship's rail, a cruel smile on his face. When I woke up my eyes were dry from staring without blinking. And Lidia was leading Signora Nardi into the room.

Signora —

Signora —

Talk in English. Talk in Italian or French or Latin, for all I care. Don't bother me. Don't stay. Don't go. Don't leave me alone. Tell me a story, Signora. I'll tell you what could happen. You tell me what did happen. Tell me that your daughter's freedom is as important to you as her safety. You let her make her own mistakes — trust being the one absolute of love.

She didn't say any of this when she sat up with me through the night. Instead, she offered me the story of her daughter as proof of the necessity of trust. See what happens when you trust someone? She is always with you, and you with her. With him. With them, Signora Murdoch. You trust them to do what they believe they have to do, even if they are mistaken, even if they try to hide their mistakes from you. They trust you to welcome them back, no matter what.

We will wait together, Signora. We will keep the lights on and tell stories to pass the time. The story of my daughter. Do you want to hear it? You must promise never to repeat to anyone what I tell you, Signora. I will tell you what my daughter told me. My daughter roaming the world while I waited for her to come home. I will tell you. My heart like a bird fluttering inside a box. If I could have, I would have ripped open my chest and let the bird fly away. I will tell you. You will understand. And when morning comes we will see what we will see.

When my brothers and I left our villa that tranquil October afternoon, we were not going to look for our father. Though we hadn't seen him for a few days, we didn't really understand that he was missing. Murray always had come back; therefore he would come back again when he was ready. And so would we. But just in case we were gone longer than we expected, Nat filled a thermos with water, and we each carried a sack with an apple, a piece of bread, and some cheese.

We set out that afternoon during the quiet hour of siesta. It was a beautiful day, the blue of the sky the pure royal tint of sapphire. Patrick, who had hunted for minerals with Carlo along the far slope of Monte Giove, knew to direct us west. As we walked along our regular route toward the path leading up the mountain, we shared the feeling that we were on the mission we'd been training for. Our games had been nothing more than practice.

Over the past months we'd learned a fair amount about valuable stones and their histories. Patrick had a list and would tell us, and when we forgot he would remind us, about diamonds weighing more than a pound, diamonds that had been stolen, diamonds that had started wars, diamonds that had been found by shepherd boys in the mud of a riverbank and sold for the price of 500 sheep, ten oxen, and a horse.

We would have been satisfied to find any gemstone that would have made us a profit of one horse. We wanted a horse. And a boat. Anyone who lives on an island needs a boat. A horse, a boat, and maybe an electric train set. We'd left our trains back in America. A horse, a boat, electric trains, and snorkeling masks for each of us so we could explore the world below the surface of the sea. It hardly

mattered that Nat and I didn't know how to swim. We could float
on an inflatable raft. We needed a big inflatable raft. A horse, a
boat, electric trains, snorkeling masks, and an inflatable raft in the
shape of a beluga.

We didn't tell anyone where we were going because we didn't
know. We just knew we were hunting for something valuable.
Something that someone else would want. The Star of Elba.

After a few days of mist and rain the air was fresh, the breeze
soft, the fields a velvety green speckled with patches of white —
perhaps orchids or fuchsia. We walked quietly, hoping to spy a
wild goat. We didn't see a goat but we saw a strange bird — a
heron, it must have been, with a black velvet stripe along the un-
derside of its long white neck and white feathers hanging from its
breast like strings of pearls. Harry spotted the black eyes of a green
lizard hidden in the grass. And we caught a glimpse of a mottled
snake as it slid across the path.

We climbed through the woods up Monte Giove and along the
rocky ridge at the summit. We rested against a granite boulder on
the northern slope of the mountain. In the distance we could see
dozens of colorful sails mingling at what must have been the finish of a regatta.

For the first time since we'd been on the island, we continued
over the peak of Monte Giove and climbed down the western
slope, out of sight of Marciana. Patrick led us into the hilly terrain
of Mezza Luna. To our east was the peak of La Stretta. We continued south, watching the ground carefully for the glimmer of a gem.

We didn't find much that was worth keeping — only a few
small pieces of what was probably pyrite and a clump of snowy
calcite. We kept walking. The heat of the sun increased as the afternoon wore on. We passed our thermos between us.

We walked west toward Punta Nera. When I was too tired to
walk, Patrick and Harry took turns carrying me on their backs. We
climbed another, smaller mountain we'd known only from the
view at the top of Monte Giove. We kept walking, following a shal-

low gully wherever it would take us. Eventually we came to a small creek that we hadn't known existed.

The valley was filled with holm oak and a green patchwork of myrtle and ferns, and there was a great scattering of huge boulders, some half cleaved with the crevices worn smooth by wind, others with buttresses and chimneys and deep openings that looked like windows. It seemed as if the rocks had tumbled down from the mountains after some great quake, as if the whole universe had shuddered over the chaos of love and picked up the earth and shook it violently, trying to force from the silent ground a confession.

Once upon a time the universe had felt . . . what? What did we know about the chaos of love? Nothing other than the evidence of its effect around us — broken stone, surfaces worn smooth by wind and rain, ancient gouges in the soil filled with green that were no less than proof of the world's ability to repair itself and endure.

Goldfinches flew between the trees, flickering like light reflecting from a tilting mirror. We inhaled the dusty smell of moss warmed by the sun. We waded with our shoes in the shallow water. We felt the silky sensation as schools of minnows bumped against our ankles. We grew giddy and loud. We splashed each other, slipped and fell, and returned to shore drenched.

We rested against the trunk of an oak and ate what was left of our bread and cheese. We finished our water, then refilled the thermos with water from the creek before moving off in different directions. Without saying it, we knew to stay within calling distance of each other, as well as to stay close to the creek. We knew that we couldn't get lost if we stayed within sight of flowing water.

Nat headed south toward Capo Sant'Andrea. Harry went in the same direction but on the other side of the river. Patrick crossed the creek and headed toward La Stretta. I headed back in the direction we'd come.

A frog began chirping and was answered by another frog. The coarse oak leaves hissed with each gust of wind. As twilight came on, the greens of the valley darkened to gray, and whatever was lighter than green became phosphorescent. White blossoms, gold birds, pink quartz — they glowed as though lit from within. Their colors mesmerized me. But when I'd try to approach, the object would disappear like a mirage.

The evening air was still warm, with a cool intermittent breeze. The sky overhead was a deep, metallic blue. Across the creek I saw Patrick's flashlight wobbling between saplings. I tried turning on my own flashlight but couldn't make it work. I tried to think a greeting to Patrick. He didn't answer. I shouted, and he shouted back, "Shut up, Ollie!" I watched him as he bent over to pick up a stone. I saw the quick arc of his arm when he threw the stone into the water. The clatter and splash scared the frogs into silence.

I'm not sure how long we searched in the darkness, but the sky had darkened to a dusky gray when we heard Harry yelling for us to come quick. I saw the beam of Patrick's flashlight on the opposite bank wobbling ahead of him and thought I saw Harry ahead of me, but it turned out to be the pale face of a rock. I tried to keep up with Patrick. When he ran ahead I called for him to wait. He ignored me. I followed the sound of Harry's voice and tried not to lose sight of the beam of Patrick's flashlight.

When I caught up to my brothers, I found Harry standing knee-deep in the creek, his face a ghostly alabaster in the glow of Patrick's flashlight. We all shared the startle of déjà vu. Once before, and now again, I followed Patrick into the creek to join Harry. The water seeped into our sneakers. We stood without speaking, staring at the wet rusty pipe that Harry was holding. We became aware of the silence. The frogs and birds were silent, the breeze was still, and we were hardly breathing. Only the little creek made any sound — the murmur of shallow water flowing over rocks. We pressed close to Harry to see what he was holding. The sky grew darker. Time passed. We might have stood there all night if Patrick hadn't finally found his voice.

"Big deal," he said. "A stupid old pipe."

"You think so," Harry retorted.

"Let's go, Ollie."

We were not playing. We were not Jakos One through Four who could make ourselves understood without even speaking aloud. We were not at all inclined to mix nonsense and different languages. Patrick shrugged. I couldn't decide whom to side with. I let Patrick take my hand in his, but still we just stood there.

"Stupid old pipe," Patrick said.

"Look, Patrick. Just look inside, will you? You dumbhead." Harry turned the pipe so one end faced Patrick and inserted his flashlight at the other end.

"Jeepers!" Patrick clutched the pipe to steady it against his glasses.

"Let me see!" I tried to shove Patrick aside. "It's my turn. Patrick, come on. Patrick!"

"Holy cow."

"I want to see!" I stomped, splashing all of us with water, but still my brothers ignored me.

"Wow!" Patrick peered into the pipe as though into the lens of a telescope. What was so amazing? Patrick was looking at a star. On the star was a colony of martians. The martians waved at Patrick. I waited for Patrick to wave back.

"It's a diamond," he whispered. Harry smiled smugly while Patrick stared into the pipe, mesmerized. I didn't know what else to do but curl myself into a powerful bundle of five-year-old fury and head-butt Harry in the stomach. He held himself upright. I slipped and fell into the water.

"Pigsnot!"

"Shitface!"

"What trash can did you crawl out of?"

I reached for Harry's ankle, he grabbed Patrick, and to my immense satisfaction they both lost their balance and fell.

I decided it was time to start crying. Harry said he'd hit me if I didn't shut up, so I cried louder. As we waded back to shore, Harry mocked me with his imitation wailing. Patrick joined in. We were all crying. We were all pretending to cry. We were laughing, the world was ridiculous, we were ridiculous, it was an October night on the island of Elba, we were soaked, the moon was shining, and we were having fun.

Patrick had held on to the pipe, but his flashlight was drenched, and when he shook it, the light flickered and went out, leaving one working flashlight between us. Patrick blamed Harry. Harry blamed me.

We took off our shoes, and while Patrick wrung out our socks, Harry let me look into the pipe.

What had Patrick said? Jeepers. "Jeepers," I said.

There was a star trapped inside the pipe. Not a star with martians. Rather, a crystalline star that absorbed the beam from Harry's flashlight but still glowed with its own light. It had no color. Instead, it emitted a mysterious gleam both from within and from the surface of the facets. A lustrous mosaic of atoms, like water frozen into ice, ice congealed by extreme conditions and transformed into a permanent, uniform substance. The star of Elba.

Harry shook the pipe gently but the star wouldn't come out. We argued about how to dislodge it. We considered carrying the pipe home and cutting it open, but we were too impatient. Harry inserted a twig into the pipe and tapped it against the crystal. The twig snapped in two. Patrick found a sturdier stick, which Harry plunged into the pipe. Nothing happened. He tried again. There was a loud popping sound, and Harry threw the pipe aside. We didn't see the splinters of glass flying out the opposite end, but we saw them scattered when Harry shone his flashlight on the ground. Glass, not diamond. Just pieces of glass, an old bottle or jar, that had been lodged inside an old pipe.

We stared at the ground rather than meet one another's eyes. Luckily, we were far away from civilization, and there were no witnesses to our stupidity. Not even Nat.

"Nat!" Patrick said.

"Where's Nat?" I asked.

Had anyone seen Nat? No, Patrick hadn't seen Nat. Harry hadn't seen Nat. I hadn't seen Nat. Where was Nat?

Strange that he hadn't been drawn by Harry's shouts or the noise of our fighting. We listened for his footsteps. We waited in silence for a moment, and then we began calling for him.

"Nat!"

"Nat, we're over here."

"Nat, come on."

"Nat, where are you?"

"Nat!"

"Nat!"

"Nat!"

We still had no idea that ever since the fever his hearing had been erratic. We assumed that if he were near enough, he could hear us.

"Nat?"

"Nat!"

We left our shoes and socks drying on the grass and headed together in the direction Nat had gone, beyond Monte Giove toward Capo Sant'Andrea. We had to walk slowly in our bare feet. I held Harry's hand. Patrick led the way with Harry's flashlight.

At one point we heard a noise of paws scrambling over pebbles. Patrick swept the light across the slope rising to our right. The beam illuminated the eyes of some animal — a wood rat or squirrel crouched in a clump of heather. The animal stared at us for a long minute, we stared back, then it slipped away, melting into the earth.

We were chasing a ghost. No, not even a ghost. The idea of a ghost. The farther we went, the more hopeless we felt. I began to feel itchy all over and kept having to pause and scratch myself. Harry tugged me along. I was hungry. I was tired. I was preparing to cry, but Harry cut me short: "Whatever you do, Ollie, just don't start crying, okay?"

Where was Nat? I wanted to find Nat and go home.

"Nat?"

We were all thinking the same thing — how right it was that of the four of us, Nat was the one who'd gotten lost. Nat's fate had always been clear. We'd always known that Nat was destined for trouble. The question we asked ourselves as we wandered along in the dark was, What kind of trouble?

"Nat!"

"Nat!"

"Nat, come on, it's not funny anymore!"

Nat, we found out later, hadn't lost his way at all. He'd followed the creek toward Capo Sant'Andrea just like he'd said he was going to do. And after twenty minutes or so, he'd heard Harry calling behind him. He was pleased to find that for the time being he could hear with perfect clarity. He heard his brother calling his name. But he also heard something else, something he recognized as the sound of someone breaking rocks, the clacking of stone against stone.

Nat headed away from the creek and up the steep bank, across an empty road, across a field, between rows of cypresses, and along a narrow footpath. At the end of the path he came to a segment of the unfinished stone wall marking our father's land.

In the center of a clearing was a wide, brackish pool. Opposite the wall, on the other side of the run-off water, beside a sheer granite wall glittering in the fading light with specks of quartz, was our father. He balanced on one knee. With a rhythmic, mindless motion, he was knocking a stone the size of a baseball against the granite.

On an island measuring 223.5 square kilometers, in the gray of twilight, in the middle of nowhere, Nat Murdoch happened to find his father breaking rocks in the woods of Mezza Luna. Nat couldn't believe what his eyes were telling him, and he staggered back in astonishment, fell into the dirt, and sat there, trying to sort out his confusion.

Only if something is possible can it be true.

"Dad?"

But reality, as our year on Elba had taught us, is full of surprises. Nat liked a good surprise. He decided that the scene of our father pounding rocks under a rising moon was more of a surprise than a coincidence.

"Dad?"

One. Two.

"Dad, hey!"

Three. Four.

"Dad!"

"Huh?"

"Hi."

"Nat?"

"What are you doing here?"

"What are *you* doing here?"

"I asked you first."

"It's late. Does your mother know you're here?"

"No."

As Murray rose to his feet, dust blew in ribbons around his ankles. He was barefoot, dressed in a T-shirt and suspenders, his left eye was swollen, the lid bruised, he had a sore crusted on his lower lip and a stripe of black bristles on his chin.

Nat started to unlace his shoes. Murray called, "Don't you dare."

"Why not?"

"Go home, Nat."

"No."

"I am your father. You are my son. Fathers tell sons what they can and cannot do."

"Yeah?"

"Yeah."

Murray slowly waded across the shallow pool toward Nat. He caught his toe against a rock, winced, but managed to pull himself out of the water. He collapsed beside Nat, who was still sitting in the dirt with one shoe off, one shoe on.

"Nat, something occurs to me."

"What?"

"I thought you had some trouble with your hearing."

"What do you mean?"

"I thought you couldn't hear."

"I can hear fine." Nat could hear fine. He could hear what he wanted to hear. Some of the time. Most of the time.

"You can hear me now. And now? And now?" Murray let his voice soften into a whisper.

"Yeah and yeah and yeah. Stop bugging me."

"I'm allowed to bug you. I'm your dad."

Murray leaned back, resting his folded hands on his belly, and gazed into the night. Nat asked Murray what he was thinking. Murray grunted. Nat stretched out beside him. After a while Murray began to speak aloud. He used the formal tone of someone delivering a lecture, though he didn't seem to care whether or not Nat was listening.

He said something about Babylon. Which made him think of Balthazar. B-words. Any old B-word snatched out of the blue.

What is Babylon? What should Nat already know, and what was Murray trying to teach him?

He rattled on about Eros and Erasmus. Epistolary jests. Expression and imagination. Something along those lines.

"Dad, umm . . ."

I-words. I I I I I.

M-words. Man. A man. Amen.

N for *no*. No . . . ah. Drunken Noah, ho ho ho.

Here was a name Nat recognized: Noah, like in Noah and the Ark!

Murray said something about Pan. Something about Proteus. Something about Pico. P-words. Something about Pico boasting that what he'd written would only be intelligible to a few. Something about parabolic fervor. More P-words. Late-antique Platonists. Mysteries cease to be mysteries when they are promulgated.

"What's *promulgated?*"

Murray told him to look it up. Nat reminded Murray that he didn't know how to read.

Murray said, "Learn to read and then look it up."

Paradigm. Purtroppo. Proud. Murray must have felt a last little stab of pride as he rested on the grass with one of his four sons beside him. Fathers and sons. It was then that he remembered that scene in Turgenev's *First Love,* where the son glances down a lane and sees his father slap his mistress.

Pretension.

"Personally I never had much of a taste for Turgenev."

"What's Tur . . . tur . . . turga . . ."

"Turgenev. Russian author of the nineteenth century."

T-words. The taming of the passions. Tripartite life. Tiresias. Trinity. Tourmaline.

"Tourmaline. I know what tourmaline is."

"You do, do you? Tell me, my young sage."

Tourmaline is unsurpassed even by corundum in variety of hue, and it has during recent years rapidly advanced in public favor. G. F. Herbert Smith. *Gemstones.*

"Tourmaline is a kind of rock you can find."

"Mmm. What else?"

"It's pretty, I guess."

"How is it pretty?"

"I don't know. It's just pretty. All rocks are pretty."

"Why?"

"Because they are."

Think about it, Murray. The beauty of rocks. The stuff of the earth, whether abundant, generally available, or rare.

Pause. Hmm. Dad was gathering himself, preparing to say something of great significance, something he'd been wanting to say for a long, long time.

"Nathaniel. Nathaniel, listen."

A subtle warning embedded in his father's tone of voice. The double click of Nat's name. Nat sat up as if on an elastic hinge.

"Nathaniel, I'm —"

Don't!

Don't what?

Our father was about to say something he shouldn't say, some-thing Nat didn't understand and didn't want to know. How could he be stopped? The best Nat could hope for was to distract him, keeping him occupied until . . .

"Dad, I —"

"— was going to say —"

"— there was this rock —"

"I have to —"

"— this rock, you know, we want to find it, well, there's lots of rocks we already found, actually Harry finds them, he finds every-thing, it's not fair, every time we're looking for something Harry finds it."

"— to say —"

"And then there was this one rock, you know, well Patrick thinks it's tor . . . ter . . ."

Funny how often a word slips from your mind when you need it. Nat looked to Murray for help. What had they just been talking about?

But Murray was trying to explain that he —

Nat interrupted, saying anything that came into his head so he wouldn't hear what Murray was trying to tell him. "And then we, you know, um, we were just, then Patrick, I don't know, that's just what he did, and Ollie, he's such a brat because, that time we found the spiders, actually it was Harry, he's always finding things, you know, Dad, but still I don't see why we have to be brothers all the time, I wish I didn't have any brothers. If I didn't have brothers . . ."

Ei fu. "What I'm trying to say . . . what am I trying to say?"

Keep talking, Nat. Don't give Dad the chance to —

"Actually there's not a law, we don't have to if we don't want to, but since, I don't know. Dad, tell me about something. Dad? Dad! I want you to tell me about, oh, any old thing, or else I'll tell you."

Able was I.

"About once, you know, when, you know, um, well, so, Dad, are you listening, you have to listen, you have to pay attention."

They kept at it long into the night. Whatever nonsense Nat threw at Murray, whatever nonsense they exchanged, was from Nat's point of view merely a way to buy time. As if — and this thought only came to him much, much later — as if, with enough time, he could succeed in paying off our father's debts.

"What'll Mom say when we tell her?"

"Maybe we don't have to tell her."

"Yeah, like she's not going to notice there's three of us instead of four."

"We can say we weren't there."

"Where?"

"Here."

We were sitting on the narrow beach at the edge of Sant'Andrea. Behind us the stack of boulders rose up steeply, though only for a few feet. At the top of the rocks was an area cordoned off by a chain-link fence, and sleeping gray gulls bordered the edge.

While we talked we picked up little stones and threw them one by one into the sea. Whatever we happened to be saying, we'd pause whenever a stone was in midflight and listen for the splash.

Cluck, chuck, silence, splash.

"Is Nat lost forever?" I asked.

"Shut up, Ollie."

This was a sadness I'd never felt before, sharp and clear and deserved. Nat was gone. Nat had been a little bit bigger than me and a little bit smaller than my big brothers. Without Nat I felt unbearably small, as small as the pebbles disappearing into the dark sea.

A sob shuddered through me. Harry shoved me so I toppled over into the wet sand. I cried louder. Patrick clamped his hand over my mouth and promised I'd get it good if I didn't shut up. Why did everyone everywhere always have to tell me to shut up?

Most of the houses on the point were boarded up for the winter, but a few were lit with a warm orange light. Wouldn't it be better if we were inside one of those houses? How would we ever get home?

Patrick took off his glasses and rubbed the bridge of his nose, a gesture that made him look ancient to me. I wondered how he had grown up so fast.

"Some day," he said.

"Some day what?" Harry prompted.

"Some day we'll remember this and it will all be like it never really happened."

"Why do you say that?"

"I don't know."

"Penso —" Harry began, but Patrick barked, "Speak in English!"

"I think we need a plan."

"Like what kind of plan?"

"Like a plan to find Nat."

"The question is, will we find him before the wolves eat him up!"

I started to cry again. Harry hit me. Patrick hit Harry. Harry said, "Race you!" I ran after Harry. Patrick just sat there. We taunted him. He threw fistfuls of sand at us.

The night wore on this way. We kept meaning to resume our search for Nat but kept forgetting about him. We fought, we played, and eventually we flattened a patch of sand to make a smooth broad bed. We stretched out side by side. As we grew drowsy we counted the stars. There weren't many that night because the moon was so bright, like a bowl of liquid light. We remembered the glass star Harry had found inside the pipe. Idly, we wondered if the real star of Elba even existed. Sometimes it's hard to tell the difference between what's real and what's fake, Patrick pointed out. I gazed at his face. He'd put his glasses on and looked very wise.

Sleep crept from our toes to our ankles to our knees.

"Poor Mom," Harry said quietly.

Patrick yawned. Harry and I yawned.

"Let's pretend we're in a war," I said.

"OK," Patrick replied. His eyes were closed. Sleep had reached our elbows. Our necks. We could hear the explosions of battle. Enemy soldiers were advancing, but we were well-hidden and well-armed. The calcite in Harry's pocket was a bomb so powerful it could blow the entire island to smithereens. Imagine that. In the place where Elba had once risen out of the sea, there would only be water carpeted with the refuse of wood and metal, flesh and bone.

As sleep reached our ears, I felt, and was ashamed to feel, that I'd always remember this night as one of the best nights of my life.

And while you all were having such a swell time, I was trying to drag Dad back into the world of the living.

Sorry, Nat.

Even if Murray didn't say outright that he was ready to quit, he was thinking it.

He'd been thinking it for a long while. He came to Elba in order to allow himself to think it. Came so he could get away. Came to escape. There he was, trapped by the wish to escape from the wish to escape from the wish.

Whatever. I was just a dumb kid and didn't put two and two together. Our old man was drunk. Really drunk. It was the first time I'd seen him this way, and I didn't understand. But at least I could tell he needed help. He'd scraped his knuckles raw, his hands were bloody, his words were slurred, and his eyes had a weird foggy glare. Turns out he hadn't eaten anything since the evening before, but he'd forgotten he was hungry. I thought if I could get him home, home to the villa first, then home to America, everything would be okay. I did my best to convince him.

What did he say to you?

I've told you what I remember, Ollie.

Nothing else?

No.

And so we're left to imagine.

That's your job.

You telling Dad what it was like to be a small boy on an island in the Tyrrhenian Sea.

Whatever.

Dad telling you about Balthazar and Erasmus and Pico.

Whatever.

You telling Dad about quartz and pyrite, calcite and tour-tour-tourmaline, Dad telling you about the Guelphs and the Ghibellines, Garibaldi and Galileo, you telling Dad that the first thing you were going to do when you got back home to America was set up your trains.

Maybe.

Dad explaining that there are things a father can say only to his son, you telling Dad about an old episode of *Popeye,* Dad telling you something about the something he'd been wanting to explain, something having to do with the Nardi girl, you telling Dad about the time Popeye went overboard with his anchor, Dad warning you about the explosion of nothing into something, all you have to do is look at a girl for the fun of it, you reminding Dad about the BB gun you'd been promised, Dad reminding you that there are confidences a father can share with his son, his wife never needs to know, no one else needs to know what the father says to his son on this balmy moonlit night on the island of Elba after too many days of rain, you telling Dad you were kind of tired, asking, Can't we go home now and if we can't go home, do you want to play Ants? Dad asking, Why the hell did we come here anyway? but you weren't sure whether he was asking why did we come here to this place in the woods or to this island, Dad pointing out that we could have gone to Mexico or Alaska or Louisiana while you tried not to yawn and to keep yourself awake you decided to explain what a periscope is, Dad cursing his Averil uncles, you reminding Dad that your birthday was in ten-and-a-half months, Dad reminding you that you were an innocent child, you telling Dad that unlike your brothers you don't actually fall asleep, you just lie in bed thinking about sleep, Dad saying that even if you didn't understand what he was saying, it sure felt good to talk, what a relief just to talk, father and son, you unable to suppress a great big yawn, Dad giving a sad chuckle of resignation and cuddling you against his chest, you hearing his laugh as a crackle echoing from the cave of his ribs, Dad shifting you a little so he could free his arm, rubbing his face as if he had a towel in his hands and were blotting his wet skin dry, you lying there thinking about sleep, Dad saying, if only, you telling Dad you were cold, though you weren't cold at all, you just wanted him to put his arm around you again, Dad saying that what he'd like right then was a scotch, you thinking lazily about blowing the fluffy parachutes from the head of a dandelion, Dad repeating, if only, you enjoying the vibrations of his voice against your ear, Dad telling himself, if only he hadn't come to Elba, getting only this far in the hypothetical, Elba being the place where his troubles began as far as he could see, and he couldn't see very far, not in the dark, not with his son asleep across his chest, not with his head aching as the evening's alcohol dissolved, not with regret fogging his vision, regret an effective cover for the terror of self-knowledge, the story he could tell himself the story of an American guy who fucked up, don't we all fuck up sooner or later, he's sorry, Claire, he's sorry, Adriana, his deception, her deception, his cowardice, Francis Cape, all of which kept him from considering his original purpose in leaving home and thus he was able to make the decision to feel nothing worse than guilt, which manifested itself visibly with the hint of a smirk, a smirk which would never entirely disappear from his face, marking him as the kind of person who, with a shrug, was always ready to acknowledge his potential for fucking up, no matter what he did he kept fucking up, sorry about that, girls, regret lit with the soft glow of virility, that radiant Y chromosome, that sexy X, the story such people could tell always the same story — Sir Winston who loved Lady Jane who loved the Duke who loved Lady Jane's sister who loved Sir Winston, never more than that, never less, you know the kind of people I'm talking about, the edge of their personality a little dulled, their eyes a little blank, ambition a little muted, and always that smirk to signal to others that they'll never be registered saints and, guess what, they don't give a damn, let someone else rise to the challenge, they can have it along with all the trouble, the confusion, the uncertainty, the suffering, the intensity of thought and feeling, no thanks, Malcolm Murdoch is going to ease himself into sleep by thinking about the only thing that really matters to a man who hasn't eaten for twenty-four hours, the antidote of food, in particular, a bloody steak just off the grill, green-bean casserole, and the well in a mountain of mashed potatoes filled with steaming gravy.

The Inconstant

M ORE THAN ONE HUNDRED ELBANS CAME TO FRANCIS Cape's funeral, though not because they'd ever cared about the Englishman while he was living. They came because they were curious. They wanted to see for themselves the body that was said to have turned miraculously into wax. Francis Cape had died of heart failure a full five days earlier, the coroner had confirmed. But instead of deteriorating with the usual rapidity, his body had remained unchanged, emitting no trace of fluids, no blood or excretions, and no foul smell, according to those who'd helped transfer the corpse to the little morgue behind the customs station in Portoferraio.

Signora Nardi paid for the service and burial. She ignored the rumors about the mummified body of il professore and went about the ordinary business of arranging a funeral. First she sent cables to Francis's relatives in London, which went unanswered. Then she contacted an Anglican minister, the Reverend Nigel Fink, who lived in Livorno. And she managed to convince the parish priest of the Chiesa della Misericordia to allow a Protestant service to be conducted in his church.

The coffin was high-quality cherry wood, but the mourners were disappointed when they arrived to find the coffin closed and Francis Cape's uncorrupted body hidden from view. Some of the guests snuck out through the side door and went home. Among the mourners who remained were Lorenzo Ambrogio and his wife, Carlo the mine surveyor, Ninanina of the enoteca and her husband, Massimo, our cook, Lidia, Adriana Nardi, our mother, our father, and of course Signora Nardi herself, who sat in the front pew beside her daughter, both of them wearing black Burano lace veils that were said to have belonged to Napoleon's sister.

The maestrale had blown in cool, bright weather for the day. White chrysanthemums lined the aisles and the base of the altar and filled the Chiesa della Misericordia with their sweet dusty fragrance. Candles cast flickering shadows on the nave columns. People blew their noses frequently, not because of strong emotion but because the winter's respiratory viruses were beginning to spread. Reverend Fink said the Evensong and read the Absolutions of the Dead in English. "He cometh up and is cut down like a flower, he flieth as it were a shadow, and never continueth in one stay." Lorenzo delivered a short eulogy in Italian in which he praised Francis for his dedication to history. He quoted Aristotle, St. Augustine, and, of course, Napoleon — "Do not be surprised at the attention that I devote to details: I must pay attention to everything so as never to leave myself unprovided."

Francis Cape had been a man of detail. In recording a small segment of history, he'd wanted to include everything that could be known. Elbans would remember him for his noble effort, if not for his accomplishments.

Too bad he was Protestant, people whispered. If he'd been Catholic, they might have let themselves believe that his body truly had been the location where God chose to work a miracle. But in fact, they pointed out, refrigeration will keep meat fresh. Taking into account the cool weather . . .

Mamma mia, what disrespect. Shhhh.

People whispered about many things. Gathering outside on the steps after the service, they whispered about the solitary professor who had been dead for days before anyone bothered to check on him. They whispered about the consequences of loneliness. They whispered about the stealth of heart disease. They whispered about our father as he and our mother walked past them, holding hands. They whispered about Americans and their love of drink, for by then everyone had heard about Signor Americano's four-day spree that had taken him across the island from Marciana to Porto-ferraio to La Pila to Sant'Andrea. They whispered about American foolishness and American greed. The rumor passed among them that Malcolm Murdoch had paid five times for his patch of Elban earth what they knew it to be worth. They speculated about when he would take his family and go home.

And they whispered about Adriana Nardi. Though she mingled among them out in the piazza, she said little about her year abroad, despite the direct, probing questions put to her. And when she was out of range the Elbans made up stories to explain her absence.

They said that she'd run away to Paris with a lover, but the man had abandoned her, as men will abandon all women who are too willing, and she'd gone on to England alone, to London, where she'd worked as a servant for a wealthy family. A Nardi working as a servant! Impossible! As a lady-in-waiting, then, yes, who knows but that she worked for the queen herself! Absurd, though it was fun to pretend. And listen to this: the lover had left her pregnant. She'd had a child — delivered it right there in the royal palace and then had given the infant up for adoption. No! Yes! You can tell from the hips of a woman if she's birthed a child, and you can tell from the look in her eyes if she's had to give the child up.

Where was the child? In an orphanage in London. Sleeping in a gilded cradle in a palace. Wrapped in a threadbare blanket in a basket left to be claimed at a train station. Adriana, what happened to the child? What did you do with the child?

Another pressing question was the identity of the lover. If not the American investor, then who? Who took Signorina Nardi to Paris? Who lured her away from Elba? Who, Adriana? Tell us his name.

People watched Adriana carefully. They watched her when she shook hands with our father and mother on the steps of the church. They eavesdropped but failed to make sense of the English words our parents and Adriana quietly exchanged. The conversation seemed cordial, though of course they all knew that courtesy could be even more effective than silence as a cover for turmoil.

The funeral procession wound down to Via del Paradiso toward the quay of Portoferraio, where Francis Cape's coffin would be loaded onto a boat bound for Livorno. Reverend Fink led the way. The coffin, blanketed with chrysanthemums, rested on a carriage pulled by Claudio Baldi's sturdy dappled pony. The mourners followed, and behind them a little boy scoured the street for coins that with any luck would fall out of purses and pockets.

Adriana was flanked by Lorenzo and her mother. Our parents joined the rear of the procession. The mourners had to walk quickly to keep up with the bright-stepping pony. Shutters flew open and women leaned on windowsills to watch. Men repairing a lamppost stopped working and took off their caps. A dog chained inside a yard lunged at the gate and barked.

One of the mourners — Massimo, the husband of Ninanina — broke off from the group and wandered up the steps of Via della Lampana. Ninanina caught him and pulled him back into the procession.

Our father and mother walked arm in arm. Although it was difficult to see in the shadow beneath his hat, Murray's eye was still discolored, though less swollen. He rested against Claire in an effort to disguise a slight limp.

He'd been home for two full days and nights and had shaved, bathed, and put on a clean suit, but still he looked haggard, with new strands of white salting his hair. Claire, in contrast, looked serene, as if she were confident that the troubles were behind her. Or in front — in the cherry-wood coffin of Francis Cape.

Clippa clop clippa clop went the hooves of the pony on the paving stones.

The story Murray told Claire when he came home was that he'd visited Francis Cape early in the morning, they'd argued, and Murray had struck him down and left him for dead. The story Claire told Murray was that Adriana Nardi had visited Francis that evening and found him still alive enough to tell her to leave him alone. Murray couldn't have killed Francis. Nor could he have done anything to harm Adriana. He was exonerated. But he felt no relief. He needed the guilt, Claire sensed. Guilt provided useful comfort. All right, Murray Murdoch, everything is your fault, if that's what you want to believe.

There went Ninanina's husband again, up through an open doorway to see what was going on inside the courtyard. There went Ninanina after him, muttering, *Merde, merde, merde.*

Clippa clop clippa clop.

The story we told Claire was that we'd gone looking for our father and had found him on the property in Mezza Luna. Since by then it had been too late to make our way home, we'd stayed the night in an old military redoubt we knew of on the road to Sant'Andrea. And we were back home in time for breakfast, unharmed, though shoeless.

The rest of the story Murray told Claire was basically true — how he'd wandered around for a while, made his way to La Pila, and for two nights and three days had earned his keep chopping vegetables in a bar. He'd left La Pila after losing at cards. He'd wandered around some more. Of the night and the day after La Pila and before Nat found him, our father remembered nothing.

Clippa clop clippa clop. Ninanina's marito had stopped to talk with Gastone of Bivio Boni, who was on his way home.

"Gastone! Come va?"

Clippa clop clippa clop clop clop cloppa! The pony shied when a small raggedy terrier ran across the road in front of the procession. Reverend Fink helped Claudio Baldi steady the pony.

Clippa clop clippa clop.

Now where had Ninanina's marito gone this time? Massimo! Had anyone seen him?

The story Signora Nardi told others was that her daughter had fallen in love. Nothing worse. Her daughter had fallen in love. Wasn't this a sufficient explanation? What else could Signora Nardi tell her curious friends? Yes, she knew the boy's name. No, he was not Italian. Yes, they would be married soon.

Clippa clop clippa clop.

Massimo?

There he was — in Armando Scarlatti's garden in a cloud of hen feathers. Why were Armando's hens plumper than everyone else's? Massimo was going to find out while Armando was inside listening to his radio.

That Massimo!

One of the mourners called, "Salve, Armando!" to alert him. But Ninanina led her husband back to the procession and planted him beside the reverend before Armando arrived outside.

Hurry up, good neighbors. Attenzione! There's a dead man in a coffin. The sacred vessel turned to wax, the contents emptied, the soul gone . . . where? A soul that through the body's senses would have taken pleasure in the shreds of clouds pasted to the blue canvas of sky, doves cooing in a garden, the two little girls swinging in a string bed. A dead man who loved this island as only a foreigner can love it. Its beauty endlessly strange to him. As strange as Adriana Nardi.

Did you ever consider, Francis Cape, that someday Adriana would be the escort for your coffin? Even if she never learned to love you, she forgave you. Is that enough?

Waxworks. The bronchial tree shriveled, the aortas crusty, the intestines hard, the veins collapsed, his skin without elasticity or temperature.

Not waxworks. Just an ordinary dead man to remind us that it's good to be alive.

Clippa clop clippa clop.

You're leaving Elba, Francis.

Ninanina's husband whispered something to the reverend. Everyone walking nearby could see that the reverend was trying not to laugh.

That Massimo!

Our father leaned on our mother's arm. He couldn't see the coffin through the crowd of mourners but he could hear the pony's hooves. He imagined himself in place of Francis Cape. He imagined waking up from a dreamless sleep to find himself nailed shut in a box. Hello, hello, is anybody there, help me, please, let me out! His voice so muffled that only Adriana, walking directly behind the coffin, would be able to hear. She'd hear him calling, and she'd ignore him. She had every right to ignore him.

Claire imagined Francis Cape alone in his hovel of a room at the moment when he knew he was dying. The pitiable man. How terribly alone he must have felt. Yet he never admitted he was lonely. Not to Claire, at least.

Clippa clop clop clop. The pony bounced awkwardly down the steep sloping road. This was the same pony that led the baldachin at the Festa di Santa Chiara every year. He was a strong little gelding, still spry at the age of seventeen, though, who knows, perhaps he felt an increasing need to prove himself capable. *Clop clop clop . . .*

Down through the streets of Portoferraio wound the funeral procession. Processions didn't usually come through the Medeceo quarter. The cemetery was in the opposite direction. Who was in the coffin? people wanted to know. Francis Cape. Who was Francis Cape? An Englishman.

Ninanina's marito started to —

Massimo Massimissimo, don't even think about it!

Adriana Nardi walked proudly — too proudly, some people thought — between her mother and Lorenzo. What secrets did she have to tell? No one really believed that she'd lived and worked inside a royal palace. But the business about the child — there must be something to it, people whispered. She'd been gone from Elba for eleven months. Why eleven months? Why not six months? Eight months? Girls who birth bastards go away from home for eleven months. And then they come back, trying to pretend that nothing has happened.

Clippa clop clop.

There would be a repast at the Nardi villa. Everyone knew and admired Signora Nardi's cook, Luisa. Luisa had been working in the kitchen for two days, preparing a feast to feed the mourners. There would be acquadelle and langostini, risotto and patate and a dozen different kinds of sweet cakes. Just the thought of it made Ninanina's husband hungry. "Are you hungry too?" he asked the reverend.

A dead man inside a coffin. Francis Cape. Who was Francis Cape? A professor of history. A scholar of Napoleon. An Englishman who once told Lorenzo that leaving England at the age of sixty-three was like checking out of a hotel. An old man who never spoke about his family. A careful man who never locked his door. A nattily-dressed man who lived in a filthy room. A solitary man. A bachelor who smoked a pipe.

Clippa clop clop clop.

Who was Francis Cape?

What do you care?

Massimo, you'd better get back into line or your wife will be —

There she goes, hitting her marito on the head with her purse again.

A dead man inside a coffin. A wooden box to signify the security of death.

Hai finito?

Sì, sì.

When will it be my turn? Murray wondered.

When will it be my turn? Lorenzo wondered.

When will it be my turn? Reverend Fink wondered.

Clippa clop clippa clop.

"Ciao, Roberto!"

"Ciao, Massimo!"

Please, people. There is a dead man present.

Who?

His name was Francis Cape.

What did he do?

Not much.

Whom did he love?

He loved the island and its history. He loved Adriana Nardi, Claire knew.

And who loved Francis Cape?

His mother, presumably. His father.

Adriana certainly didn't love him. Adriana was in love with a boy her age. Good for her. She would marry and have children, molti bambini to fill the Nardi villa. Good for her. And while she's at it perhaps she could give the archival material to a museum for safekeeping. An antique cup that once belonged to Napoleon did not belong in a house full of children.

Ninanina's husband pointed to the butcher's shop. In the window was a pig's head wearing sunglasses and a bright red visor. Bravo!

Massimo, stop it! Attenzione!

The mourners had never processed in a procession like this.

Down toward the quay instead of to the cemetery at San Giovanni. For a Protestant, no less. Mother of God, spare us.

Who was Francis Cape? A man who felt obliged to explain to the fishermen of Marciana Marina that what the ancients thought were the voices of sirens were, in truth, the cries of the gabbiani echoing in the Cove of Barbarossa at twilight.

Clippa clop clop clop.

The procession slowed to a halt. They'd reached the quay, where there should have been a boat waiting to transport the coffin and the reverend to Livorno. There was no boat. Massimo, Lorenzo, Carlo, and a dozen other men gathered by the harbor master's hut to argue about what should be done. Children approached the coffin. One girl took off a chrysanthemum and put it in her hair, but her older sister plucked the blossom free and returned it to the coffin. The mourners stood quietly, waiting for Reverend Fink to indicate the next course of action. The reverend looked at Signora Nardi for a suggestion. Signora Nardi blinked, startled at the awkward situation. People thought she looked vulnerable and gentle, and they were reminded of how much they had admired this woman over the years.

But it was time for the mourners to go on to La Chiatta. Motorcycles and bicycles suddenly appeared out of nowhere. A couple of taxis started their engines. The mourners bid Francis Cape a safe journey to his final destination and began to disperse — and then stopped, for they noticed, or were told to notice by their friends, Murray and Claire Murdoch, i signori Americani, approaching the coffin.

The Nardi women were standing nearby. Our parents had already let it be known that they would not continue up to La Chiatta for the meal. They had to get back to their children.

"Arrivederla," said Claire softly. People watched as Signora Nardi and Claire exchanged a warm three-point kiss. They watched as Claire and Adriana kissed twice. Murray just stood there. Signora Nardi offered him her hand. He pressed it weakly. Adriana offered him her hand. He held it. People watched as Adriana and Signor Americano politely shook hands. They watched as Murray bent to whisper something in Adriana's ear while Signora Nardi and Claire stood by, patient and expressionless. They watched Adriana give a slight nod, indicating plainly that she understood. They watched as Murray kissed her lightly on the cheek and then turned toward Francis's coffin. He bowed his head, touched the wooden lid with his fingertips.

"Good-bye, my friend."

A tear shed. A touch of sarcasm visible in that shadow of a smirk. Claire put her hand over Murray's, held it against the wood as though she wanted him to feel a heartbeat.

Good-bye, Francis Cape.

Our parents took a taxi back to Marciana. The rest of the mourners made their way up to the Nardi villa. The Nardi women waited with the reverend and Lorenzo while the harbormaster found another boat willing to take the coffin as cargo. Reverend Fink himself had to help carry the coffin, unadorned by flowers now. It was a difficult effort with only four men, and at one point the reverend lost his grip and the back end of the box banged down on the pier, splintering the wood at the corner. The harbormaster came to help, and the coffin was loaded onto the boat.

At last, Francis Cape was leaving the island.

From henceforth, blessed are the dead which die in the Lord: even so saith the spirit; for they rest from their labors.

Good-bye, Francis Cape.

He did not want to go.

Good-bye, Francis Cape.

Later that evening Nat and Harry and I were in the bedroom building block towers. Patrick, hidden in the darkness of the hallway, was spying on our parents, who sat across from each other in the living room, sipping wine and talking in quiet voices that grew more animated as the evening wore on. When he'd heard enough he returned to the bedroom.

"Hello, I have an announcement to make." Patrick stood in the doorway, looking imperious.

"We're going home," guessed Harry.

"I was supposed to say that," Patrick wailed. Harry smiled wickedly. Patrick jumped on him. Nat jumped on Patrick.

I realized only then how tired I was. I pulled my pile of blankets to the corner, planted my thumb in my mouth, and watched my brothers fight.

I don't remember who broke up the fight or put me to bed. I woke once to throw off a blanket and then went back to sleep, tumbling into the middle of a dream that seemed to have started without me. I found myself alone, lost in the woods — not in the pineta of Elba but in the suburban woods of Connecticut. It was winter, cold enough for my breath to cloud in the air, and though there was no snow the grass was brittle with frost and the brook I came to had a fringe of ice. I remembered my brothers telling me that if I followed flowing water I'd always get somewhere, so I walked along the bank through the woods. Eventually I came to a yard, which after a moment I recognized as the backyard of our old house. The lights were off, everyone inside already asleep. I went in through the kitchen door and up to the bedroom I shared with Nat and climbed into bed with him. I fell asleep.

That night Nat dreamt that he was asleep in our old house in Connecticut. A loud bang woke him. He climbed out of bed, careful not to disturb me, and went to the window. The moon was out, shining brightly, yet gale winds were shaking the trees. He tried to close the window but couldn't budge it. The wind blew into the room, swirling papers and books and clothes into a funnel.

Harry dreamt that he, too, was in our old house back in America. It was late at night when he heard the crash of books in our bedroom. He tried to open our door but found it locked. He heard Nat shouting for help inside. He ran to our parents' bedroom, but though the spread had been pulled loose and the pillows dimpled, our parents weren't there. He ran through the house looking for them.

In Patrick's dream, he was reading a book in bed when he heard the branches scraping against the house. He looked out. The moon was shining, the wind blowing. He saw Nat blow by like a cobweb being sucked into a vacuum. Patrick watched him disappear above the trees, then he returned to his book.

In my dream, I woke up and found the room in terrible disarray, as if it had been turned upside down and shaken hard. Nat was gone. I started to cry.

In Harry's dream, he heard me crying and ran back upstairs. He banged on our bedroom door. He called to me, told me to unlock the door. On the other side I pulled and banged the knob, but the lock was jammed.

In Patrick's dream, he was reading a book about wild horses roaming the hills of Wyoming. The thought of Nat flying across the sky filled him with envy. Lucky Nat, he figured, had gone to Wyoming.

In Nat's dream, he sailed through the air high above the town. He felt gripped by both fear and pride. He shouted. He wanted witnesses.

I was woken by Harry pounding on the bedroom door. Harry said he'd been woken by my stupid crying. Patrick said he'd been woken by Nat's shouts. Nat said he'd been woken by the whistle of wind as he plummeted from a great height toward the earth.

At breakfast we whined and protested when Claire told us we would be going home soon — home to America, home, hopefully, to the very same town in Connecticut where we'd lived before Elba. We said we didn't want to go home. Harry told Claire about his nightmare. I was going to tell her about mine next but was silenced by her response to Harry.

"A dream," she grumbled. "What are dreams? I'm sorry, puffin, but I don't want to hear about dreams for a while."

MURRAY WENT ON AHEAD of us by train to Paris and by plane from Paris to New York, where he would immediately start looking for a job. Once he found an adequate job, he'd find a house to rent. Once he found the house, he'd send for us.

Our cat had returned after wandering off. Harry found her in the old cantina on our property. She'd made a nest for herself with a bundle of tarp behind a rusty vat, and she was nursing four new kittens. They were longhairs, with wisps of blond woven with red and black — odd offspring for our sleek, dignified seal-point Siamese.

Before we left Elba we gave the three surviving kittens away — one to Lidia's ten-year-old niece, one to a neighbor, and one to Francesca. Meena, in outrage, would sit outside in the yard and yowl through the night.

In the weeks remaining, we returned to Monte Giove at every opportunity. Although our mother had given Francesca strict orders to keep us in her sight, we took advantage of the long pause of siesta, when all the adults closed themselves inside their shuttered rooms. We promised to stay inside, too, but as soon as the house was silent, we went outside.

Up the dirt path behind the villa, up into the woods, then off the path and up the rocky slope toward the summit. The gulls drifted lazily overhead. We discovered that if we made the right scratching sound with our fingers in the gravel, the lizards would stand still for us. We always saw the same lone blackbird perched in the bare branches of a dead cork tree. It would watch us with a look that suggested it was only reluctantly giving us permission to pass. One day Nat cawed at it, and the bird squawked back in obvious indignation, then flew off with a noisy, heavy flapping.

Jako One, smettila!

No!

Our attempts to revive the magic of our game was halfhearted, our success limited. Were we hearing what we expected to hear, or were we still able to hear the sound of thought? We hardly cared. We knew we couldn't take the magic of Monte Giove away with us. We were going home. We belonged to our parents, not to this island.

One afternoon we climbed up to the shade of Madonna del Monte, to a stone table and blocks of granite seats where, according to a sign, Napoleon had sat during his year of exile.

"What's the big deal about Napoleon?" Nat asked. Nat the bird. I wondered if he would ever fly again. I didn't wonder if he could hear us when we spoke to him because I'd never known that he'd had any trouble hearing. The mysterious problem had resolved itself, and he could hear perfectly well. We didn't realize anything had changed.

Harry shrugged. Patrick began to reply, "He was . . ." and then fell silent.

"What?" Nat asked.

"I'm not sure," Patrick said.

I thought about this. I thought about other things I wanted to know.

"Why don't we come back next year?" I asked. My brothers gave me looks implying that my stupid question couldn't possibly have an answer.

I meant to urge them to reconsider and started to say, "Hey, Jakos," but somehow it came out "Jackass." My brothers hooted with laughter. Harry laughed so hard he fell off the stone bench. Harry lying splat on the ground with his feet in the air was something I could laugh at. I joined my brothers.

What was Napoleon? He was. Heehaw, heehaw!

Four little jackasses, our ears forever tipped with fur. Four little jackasses on the terrace where the king of Elba once sat, writing the future in airy words above the sea.

Those were serene weeks for our mother. After helping Signora Nardi dismantle what was left in Francis Cape's apartment and put his belongings into storage, she began sorting through our own accumulations. What we wouldn't take back with us she planned to disperse between Lidia and Francesca — except for the various minerals Murray had brought home, most of which he'd never even bothered to identify. These she'd give to a collector Signora Nardi had told her about, a man up in Sant'Ilario.

Claire and Signora Nardi spent most afternoons together, both of them relishing each other's company with an energy neither could explain. They talked at length, in private, about Adriana. The great consuming love that the mother felt for the daughter was returned by the daughter in her abiding loyalty. That Adriana hadn't come to her mother for help remained a source of deep pain for the Signora. No matter what her mother could say to reassure her, Adriana would always believe that she should spare her mother from her own troubles. In the girl's scheme, secrecy was protection. Adriana, like so many people who know they are beloved, was determined to be happy for the sake of someone who wanted her to be happy.

And now she was happy. Happy to know she had the freedom to go away and always to be welcome at home. Happy to have fallen in love with a good man, a young Englishman who arrived on the island in the last week of November.

"Piacere, Paul."

A man who would never hold her past against her. You could tell by the way he looked at Adriana, the way Adriana looked at him. Love enriched by some secret understanding of what each had endured. The secrets children try to keep from their parents,

Claire thought, watching the two of them sitting without awkwardness or the performance of affection on the sofa in Signora Nardi's living room. They were in love. Love born from heartbreak. Love repairing the damage of love.

If Claire stayed, she and the Signora would teach each other the nuances of their languages, the energy of their friendship opening up the subtleties of words. But she wasn't staying. Signora Americana was going home, and though she promised to write, she knew their letters would be too formal to sustain this intimacy.

As they kissed good-bye, Claire's premonition of this friendship fading with the rest of the past — life going on, memory blurred by experience — sharpened into understanding of the way fierce love provokes loyalty. The daughter's loyalty to her loving mother had cast a veil of secrecy over her life. Adriana feared disclosure, not because it could lead to accusation but because it would lead to sympathy. The mother's protective love for her child would continue to generate the daughter's determination to protect her mother from pain.

The mysterious nature of love and all its unpredictable outcomes. Now we know better, you and I, Signora, how to be patient. Both of us a little wiser, Claire told herself, comforted by the cliché, resisting the urge to turn around as she walked away from Signora Nardi, and then giving in to the urge, turning, facing the Signora, who was still standing at the door, and declaring, "Tu sei magnifica!"

Two taxis came early in the morning to take us to the ferry. It was a gray day, though not yet raining. Nat refused to get dressed, and Francesca had to hold him while Lidia pulled his clothes on. Harry hid in the cantina. He was found and dragged back to the house by Francesca's fiancé, Filiberto, who would accompany us as far as Genoa to help with the luggage. Patrick appeared with a pillowcase filled with rocks.

Four boys — Oliver, Nathaniel, Harold, and Patrick. Sir. All accounted for, Sir. Ma'am, rather. Here we are, Mom. All four. All of us except —

"Meena!"

It was my fault. My crime. My stupidity. One of the many foolish acts I've never been able to live down. I'd opened the door of Meena's cage to give her some grass. Good Elban grass. She needed some grass for the long journey ahead, I'd decided.

Spark of tawny fur, black tail whipping through the air, paws outstretched, body low to the ground as she wound up the path toward Monte Giove, and she was gone.

"Meena!" Patrick ran after her. Harry ran after Patrick, Nat after Harry. Francesca kept a firm grip on me.

"Boys, get back here! Filiberto, help!"

Filiberto Boschi to the rescue. Filiberto Boschi and his dog. "Vai!" The dog racing up the slope past my brothers, up along the path where Meena had gone, up Monte Giove. Look, there she is! A glimpse of cat, a dog, a dog chasing a cat.

"No, no, Rosella, vieni qua!"

A big dog chasing a little cat up into the mountains of Elba while my brothers shouted in desperation. It was no use. They'd never catch her. They headed back to our garden while Filiberto raced past them.

"Rosella!"

My brothers and me — the four of us. Attenzione! Was there ever a kid as stupid as me? My brothers, our mother, the taxis and their drivers, Francesca, Lidia, and, at last, Filiberto with his panting, slobbering hound named Rosella. The bliss of pursuing a creature smaller than yourself. Proud Rosella.

The grownups clucked and called in a pathetic attempt to lure Meena home, but she was gone, and we had a boat to catch. We were herded, sobbing, into the taxis. We weren't going to leave Elba. We vowed to jump off the ferry and swim back to the island.

We insisted that we couldn't leave without our cat. We couldn't. We just couldn't.

We did — traveling to America on a ship called the *Roma* in another first-class cabin paid for with borrowed money, because Murray said we deserved the luxury after all we'd been through. We were home in time for Christmas.

LOOK AT THE SURFACE of the water. Look carefully. Look at the words on this page. Look at the tip of your pen. Look up at the clouds. Look down at the clover growing in the cracks of the sidewalk. Look at your hands. Look at a map. Look at a painting. Look at a clock. Look at the ceiling, the wall, the floor. Look at a piece of honeycomb. Look at a sign. Look at these photographs, Ollie. We've looked through them before, I know. But I want you to look at them again when you have a chance.

Here I am — 1956, in Marciana Marina, framed by the lens of the camera your father held. It must have been September or early October.

Look at me. My hair pulled back in a ponytail, my glasses propped above my forehead, a bra strap showing where the sleeve of my dress has slipped down my arm, my lips dark with what must have been plum-colored lipstick.

I don't remember me. I don't remember what I was thinking when Murray took the photograph. Probably I was thinking I wanted to look better than I knew I looked, but I'm not sure.

Look at me, Ollie. What do you think I was thinking?

Here we are, the six of us, on the beach. Lidia or Francesca must have snapped the picture. Your father in his striped boxer suit. You, Ollie, plump and brown and naked, straining to pull away from the grip of Patrick's hand around your arm. Harry looking at something to the right of us. Nat making a silly face.

Here is Lidia, stern, stout Lidia. We could never get her to smile for the camera.

You and Nat in the little wooden cart Lorenzo's farmhand Nino built for you. You're on the terrace of our first house, the one in Le Foci. I think that's Francesca's arm cutting across the picture, reaching over to steady you, Ollie.

Look at you. What were you thinking? What are you thinking now?

Here's the picture I thought we'd lost. A little blurry, but it gives you an idea of what our Mezza Luna property consisted of. Not much more than thick sloping woods surrounding the pool of run-off water and the gouged granite rockface in the background.

Here — these are out of order — a picture of the four of you eating gelato in Piazza Signoria in Florence. Look at all of you. Your faces masked with chocolate. Look at how happy you were.

This is Francis Cape. Old Francis Cape on our terrace in Marciana. He looks startled, doesn't he? As though he wasn't expecting the pop of the flashbulb.

This — oh, this is Mom and Jill on a trip to Niagara Falls. How did this one get in the box?

Here you are asleep on Murray's lap. Murray is asleep, too. No, he was only pretending to sleep, if I'm remembering correctly.

The four of you dressed in your darling pinstriped jackets and shorts. We didn't go to church while we were on Elba, and I'm not sure why you were dressed up. Maybe so we could take this photograph.

This — your father and me in a restaurant. Our faces lit from the glow of the candle in the cake. It must have been my birthday.

This is the view of the island from the castle at the top of Volterraio.

This is our garden in the second villa. The wall of sunflowers, the jungle of Lidia's tomato plants. We had fresh tomatoes all year round.

Tomatoes. Fresh mozzarella from white oxen. Anchovies and

octopus and squid. The kitchen counter covered with squids turned inside out. Your father couldn't stand the sight of raw squid. Or fresh blood. Both made him weak-kneed.

Here's one of Murray with his eyes closed, rolling a cigarette. He could roll a cigarette blind in eight seconds.

Meena and her litter of kittens. They are, count them, they are all there, all four. I don't remember which one Patrick accidentally squashed. Do you?

Now this group includes Lorenzo, our padrone, and his wife. That's Francis Cape again at the end of the table. The others I don't recognize.

This is the mossy statue of Napoleon in the garden at his Palazzina dei Mulini. And here I am with Murray standing on the steps of the Roman villa above Portoferraio.

And here — this is another one of you boys at the top of Volterraio. I remember this day. Murray brought all of us to Volterraio in January to look for diamonds. It's one of our few pictures of the island in winter. The bare vines below look like fishing nets spread across the fields, don't they? That's snow on the peak of Monte Capanne.

Here I am wading back to the beach after a swim. I'm lingering in the water so my legs wouldn't show in the picture.

Here's Nat on the *Roma* with the Statue of Liberty behind him.

Did you know that since Elba, we never successfully paid off a loan without taking out another loan?

Did you consider what we would owe in back taxes, if that deed to the Mezza Luna land was valid?

For you, Ollie, Elba has stood in your memory as the paradise you lost because your father bungled the situation. But I'll tell you, I was relieved to leave that island behind and to have made it home, our family intact, across the ocean and into a house with a washing machine and drier and a fenced yard. I was relieved that Murray found a job and I needed only one course to become certified as a teacher, so I'd be ready to find work when Murray was unemployed again. I was relieved that you children took pleasure in friends and books and the puppy we gave you that spring. I was relieved that though Murray kept on drinking, I knew he would never turn into one of those monsters who, after too much booze, will crash through the door you've locked against him and grab you by the throat. We had many years ahead together, and I was relieved that I had no reason to doubt his word anymore and could keep the old suspicions hidden in the dark stony place in the soul where love mingles with fear.

Now don't I sound grand.

March 1, 2001

To the west, behind the hills, the granite cap of Monte Capanne a shadow in the mist. To the east, the peak of Volterraio crowned by its ruined castle. In the fields, rain soaking the purple tips of lavender. In Portoferraio, the swollen sea lapping at the quay. Straight ahead, an archway leading to a piazza; from the piazza, steps rising, crossing narrow terraces of streets. Water streaming down furrowed stones. Clack of a woman's heels. Wet tires. Someone standing inside an open doorway, whistling for a dog. Yellow paint on stucco. Terra-cotta trim. A pot of red geraniums. A box of white cyclamens. Another set of stairs. A man with a cane. Tap of the cane. Rise of one shoe and then another. A man with thick glasses and a useful cane.

Dopoguerra: "Poi, come per un miracolo, ecco che il successo turistico fa affluire denaro e benessere, grazie a ciò che da sempre queste isole avevano subito: l'invasione dei continentali!" — *Guide d'Italia de Agostini: Isola d'Elba E Arcipelago Toscano*

I am here alone. From my hotel window I can see over the roofs of the bungalows and across the bay to the water. The sea is gray today under a gray sky, though yesterday, seen from the top of Volterraio, the sky was clear and the sea was the blue of blue tourmaline.

I can hear the hum of my computer, the buzz of controlled ventilation, and the television in the room next door. I have my own television on, tuned to CNN, but the volume off.

My brothers and I have always wondered what would have happened if we'd stayed another year or two. What we could have found. What we could have done. If only we'd dug a little deeper, gone a little farther into the hard earth. If we'd been more persistent.

In order to secure the finest optical effect in a cut gem, certain proportions are necessary. I forget the exact formula. The base must be twice as wide as the crown, the table half of the whole stone. Something like that.

The weather: nuvoloso domani, e molto nuvoloso dopodomani. The sun is shining in Tunisia. It is snowing in Milan. The ice cap on Kilimanjaro is shrinking at the rate of 508 feet per year.

Elba was the joke we grew up with. Whenever we wanted to make fun of Murray, we reminded him of Elba. Of Napoleon and Lambrettas. Of black and pink and blue tourmaline. Of uninhabitable acres of rocky earth. Of land that cost more to sell than it did to buy. Once upon a time our father had brought us to Elba, and he was in debt ever since. His last great gamble, from which he never recovered.

What he would call a "nonevent, Ollie, for Christ's sake."

Why bother to write about Elba? Make it up, for Christ's sake. Stick to the imagination.

I've changed the names, haven't I? I can't help but take some liberties. It's in my blood, this inability to tell the simple truth. Though it's true that I'm sitting in a hotel room on the outskirts of Portoferraio on the island of Elba, it's the first of March, 2001, and I was in Siena last week. It's true that I have the television on "mute." It's true that I had a pastry and cappuccino for breakfast.

Untrue is the attribution of Napoleon Bonaparte to the graffito at his palazzo in San Martino: "Ubicunque felix Napoleon." The author is anonymous.

The man with the glasses and cane is eager to talk, if you have time to listen. His brother, a barista in Rio nell'Elba, was in the navy and has been to Montreal, New Orleans, Norfolk, and San Francisco. But this man, standing on a stone landing in Portoferraio, has had poor vision all his life, and the Italian navy didn't want him.

He'll tell you about the difference between the wines of La Chiusa and Acquabona. He'll tell you where to buy olive oil and what to expect from tomorrow's weather. He'll tell you about his cousin, who is selling her house in the village of Marciana. He thinks she's foolish to sell it. Her son will want the house for himself someday. The son has a tumor — tumore, capito? — and goes to Firenze for treatment.

What writer committed to factual representation doesn't miss the freedom of fiction? If I were writing a novel, I'd be writing about coming to Elba in winter of the year 2001 and visiting the Nardi villa. I didn't look for it my first visit, and I couldn't find it when I was here last April. But the other day I found it exactly where my mother told me it was: along the road to Magazzini. I'd describe the villa and its fresh orange stucco, the moss darkening the roof tiles, the terraces of olive groves behind the house — the surrounding land and buildings unchanged for almost fifty years, only the traffic on the street, the automatic gates, and, inside, the satellite channels on the television, to remind the occupants of the modern world.

The gate had been left open. There was a doorbell, but out of timidity I knocked — softly at first, and again with more force.

The truth is, the woman who answered the door was named Elisa Vivaldi, she was the daughter-in-law of the owner of the Vivaldi Hotel in Procchio, she came from La Spezia, and she'd never heard of the Nardi family. Which left me nothing much to do but thank her for her time and excuse myself.

If, instead, Adriana Nardi still lived there —

Buongiorno, sono Oliver Murdoch. My father owned land in the Mezza Luna region.

Sì, prego.

She'd be, what, sixty-six years old, with thin white hair, subtle blue shading around her eyes, deep red lipstick. Her clothes — black slacks and a pink wool sweater cuffed with bunched silk — would be comfortable, bright, unpretentious. Her manner would be relaxed. She'd invite me to come in. She'd offer me something to drink.

The man on the landing will compare the virtues of Portoferraio and Porto Azzurro. He'll tell you about Marciana, if you're interested. Have you been up to Marciana? His cousin is selling the house she grew up in, the house where his whole family hid during the night of violence in June 1944, the night the Allies met the Germans on the island of Elba. The stories this man could tell, you wouldn't believe.

My name is Oliver Murdoch. My father owned land here in the 1950s.
     Yes, come in.
     Grazie.
     Would you care for something to drink?
     A glass of water would be fine.
     Have a seat. Those pictures, by the way, the ones on the credenza, they are of my two grandchildren, Camilla and Philip. They live in London. My husband and I have a house in Redding. We're only here to prepare our villa for summer tenants.
     Her voice comes from the kitchen. For a moment I forget that she is Adriana Nardi and mistake her for her mother, though her mother has been dead for more than thirty years.
     She brings me a glass of water. Just water. Secretly, I was expecting a tray piled high with meringues.
     Now how can I help you, Signor Murdoch?
     What would I say to her? Why was I there?

I am sitting in a hotel room, looking out beyond Punta della Rena at the sea, imagining the story I would write if I were going to start over. The story of Adriana Nardi — a novel based on truth, truth based on hearsay, gossip, rumors, secondhand accounts, and dreams.

Won't you tell me about the guard who worked at the prison on Pianosa? The professor from Bologna? The exact nature of my father's involvement? Your four days in Portovenere? Tell me about Paris. How did you find a willing doctor? Was he really a doctor? How much did he charge? How long did it take? How did you get back to your hotel afterward? Were you alone?

How dare you, Signor Murdoch!

How dare I ask to hear about what this woman endured. My prurience. Her dignity. My disrespect. Life diminished and falsified by the simple act of transcription.

The American Express Travel Guide to Tuscany and Florence
SIGHTS AND PLACES OF INTEREST
PALAZZINA NAPOLEONICA DEI MULINI*
NAPOLEON CREATED HIS RESIDENCE IN EXILE FROM TWO OLD WINDMILLS ABOVE
THE CITY NEAR FORTE DELLA STELLA. THE FURNISHINGS FOR THIS DELIGHT-
FUL LITTLE PALACE WERE COMMANDEERED FROM HIS SISTER ELISA'S HOUSE
AT PIOMBINO; THE PLATE AND LIBRARY WERE BROUGHT FROM FONTAINEBLEAU.

I was just wondering if you remember my father.

He's not easy to forget.

He had liver cancer and passed away in the summer of '92. Actually, he died of pneumonia following surgery.

I study her face, watching for her unspoken reaction, but what I see I can't decipher.

I think, Signora Nardi, that he was very much in love with you.

I know, Signor Murdoch, that he loved his family.

The truth of love being its power to corrupt and divide and destroy.

Your father considered himself a lucky man. Perciò era molto fortunato.

Portoferraio in a soft winter rain. Hiss of steam frothing milk in the café. The man on the landing is wearing a hat and rarely bothers with an umbrella. This man will keep talking, if you don't mind getting wet.

First the Germans. Then the English and French and Senegalese. And then the Americans arrived with their gifts of clothes, shoes, chocolate, peanut butter. What do you do with peanut butter? And meat in a can?

Capsized dinghies clogging the harbor, rubble blocking the streets, and all the Americans wanted to do was play football on the beach at Le Ghiaie.

You want to hear about the war? His own father, a shepherd from San Piero, bringing pecorino and fresh milk to the group of English soldiers camped on Monte Capanne.

Though it is damp and cold today, I'm told that Elba has had a mild winter this year. It is only the beginning of March, and finches and sparrows are singing in the hotel garden, the almond trees have already shed their blossoms, and the vines on the trellis are budding. I've opened my window a crack to let in the fresh air.

Still, the island at bassissima is like a theater before a show opens. Elbans are waiting for their audience, and those of us who are tourists are treated to a gentle bemusement. Why have we come to the island in winter? Don't we know any better? What sort of people are we who at this time of year are able to leave jobs, homes, families, and come to Elba to do nothing? How did we earn such a ridiculous privilege?

Of course I remember you. You had a rock named King George.

A what?

The first time I met you, you took me into your room to show me your rock. You'd named it King George, and you kept it in a shoebox lined with black tissue paper. You'd made a little cardboard throne and filled it with chalk dust. You used a piece of wood for a table, dried leaves for the plates. King George was a piece of rose quartz.

Really? I sip my water. She smiles at me. I think about the murky passage from infancy to childhood, when the experiences we survive become confused with experiences we imagine.

Of course I remember you. Everyone who was on the island at that time would remember you and your brothers. You couldn't have realized it, but we were looking out for the bambini Americani, making sure you didn't get into any harm and didn't cause too much trouble.

In Florence last week, as I crossed the piazza to enter the Baptistery, a young boy — he couldn't have been older than seven or eight — stuck his hand in the back pocket of my jeans, searching for my wallet, which I keep in the inside breast pocket of my jacket. I grabbed his arm, pushed him away, we exchanged a glare, and that was that. He went looking for another stupido Americano, and I went into the Baptistery.

"At lower right, near some open trap doors, a red devil is tormenting some of the damned. He has a robust hairless body, claws instead of feet, and bat's wings; his face is not strongly characterized but it is an animal's one with a few human features. Goat's horns emerge from the nape of his neck." — *Devils in Art,* Lorenzo Lorenzi

During my second visit to Elba, last April, I found a zebra spider in the crumbled stones of the castle at the top of Volterraio. On that same trip I saw specimens of blue and pink and watermelon tourmaline in the mineralogical museum. The day before yesterday, a group of children threw flour at me when I was wandering through Porto Azzurro.

When my brothers and I were growing up in a series of rented houses in various communities in the northeast, we remembered Elba as a place of refuge and magic, and we never stopped longing to return. We had a sense that our father was responsible for giving us the experience of the island, but we also knew that he'd made it necessary for us to leave. We were ashamed of him, even though we didn't know what, exactly, he'd done wrong.

In the years that followed our stay on Elba, up until the time he fell ill, Murray was always struggling either to find a job or to hold on to one. After he quit the job he'd found upon returning from Elba, the Averils would have no financial dealings with him. His mother's death in 1968 ended all vestige of connection with that side of the family. From then on, Murray clung to us, his children and wife, like a man adrift after a shipwreck.

I don't think I'd offend him with these words. He never pretended that he didn't need us. And he was far more forgiving than I will ever be.

Mi scusi, non mi ricordo di lui.

Murdoch. My father owned property on Elba back in the 1950s.

Murdoch . . . Murdoch . . . no, I'm sorry, I don't remember the name.

I imagine a young Elban woman sitting by the window on a train, traveling from Genoa to Marseilles. None of the other passengers tries to speak to her. They can tell that she is deep in thought.

She is thinking about the man, her lover, the guard on Pianosa.

They used to meet in a room in Marina di Campo, a dusty little room overlooking the tin roofs of storage shacks. He was at the window, pulling the shutters closed, when she told him she was pregnant. He gave a nervous laugh and started buttoning his shirt back up. He might as well have smacked her.

Now she is heading toward Marseilles, toward Nice, toward Paris. She feels desperately lonely, wants to weep, would start weeping if there weren't strangers sitting across from her, had cried herself to sleep for three nights in a row back in Portovenere. But loneliness doesn't make her any less determined.

Our house in Le Foci is no longer standing, but I found our Marciana residence on my first visit to Elba. With the help of a map my mother had marked, I made my way from the hotel to Procchio, from Procchio to Marciana Marina, and up from the port into the valley.

The house is below the village of Marciana, situated in the upper slope of Valle Grande. The shutters were closed, the drive empty, the front gate locked, and no one answered when I rang the bell.

The road to the house cuts between terraces of vineyards and olive groves. I parked along the verge and climbed over the wire fence and up through the vineyards until I had a good view of the house. It was smaller than I'd expected, though it looked well-kept, with cyclamens blooming in pots along the windowsills and the soil around the olive trees freshly turned over.

I kept climbing up the eastern slope of Monte Giove, along a footpath that wound through cobwebs of dead pine. Goldfinches and woodchats flitted about, and at one point I heard the scrambling noise of some large animal retreating further into the woods. I was surprised by how far the sounds of the island travel. I heard dogs barking all the way from Marciana Marina. I heard cars on the road leading into Poggio. I heard roosters crowing in the valley.

After an hour or so I reached the ridge connecting Uomo Masso with Monte Giove. This area is part of the park system, and I found myself on a well-marked path leading to Marciana. Just outside of the village I turned off on a cart road and made my way to Madonna del Monte. The doors of the church were locked. I took in the view of the sea sparkling beyond the outcrop of Capo Sant'Andrea and then followed the path that led to the stone table and benches.

I thought I remembered that it was right here where I'd seen my brother Nat float in the air, and this was the reason we'd all been laughing — laughing so hard that Harry fell off the stone bench.

Over the last year I've had to trace and retrace memory through conversations with my brothers and mother. I admit that I'm still not exactly sure what is true.

If you keep listening, the man on the landing in Portoferraio will keep talking. He was telling you about the English soldiers on Monte Capanne. And then the Americans and their laughter, as if nothing had happened. They came to bring gifts of clothes, shoes, food. They were always laughing, having fun, playing football on the beach, bathing in the sea. They stayed for a month. They didn't want to go back to the war.

I can see on the television the American news I am missing. Interest rates are falling. There was an earthquake in Seattle. No one was killed, but damage is extensive.

A woman's voice blurs in echo in the courtyard. Tires squeal when a car brakes on the hotel drive.

"You're going to Elba *again?*" Of all my brothers, it's only Nat who has come right out and called me an idiot for writing about our family. He'd rather remember our time on Elba the way he wants to remember it, without the interference of uncertain history. He tells me that if I have any doubt about what happened, I should keep it to myself.

Murdoch, you say? Mur . . . doch? Ah, yes, of course! Signor Americano. He bought land in the Mezza Luna zone. He should have stayed and built a hotel. That's the way you get rich on this island.

Truthfully, the only person I've met on Elba who remembers my father is a bald little man of ninety who has lived in Sant'Ilario his entire life in the same little house where he was born. I met him last time I was here, after having read about his mineral collection in one of the guidebooks. His living quarters are upstairs. He's given over the downstairs rooms to his collection, which includes more than five thousand specimens of semiprecious stones.

Behind the dusty glass of a display case, there is a white opal with a vibrant rainbow surface. There is a black opal striped like a painted egg with blue and green. The specimen of alexandrite is greenish gray by daylight but turns, as he showed me, a beautiful maroon under a fluorescent light. The man has many specimens of lapis lazuli, cat's eye, and almandine. And though he has no diamonds, his prize is an amethyst geode the size of a basketball.

When I told him about my father, he took me into the back room, where the less valuable minerals are displayed, and showed me a large chunk of schorl dated March 1957. This, he said, came from my father's property, along with quartz crystals and a piece of acquamarine, the rest of which he had to keep in a drawer because, as I could see, he didn't have the space to display everything.

He is a bony, frail man, yet he is surprisingly nimble. When I returned to his house for a second visit a few days ago, I asked him, "Signore, come sta?" and he replied, in English, "I am still here, no?"

Though he remembers that my father was the owner of the land where the piece of black tourmaline was found, he does not remember ever meeting my father. He remembers my mother, though. He remembers her carrying a box of stones weighing ten kilos into his house. He remembers her saying that she thought the stones were worthless but he could have them if he wanted them. He told her that no stones are worthless.

I imagine a girl lying alone on a bed in a boarding house in Paris. She is bleeding heavily and has already gone through three sanitary napkins in the course of two hours. She'd been warned that she would bleed. But how much blood is too much? How can she know?

The phone out in the hallway is ringing. No one answers it. She falls asleep and dreams only of the sound of the ringing phone. When she wakes up half an hour later, the phone is still ringing, and she drags herself out of her room to answer it.

Pronto? She means, Hello. She means, Bonjour.

It is the ragazzo she met the other day at the carousel in the Tuilleries. He wants to take her to dinner. She wants to cry with joy, she is so desperate.

How can you presume to know what I went through, Signor Americano?

How can I presume to know about a twenty-one-year-old Italian woman who in 1956 went to Paris to terminate an unwanted pregnancy?

I dunt know nuttin about nuttin, our father used to say, holding up his newspaper to shield him from us — his strategy for forcing us to complete our homework without his help.

The last mine on Elba closed down in 1982. Rio nell'Elba is one of the island's starkest villages, and the surrounding land, the iron-red earth gouged and abandoned by the mines, has been devastated repeatedly by brushfires.

I walked through gritty, empty Rio nell'Elba the other day. I stopped at a bar for a caffè and had a short conversation with the barista about America. He had been in the navy and traveled to Montreal, Norfolk, New Orleans, and San Francisco. We talked about the winters in upstate New York.

After leaving the bar, I walked out of town up the road toward Volterraio. I picked some lavender as I walked along. I collected colorful pieces of quartz. I saw a white horse grazing on the marshy grass beside a creek.

I imagine a young woman sitting beside my father in a room lit only by moonlight. She has come to ask for help. Signor Americano might know of a doctor. Signor Americano might even loan her money.

She can't find the words she needs to explain her situation. She can hear my father's nervous breathing as he shifts his position on the sofa. He reaches for her, and all at once she perceives his mistake: he thinks she wants to lure him away from his family. She regrets having provoked such misunderstanding. Or else she doesn't regret it at all.

Last night I was woken by a storm. I got up and stood at the window for a long while. Palm fronds blew about like ribbons in the wind. Wisps of fog floated between the sea and the dark bed of clouds. Water spilled from the drainpipe extending out over my terrace. The noise of the wind, a low steady humming, was the sound of memory returning.

In 1944 Elbans gave Americans gifts of amethyst, agate, quartz, hematite, and tourmaline. Blue tourmaline lodged in a block of granite, the spiked blue inside the transparent crystal the exact blue of the Tyrrhenian Sea on a clear afternoon. Take this, keep it so you won't forget. Come back and visit us. We will welcome you. We will share our treasures.

I picture Adriana Nardi on the ferry bound for Piombino. It is a cool, bright autumn day. Fluffy cumulus clouds drift lazily from the open sea toward the mainland. The water is tinted maroon through the lenses of the young woman's dark glasses. It is the same color as her fingernail polish. She is wearing a camel-hair coat and a beret to match. She has wound her red silk scarf twice around her neck, leaving the ends loose to flutter in the wind. Her leather purse is a paler red. Her shoes, made in Florence, rise on two-inch spindly heels. Her net stockings are black. Black cuffs of her lambs-wool gloves, a Christmas present from her mother, peek out from her pockets. Her earrings are simple ruby studs. The rest of her jewelry, packed in her suitcase, she intends to sell.

Surf churning against the headlands of Polveraia. Rain turning the cart ways of the old open-cast mines to mud. Vine stumps sprouting. Cormorants diving in the harbor of Marciana Marina. Smoke puffing from stovepipes. Cars slowing to round the bends of mountain roads. Rain disappearing into the tangle of genista and broom. The rich fragrance of wet moss. Boulders frozen midway in their tumble to the sea.

JOANNA SCOTT is the author of six previous books, including *The Manikin,* which was a finalist for the Pulitzer Prize; *Various Antidotes* and *Arrogance,* which were both finalists for the PEN/ Faulkner Award; and the critically acclaimed *Make Believe.* A recipient of a MacArthur Fellowship and a Lannan Award, she lives with her family in upstate New York.

Also by Joanna Scott

Make Believe

"Wonderful.... There are things in this novel that take the breath away.... As is made dazzlingly clear in *Make Believe,* Joanna Scott is a Michael Jordan: she has talent to burn.... Scott inhabits the souls of the least articulate characters and makes them sing.... What we get is one of the most convincingly impressionistic versions of a difficult childhood that I have ever read.... There are occasions when the author's ingenuity and command of her craft make you want to laugh with pleasure.... One cannot help urging anyone who loves writing to read this book." — Nick Hornby, *New York Times Book Review*

"Elegant, rich, and completely spellbinding." — Deborah Sussman Susser, *Washington Post Book World*

"A powerful novel.... As *Make Believe* builds in emotional intensity to its dramatic conclusion, Scott's narrative probes the psychological states of her characters and explores how a single decision can completely change lives." — Joan Hinkemeyer, *Denver Rocky Mountain News*

"Scott masterfully balances the perfection of the child's imaginative interior world with the errant turbulence of adult life.... Her brilliant prose resonates with awe at the wondrous 'ability of life to sustain itself.'" — Trey Strecker, *Review of Contemporary Fiction*

"The opening sections of *Make Believe,* which depict Bo's experience of the car accident that killed his mother and his new life with his paternal grandparents, are as powerful as anything the gifted Ms. Scott has written. They possess the unsettling intensity of Benjy's interior monologue in Faulkner's *The Sound and the Fury*.... The penultimate chapter, which sends Bo's life skidding off in yet another direction, contains a dazzling set piece that showcases all of Ms. Scott's virtuosic skills." — Michiko Kakutani, *New York Times*

BACK
BAY
BOOKS

Available in paperback wherever books are sold